Unwanted

ASHLEE ROSE

First Edition

Cover: Irish Ink Publishing
Formatting: Irish Ink Publishing
Editor: Lindsey

For my husband, thank you for everything.

For pushing me and always telling me not to give up on my dreams, even when it gets tough.

If it wasn't for you, these books would never of happened.

I love you x

Other Books
BY ASHLEE ROSE

Entwined In You Series:

Something New

Something To Lose

Something Everlasting

Before Her

Without Her

All available on Amazon Kindle Unlimited

Only suitable for 18+ due to nature of the books.

LUNA

I sat in the bridal suite, waiting for the last touches to be done to my hair and makeup. I took a minute to take all this in, this moment, before I married my childhood sweetheart.

I met Josh in high school and we hit it off. He was captain of the football team, I was head of the cheerleading team. So, cliché I know, but it was love at first sight.

We were inseparable ever since.

But what was about to happen on our wedding day, I could never be prepared for.

Chapter ONE

I stood and looked in the mirror as the make-up artist finished my make-up, the light dusting of nude eyeshadow that was brushed over my lid made my green, bambi eyes pop. I had light pink blusher swept across my visible cheek bones, giving them a *just bitten* look. My full lips were glazed with a light pink lipstick. I didn't want to go over the top. I had china-doll-white skin, which luckily still tanned once the sun touched it.

I looked down at my Vera Wang 2005 wedding gown, the same one that Kate Hudson wore in the film Bride Wars. I needed it, and of course Daddy delivered. I made sure I had the three things every New York wedding needed;

Vera Wang Gown
The Plaza
Sylvia Weinstock Cake

I ran my hands over my petite waist, running the ivory silk bow through my fingers. I had to have a lot taken off the dress as I was only five-foot-two. The sculpted bodice made my already tiny waist somehow seem smaller.

My mum approached behind me, pulling me from my thoughts.

“Darling,” she cooed. I watched as tears pricked her emerald eyes. If it wasn’t for the tears, you wouldn’t notice any emotion on her freshly botoxed face.

“You look stunning. Josh is extremely lucky,” she said as she lifted my long veil above my head before placing it delicately onto the top of my head. She then brushed my long tumbling, blond curls over my shoulders.

“Perfect, you look like an absolute princess,” she said as she stepped away, her hands finding her mouth as she looked at me with so much love.

I heard the photographer snapping away, then the door opened and I turned to see my dad walking towards me, looking as handsome as ever in his black tuxedo and dickie bow, his greying hair pushed back away from his face. Emotions consumed him, which set me off.

“Oh, Luna, you look like the princess I always knew you were,” he said, choked. He walked over and took my hands in his, his crystal blue eyes glistening as the tears brimmed in them.

"Daddy, thank you for all of this," I said as I leant into his large frame, feeling his arms wrap around me as he embraced me.

"Your happiness means everything to me," he said into the top of my hair.

I forgot where we were for a moment, standing in the impressive bridal suite in the Plaza, New York. Of course, I wanted to get married here. My dad flew our family, Josh's family, and all of our friends out to celebrate our magical day.

I pulled away from my dad when I heard the suite door open again, and this time my three best friends and my brother walked in.

The girls looked amazing in their black gowns. They were sweetheart necked, the satin material clinging to their bodies. I was so grateful I had Brooke, Ava and Vanessa.

My brother Chris had a look on his face that I would never forget. The girls were fidgeting and looked uncomfortable, and the panic started to rise from the pit of my stomach.

"What's going on?" I asked quietly, and they all looked back and forth from each other. My dad took my hand in his and squeezed it tight.

"WHAT IS GOING ON?" I shouted, my throat burning as the lump in it started swelling in my windpipe.

"It's Josh," my brother said with a whisper, before

walking towards me.

"What do you mean, 'it's Josh.'" My voice quivered. "What's happened?" I asked again, this time not as angry.

"He isn't coming," he said quickly and bluntly.

"What?" I asked in disbelief.

This must be some sort of joke. I know what Chris is like, he loves a joke.

I started laughing, delusion lacing it. "You're winding me up, aren't you? Good one, Chris," I said, continuing to laugh as I grabbed my all-ivory bouquet.

"Tink, I wish it was one of them, trust me," he said, using my childhood nickname he gave me because of my pixie like features; he always said I resembled Tinkerbell.

This time I searched his face, his green eyes were dull and flitting back and forth to mine. That's when I realized he wasn't lying. This wasn't one of his pranks.

"He isn't coming?" The realization was apparent in my voice. I didn't take my eyes off of his.

I felt my dad's hand leave mine as he stormed out of the room.

The girls rushed to my side as I took the news in, a million questions were swirling around my head. I clung to my stomach through my dress, I couldn't breathe.

I felt my legs buckle beneath me as I fell to the ground.

"I need this dress off me, get it off me!" I screamed as I felt like I was being suffocated by my own wedding dress.

How could he leave? He was fine last night at the rehearsal dinner.

What have I done wrong?

I came back round to the girls unbuttoning the back of my dress, then pulling me to my feet and supporting me. My mum started rolling my dress down my slender frame before taking my hand and helping me step out of it.

"Brooke, pass me my phone," I demanded.

"Okay, babe," she said, her long ginger hair swishing as she spun on her heel to get her bag. She held her hand out with my phone as I snatched it from her grip.

I had a voicemail.

Maybe it was Josh? Maybe it was him telling me that he made a mistake?

I pulled a dressing robe on and put the phone to my ear. My heart broke as I heard his voice playing. I pressed one to listen to the message again, this time, taking it in...

Baby, I'm sorry. I never wanted to hurt you, I have loved you for ten years. But this, this was never me, never the life I wanted.

I can't be the prince charming you want me to be. I lost my head. Whilst you were sleeping last night, I crept out the hotel, ended up in some dive of a bar and turned to the bottle.

Panic started setting in that this was going to be my life. My life with only you in it.

I'm twenty-five, I'm not ready to settle down.

I love you, my little dove, I always will, but I can't do this.

Don't hate me, please forgive me.

I hit one again to listen one last time before Vanessa stepped in and took my phone away from me. I stared at her, her honey eyes full of sympathy for me. Her tanned skin glistened against the black satin dress that she was still wearing.

I needed to get out of here.

I ripped the veil from my hair, throwing it to the floor and sprinting out of the room. I didn't know where I was going, but I needed air. I needed the fresh air to fill my lungs.

I needed to breathe.

I felt like I was being smothered in there by the sad looks, sighs and sobs that filled the room. I didn't even feel like I had any tears to shed, my heart had been obliterated by my soulmate, yet I couldn't cry for him.

The shock consumed me, his message playing around my head. I ran into the main lobby, watching my wedding guests make their way into the grand ballroom where we were meant to be getting married in half an hour.

Half an hour, when my happily ever after was meant to begin.

Yet, I am about to run out onto the streets of New York in my wedding underwear and gown after being left at the altar by the only man I have ever loved.

As I get to the front Plaza steps, the crisp autumn air hit my lungs. Autumn is my favourite time of year, the red, yellow and orange burned leaves falling off the trees. I always felt like autumn was the start of new beginnings, the leaves fall to the ground, then the white blanket of snow covers the ground before spring blesses us again with hopeful new beginnings.

I opened my eyes to see Josh standing on the steps in front of me wearing jeans and a T-shirt, staring up at me. He wasn't even dressed. He really wasn't coming.

"Luna..." he said exasperated. Before he could say anything else I charged at him and pushed him.

"I hate you," I screamed at him. I didn't care who was looking at me.

"Luna, please," he begged as he grabbed my arms tightly trying to stop me. I wrangled my arms from his grip as I started pelting my hands on his chest, whilst screaming my hurt and embarrassment out to him.

"I. Hate. You," I said slowly, as the tears started to fall. The lump burned my throat as if I had swallowed hot coal. I felt exhausted.

I dropped my arms from his chest and my head in

disbelief.

I patted his broad chest one final time as I lifted my head to look up at him. He towered over me, but I loved that I was so small in comparison to him.

I took one final look at his deep blue eyes, his mousy blond hair, and every single detail of his face.

I turned to walk away, when he called after me and started to follow. "Don't!" I said abruptly.

"Don't fucking follow me," I snapped as I ran back into the Plaza.

I walked back into the room, physically and mentally exhausted. I couldn't even be angry. I was just broken.

I flopped down onto the chaise lounge as the girls swarmed me. My dad and Chris were still in the room. God knows where my dad went when he ran out. My mum was nowhere to be seen, but to be honest, she was useless in these kinds of situations.

"Luna, I am so sorry," Ava said as she sat down next to me, taking me into her embrace.

I just nodded quietly as I looked up at Vanessa who was now crouched down in front of me, placing her hands on my knees.

"We will get you through this, babe," she said in a comforting voice.

Brooke stood next to me as she placed her hands on my shoulders.

"Whatever you need from us, hun, we will be there," she muttered in agreement with Ness.

I was so lucky to have these three girls in my life. We have known each other since high school.

Vanessa was always the popular one of our group, she was drop dead gorgeous. Her tanned skin was radiant, her honey eyes drew you into her soul. She always knew what to say.

Brooke was the fiery one, her red hair suited her personality. She was similar skin tone to me; her creamy complexion suited her green eyes and red hair.

Then my darling Ava, she was the mother of the group. Her short brown hair sat bluntly on her shoulders, her brown eyes so dark they looked black. She was the most level headed out of us all.

My dad and brother lingered closely. I knew I could always rely on them to be there.

I blinked through my fresh tears as I looked up at my stunning Vera Wang dress... What a waste.

"What do you need?" Ava asked.

"A drink," I scoffed. Before I could look up, I had a glass of champagne shoved into my hand.

"Drink it," Vanessa said. I did as she said and knocked it back in one.

"Another," I said quietly. No one questioned it.

I saw my dad and Chris exchange looks, but they didn't say anything. Vanessa passed me another glass before I drank it down quickly.

"I need to sleep. I need to escape, to try and forget what happened this afternoon," I said as I crawled up the bed that was situated behind the chaise lounge that I had been sitting on. I snuggled into the Egyptian cotton sheets and pulled the duvet over my head.

"Shut the curtains," I groaned from my safe place.

I heard soft mutters before giving into sleep. I just wanted to wake up and for this to have never happened.

Chapter TWO

I was so glad to touch down at City Airport. My dad flew home the next day after the wedding with my mum, after he settled the bill at The Plaza and explained a short, brief reason as to why the wedding was cancelled. I know he would have told them the truth, but I think he just needed to be straight up instead of giving them the sugar-coated version that I know he would have done.

Me and the girls stayed for a few more days so I could try and get my head round what had happened, but it didn't help. Truthfully it made it worse. Josh was still calling three times a day, but I wasn't answering. After the grovelling voicemails, it then turned to text messages. To be honest it was a lot easier to ignore the text messages than hearing his pathetic, begging voice on a voicemail.

"How are you feeling now you are home?" Ava asked me. I heard Brooke tut at her question, and I rolled my eyes at her rudeness.

"Not great, but better now that I've left America

behind," I said as we stood waiting at passport control.

I looked down at my naked left hand. I've had an engagement ring on my finger for four years, and now, nothing. It's as empty as my heart. I honestly don't think I will ever fill it again.

"Oh shit," I groaned as we waited for luggage. "How have I only just remembered about our honeymoon?" I threw my head back and moaned out loud. "Room for one in the honeymoon suite please," I said sarcastically.

"Cancel it," Brooke said.

"I can't, I'll lose all my money. I stupidly put it on my credit card to surprise Josh. He didn't know where we were going, just that we were going away." I sighed.

"I can sort it, I was the one that booked it," Ava piped up, reminding me that it was her idea, plus she had her own little travel agents that had been passed to her from her family.

"I know, hun, but it's a lot of money to waste, isn't it?" I pathetically argued back. Truth was, I didn't want it cancelled, I wanted to go, but I wanted to go with Josh. I wanted us to go away on the holiday that I had paid for.

I stood in a daze for a moment when Brooke came and wrapped her arm around me.

"So, me and the girls were thinking, why don't we go away? We can either stick with Hawaii which was your honeymoon destination or go somewhere else? Ava has said she can sort it," she said excitedly whilst gripping onto my shoulder a lot harder than she was before.

"I don't know, guys..." My voice trailed off.

"Why shouldn't we?" Vanessa piped up. "You bloody deserve a holiday, and so do we."

"She is right, you can't argue with her," Ava agreed. "Plus, I think Hawaii is our best bet. It's still warm, we can take each day as it comes, or we can go somewhere a bit more 'girly holiday' place."

"Like Vegas!" Ness shouted out.

"Oooh, Vegas, I like the sound of that," Brooke said, still with her arm wrapped round me.

"Can I think about it please? Let me just get home to my own bed and sleep on it." I said in a pleading tone.

"Of course," Ava said. "Either of the destinations are good weather wise for late October." She beamed at me as she grabbed the last suitcase off the belt.

We walked in quiet chatter as we made our way through to the arrival lounge and saw my dad's driver waiting for us all. We all lived in London, different postcode areas, but nothing a short train or taxi ride couldn't fix.

I lived in Mayfair with my parents. Me and Josh had been saving for our own house, but that was a distant memory now. My dad owned a large international bank right in the heart of London's Oxford Street. His father came from a line of bankers and inherited Smiths International. Then once my grandad was of an age where he could no longer work, it was passed down to my father. He has given us a life that most dream of, and I am forever grateful for the life we have had. Don't get me wrong, we haven't had the easiest of rides, like any family.

I own a small florist and cake shop called, Cakes & Roses, which I love. I love that I have two creative things to help keep my mind busy. Some days I choose flowers, others it's cakes.

As soon as we left school, it was either university or work. I chose work. I was fortunate enough that my parents had been saving since I was born, so I used a chunk to buy and open my business.

My brother Chris was in the stock market. He loves it, but I couldn't cope with the hustle and bustle of that life. I think my father was still hoping that Chris would run Smiths one day, but Chris ignores that responsibility for now.

I still have the London life, just not with the stress like he does. Chris isn't married, he is three years older than me and loves being single. He lives in a beautiful pent house in Chelsea. I get frustrated that I still live at home, but I will fly the coop once I am ready.

I sat thinking about the conversations I am going to have to have with people at work. I shake the thoughts away. I have a couple of days before we are due to go away, so have a few weeks before I have to face them.

I would let Ava know in the morning what I wanted to do. A girl's holiday would be nice, not what I had planned obviously, but a bit of one-on-one time with the girls would do me the world of good.

I pulled my compact out of my Louis and looked at my face. I looked paler than usual. I had deep insets under my eyes, making my dark bags look worse than they were. My hair was pulled onto the top of my head like a bird's nest, but I didn't care. I didn't care what I looked like, I just wanted to get home.

After dropping Brooke off, I was finally on my way home. I couldn't wait to see my dad and mum. It had only been a few days, but I missed them. I wanted to get home to what I knew.

I sighed when we finally pulled up outside our luxurious townhouse. I was filled with mixed emotions. When I left here a week ago, I was excited and in love. I couldn't wait to start my new life with Josh, but that wasn't meant to be.

Now, here I am, outside, single, broken and wrecked. I was a ghost of myself. I am normally so upbeat and positive, but I just couldn't find that side of me at the moment.

Baxter grabbed my bags out the boot of the car and opened my door.

"Thank you, Baxter," I said quietly as I followed him up the stairs to our front door. I instantly felt better as soon as I stepped into our entrance hall. There really was no place like home.

"Darling," my mum called out as she walked down the hallway in her vintage Chanel pant suit.

"How was your flight?" she asked as she ushered me through to the kitchen where a cup of tea was waiting for me.

"Long." I sighed. "Just wanted to get home." A small smile appears on my face as I take a seat on the sofa, which is placed in a large space at the side of the kitchen. I tuck my legs underneath me as I cradle the hot cup of heaven.

"Have you decided what to do with your honeymoon?" Mum winces slightly as she asks.

"Not sure yet. Ava has suggested us all going on a girl's holiday, still to Hawaii, or changing it to Vegas or something." I shrugged, staring at my cup the whole time.

"Well, I think that's a brilliant idea. A nice holiday with the girls. Just what the doctor ordered," she chirped.

"I said I would think about it," I said quietly. "To be honest, I just want it over with." I shook my head. "How the hell has this happened?" I voice my thoughts.

"I don't know, but your dad is furious. He has already called Josh's father Carlisle. A few strong words were exchanged, but that's all your father has told me," she said as she continued to clean our already spotless kitchen.

"Oh," I said.

"Don't worry, sweetie, it'll be fine. Daddy is just

upset with the situation, and of course Josh. After everything Daddy has done for him and his family. He is disgusted." She shook her head.

Josh's family are very well off as well. My dad got them some of his biggest clients for their law firm. I know my dad would wash his hands with him if he could, but it's not that easy.

I cuddled my knees as the familiar pain shot through my heart as I thought back to my Josh. *My Josh.* He didn't show any signs of being unhappy, I don't get it.

I pulled myself from the sofa and placed my empty cup on the kitchen side.

"Thanks, Mum, I'm going to have a shower," I mumbled before taking myself upstairs. I was always in awe of our home, it was stunning. I felt very lucky to have grown up in this beautiful home.

I walked into my large bedroom. I wanted to crawl into my queen sized bed, but I needed a shower. I was jet lagged and I was sweaty.

I pulled my long, blond hair out of its messy bun and let it fall down my back. I twisted the shower knob and left the shower running warm. I peeled my grey leggings off my legs and put them into the wash basket before taking my matching lounge suit jumper off.

I stood and looked at myself in my large bathroom mirror. My pale, porcelain skin looked almost transparent, my emerald green eyes lifeless. I ran my fingertips across my full bottom lip as I reminisced Josh's lips on mine the night before our meant-to-be wedding day. His thin lips somehow consumed my extremely full ones, I never understood how. His kisses were like heaven, his lips felt like the inside of a rose. They were always so soft.

Even when we got down and dirty, he was always still so soft and attentive to my needs. I traced my fingertips across my visible collar bone and down the side of my full breasts. For someone who had such a tiny, petite frame I was blessed in the breast department. I always felt I was too small and skinny, but it didn't matter what I ate, I didn't put any weight on. Some would say I was fortunate. I don't agree, but I have to appreciate and love the body I was given.

The shower room was slowly filling with steam from the scalding shower. I didn't think twice as I stepped underneath it, the hot shower burning my skin a crimson red as it hit me.

I left the shower like a zombie, wrapping myself in my luxurious, fluffy towel. I fell onto the bed, staring at the high bedroom ceiling, my champagne-crystal chandelier catching my eye.

I felt myself go into a stare off with the crystals dangling down. I felt like I needed to cry, like full on ugly cry, but I couldn't. I sobbed for days after he left me. I cried on the plane, but then as soon as I was back in London I stopped, and I haven't been able to cry since.

I feel like I have the burning lump in my throat, threatening to release my tears, but something is stopping them, and I don't know what.

I pulled myself up and sat at my mirrored dressing table. I reached over for my phone to check the time. Eight pm. I felt exhausted but didn't know if I could sleep or not. I rubbed the towel over my hair, trying to get it as dry as I could before having to get the hairdryer out. It took forever to dry where it was so long, and everything felt like an effort.

I heard my bedroom door handle go, and I saw my mum. I smiled at her.

"Hey, angel, how you feeling after your shower?" she asked as she walked over and took my hairbrush off my dressing table top and moved behind me, before brushing through my hair. I instantly relaxed knowing she was here and looking after me. It really didn't matter how old you were, you always needed your mum. Okay, I was only twenty-five, but I was so grateful I had a good relationship with my mum. Well, when she wanted to be *that* mum.

"A bit. I just feel so tired, but don't feel like I could sleep," I said as I closed my eyes as she continued to brush my hair, then leaning down to one of my drawers and pulling my hairdryer from it. She bent down and plugged it in before standing back up straight as she clicked the button on.

We didn't say anymore, she just started blow drying my hair and taking care of me like I was five years old again. After half an hour of my mum pampering me, she placed a kiss on the top of my head, then tilted my head back to look at her.

"I love you, and this will get easier. The pain will pass, and you will find a wonderful man who can't wait to spend the rest of his life with you," she said with emotion clearly lacing her voice.

"Now, get some sleep, I will see you in the morning," she said softly as she walked towards the door of my bedroom.

"Thank you, Mum. I love you too," I said quietly to her.

She smiled at me before leaving the room and closing the door behind her. I hung my towels back in my bathroom and grabbed an oversized tee out of my drawer before pulling it over my head and slipping into my bed. Oh, it felt good to be back in my own bed. I was going to put the tele on, but as soon as my head hit the pillow, my eyes fell heavy and I couldn't fight it.

Chapter THREE

I woke feeling more refreshed. I had slept a solid fourteen hours, and I felt so much better for it. I needed to work out where we were going on our holiday in four days, Hawaii or Vegas? I called Ava as soon as I was downstairs.

"Hey, hun," I said in a soothing voice.

"Hey, you, how you feeling?" she asked. I was sick of that question.

"Yeah, not bad, been better," I said with a hint of a smile in my voice.

"That's good to hear. So, have you decided what you want to do? Because if you want to change Hawaii, I need to do it as soon as possible," she said.

"I think I want to stay with Hawaii. I booked it for a reason. All I ask Ava, tell them I don't want any fucking honeymoon shit in our room."

I hear her laugh. "Okay, boss, noted. I'll deal with it." She giggled. "Right, I'll call you back in an hour or so."

"No worries, speak to you soon," I said before cutting her off.

I tiptoed down into the kitchen to see my mum and dad sitting at the breakfast bar.

"Morning, darling," my dad said as he patted the empty seat next to him as my mum stood to put the kettle on and start breakfast.

"Morning, Daddy." I smiled at him as I took my place next to him. As soon as my bum had hit the seat he placed his hand over mine. My dad was a bigger built man, he never used to be, but I suppose with his age and his slowing metabolism it was to be expected. Him and my mum loved the gym, they encourage me to go when I feel like it, but to be honest, I find it hard to find the motivation.

"Have you decided what you are going to do in regards to the honeymoon, sweetie?" my mum asked as she slid the cup of tea over then went back to making pancakes, my favourite.

"Yeah, I have. I spoke to Ava this morning and decided to stick with Hawaii. It's a five-star resort, plus I paid a small fortune on my credit card for it." I grimaced as I felt my dad's eyes on me.

"Why did you use your credit card, Luna? You have money in the bank." He tutted as he shook his head, disappointed.

"I know, but you know, credit card protection and all that." I shrugged and gave him my best smile. I was always told my smile lit up any room and was my best feature.

"You have me wrapped round your little finger, Luna," he cooed. My mum placed my pancakes in front of me, my belly rumbled loudly. I couldn't remember the last proper meal I had. It must've been the rehearsal dinner. I started eating so quickly that I forgot my table manners.

My mum tutted at me. "Luna, please."

I looked up at her guiltily. "Sorry, forgot myself for a moment," I admitted as I took a napkin and wiped my mouth softly whilst keeping my eyes on hers the whole time.

"Anyway, talking of protection," my dad piped up, clearing his throat, "I am hiring a bodyguard for you," he finished bluntly, then looked down into his lap, knowing full well what was about to happen.

"What do you mean a bodyguard?" I snapped, dropping my fork onto my china plate. I winced when I saw my mum jump. These plates weren't cheap.

"I just want someone there watching you. Carlisle would have done the same if you and Josh were going, he is worse than me," he tried to justify himself.

"I don't need a bodyguard, and Carlisle wouldn't have done that, so don't try that one," I said as I stood from the breakfast bar.

"This is not up for discussion, Luna. You are having

a bodyguard and that's final. If you don't want one, then you don't go. It's that simple, now end of discussion," he said as he inhaled deeply. "I've got to go to work. I'll start interviews today." He walked over to my mum and kissed her before walking out of the kitchen.

"Mum, he can't be serious?" I asked.

"I'm sorry, it is what it is. I know it seems a bit extreme, but he is doing it to protect you," she said, defending my father.

"I don't need protecting! I am big enough and ugly enough to look after myself. Plus, I'll be with the girls. Brooke wouldn't let anything happen," I pleaded, trying to get my case across.

"Luna, you are wasting your breath. Your father will *not* allow you to go without a bodyguard. And yes, agreed, Brooke would have your back but that's not enough. Please, do it for your dad. He is so stressed with work, it'll just help him relax." I could hear the desperation in her voice, I couldn't bear to argue against her anymore.

"Fine," I said exasperated. I gave up.

"Thank you," she said as she took my plate from me. I didn't stick around, I made my way upstairs and threw a pair of jeans on with an oversized grey jumper and my grey Ugg boots. I ran the brush through my hair and applied some mascara and lip balm to my lips before bracing the cool autumn breeze.

I aimlessly walked towards the train station and

jumped on the jubilee line before jumping off at London Bridge and walking towards St Katherine's Dock where Vanessa lived.

Vanessa was a well-established wedding planner and lived in a luxurious two-bedroom apartment with a stunning wrap around terrace that overlooked the harbour. I always felt like I was on holiday while I was there.

After a short walk I approached the dock, taking a deep breath in as I walked along past the boats and yachts. I opened the small gate and walked up to the main communal door, then buzzed on the intercom.

"Hello," I heard Vanessa's sweet voice through the speaker.

"Hey, buzz me in, I'm freezing," I said back, a little agitated.

"Okay, stress head," she replied as I heard the door unlock. I ran up the first flight of stairs and walked straight into the open front door.

"Hey, Agg, what's up with you?" Ness said from her open-plan kitchen.

"Ugh, I'm fed up. So, I decided this morning with Ava that we would stick with Hawaii," I said, flustered as I took my coat and hat off and threw it over her stunning sofa whilst taking in the views of the dock, the sun bouncing off the glistening water.

"Right," Ness said distracting me and handing me a

cup of coffee.

"And my dad pipes up telling me he is getting me and us a bloody bodyguard." I shake my head as I feel the anger and distrust fill me once more.

"Can you actually believe it? A bloody bodyguard," I snap.

"Oh dear, that's not what you need, is it?" she replied sympathetically as she took a seat next to me and curled her legs underneath her. "But, Carlisle would have done the same if you and Josh were going. Him and your father are powerful, wealthy men who will always have enemies. I'm not saying that's why he is doing it, but I don't blame him." She shrugged before taking a mouthful of her coffee and smiling as the taste hit her taste buds.

"How can you defend him?" I said, my back clearly up.

"I'm not defending him, I am just saying I can understand why. What if something was to happen to you? At least your dad can relax and know you are safe," she argued back.

"I just wanted a girl's holiday away, with you, Ava and Brooke." I sighed. "And now I have to go away with a glorified, bulked up babysitter." I scoffed, Vanessa breaking into a giggle.

"It'll be fine, we will just ignore him, or her. We are assuming it is a him," she added then shrugged. "But it'll be fine, we have just under a week until we go, and I can't wait for some sunshine on my skin."

"Me neither. I love the autumn, but I do need some sun. My pale skin needs a bit of colour." I rolled my eyes as I held my arm up next to Vanessa's tanned skin.

"Have you heard from Josh?" she asked changing the subject from the bodyguard situation.

I sighed at her question before answering, tears threatening my eyes.

"The odd text here and there," I said quietly. "I just can't bring myself to message him back. I thought he would have been banging my mum and dad's door down, I thought I was going to have him grovelling on his knees, begging for me back with a huge bouquet of peonies in his hand, telling me it was all a mistake, but no. I get lousy messages. He obviously wasn't that into me. I've played the voicemail over and over in my head, I just don't know what happened. What changed his mind?" I hadn't realized it, but I was crying, and it felt so good to let them flow.

Vanessa swooped me into her arms and held onto me tightly, not letting go until I was ready

"I can't do this," I sobbed out. "How can you hate and love someone at the same time? The last time I saw him I told him I hated him, I hit him and lashed out." For some reason, I felt disgusted with myself for treating him that way, even though he broke my heart within minutes.

"That's a normal reaction, babe, I would have done a

lot worse and I'm not even the angry one of the group. Imagine what Brooke would have done to him," she said, raising her eyebrows as if she was imagining exactly what would've happened if it had happened to Brooke.

We both started laughing, and it was just what I needed to turn off the horrible feeling that had consumed me.

"So, when is daddy dearest sorting your protector out then?" she teased.

"Next few days, apparently." I rolled my eyes. "I am dreading it. Going to have some old man named Bennett or something following me around." I shook my head and started laughing again. "Can you imagine though, Ness, like it'll be awful."

Vanessa started laughing along with me. "Oh, Luna, it won't be that bad. He could be a right hottie for all you know," she said, giving me an elbow.

"Stop it, I wouldn't be that lucky." I laughed back at her. "Hey, I'm hungry. Can we get take out? What time is Madame Brooke home? Or is she out after work living the single life?" I teased.

"God knows, she doesn't normally let me know until the last minute, but yeah, let's get takeout. Pizza or Chinese?" she asked as she stood from her cosy spot on the sofa to fetch the menus.

"Oh, tough choice... Pizza... It's easier, isn't it," I said as she came and sat next to me and handed me the menu.

I could have eaten the whole menu, I felt starving all of a sudden.

"How about Hawaiian? Seeing as we are going Hawaii in a few days," I said a little more excited than intended.

"Of course, I'll grab some sides as well and put a bottle in the fridge," she chirped as she walked through to order the pizza.

I couldn't believe the day had gone. It was early evening by the time the pizza arrived, and we were already a bottle of wine down when we heard Brooke walk in.

"Hello," she called out as she opened the front door.

"Hey, you," I shouted out as the second bottle had just been opened.

"Oh, hey, you," Brooke chimed as she dropped her bag to the floor then sat next to me, clicking her fingers for Ness to bring her a glass of wine. I shook my head at her boldness then got frustrated when Ness came at her beck and call.

"How was work?" I asked Brooke as Vanessa sat next to me and gave me a soft pat on the knee

"Work was okay, same old, day in, day out," she whined. "But, my boss, Ryan, makes it so much more pleasant. He is soooo hot." She started fanning herself. "Suited and booted, tight butt, ripped body and so rugged," she carried on. "Honestly, he wants me as well, I can tell. I feel like just putting it on him and seeing what reaction I get." She started giggling.

"Oh yeah, that's good, put it on your super-hot, rich boss and then get your arse fired," Ness snapped but in a joking manner.

"You win some, you lose some, right?" she teased back at us both. "Anyway, enough about him otherwise I am going to have to go into my bedroom and have a date with Mr Rabbit." She winked at me as she said it. "Let's plan Hawaii."

We all clinked our glasses and started chatting about our week away. It couldn't come soon enough.

Chapter FOUR

I sat in our large lounge waiting for my dad to introduce me to my new, personal bodyguard. My dad pacing up and down as his impatience was kicking in. It was only two-fifty pm, they weren't getting here until three pm.

My mum pottered about fixing her already perfect appearance in the mirror and giving her pillows one last fluff.

Then there was me, sitting here angry and nervous at the same time that this was still happening. My dad's face lit up when he heard the doorbell go, looking at his watch, clearly impressed with the new bodyguard's timekeeping.

I knotted my fingers together as the nerves started again. We flew in two days, so I would have to have them following me tomorrow whilst doing my last bits before we left. I heard my dad's voice bellow through the large entrance hall as he greeted his guest. My mum sat next to me and patted my leg as if she was trying to reassure me.

It had me wondering whether she knew who it was or if she was completely unaware, the same as I was.

"Follow me through here, my wife and daughter are in the lounge ready to meet you," I heard him say, his footsteps getting closer as he walked down the hallway.

My heart was thumping so hard, I'm sure you could see it through my chest.

"Just in here," I heard him say as him and said bodyguard walked into the room.

My heart felt like it had stopped, my eyes ran up and down his body taking every inch of him in.

My mums grip on my knee tightened as she must've been thinking the same thing as me. My god, he was something else.

"Luna, this is Sloane, Taron Sloane," my dad said proudly as he introduced my bodyguard. My legs felt like they would buckle if I stood, but somehow, I managed. I took a few steps over, so I was standing in front of him.

"It's nice to meet you, Taron," I said quietly, my eyes studying his features.

He towered over me, he was easily six foot six. I thought Josh was tall, but he had nothing on this guy. He had jet black hair that was styled perfectly off his face, it wasn't short, but it wasn't too long, it was long enough for me to run my fingers through and grab. His eyes were dark brown, but so dark they looked almost black. I could feel myself losing myself in his pools already. He literally made my knees weak just staring at him.

He had a noticeable rugged look about him, his stubble apparent on his face. I wanted to run my hand across it just to feel the friction on my skin. His lips were full, his bottom fuller than his top. I had to stop the thoughts of myself biting down on it. His glorious sun kissed skin glowed as he radiated the room. I don't know what had come over me, I felt like a giddy school girl in front of her crush.

"It's a pleasure to meet you, Luna." His eyes flitted back and forth from mine, and that's when I realized he had a slight accent.

"Will I know you are there?" I asked abruptly. I knew it sounded like a silly question, but I meant, would I know he was there as in being right by my side constantly.

"No, unless there was a threat and I needed to be close," he said, his voice cool. "I promise, I will be with you the whole time, but I won't be stuck to you like glue." He smiled at me.

"Right," I said quietly as I took a step back. I studied him for a moment, he literally glowed. I had to try really hard to pull my eyes from his, then looking at my dad I said, "So, is this it now? He is with me from this moment?"

"That's right." He nodded.

"Okay," I said taking a breath. "Well, I'm staying here for the rest of the afternoon, but tomorrow I need to go and get some last bits for holiday. So Taron, or is it Sloane?" I asked.

"Taron is fine," he said with a smile on his face.

"Okay, cool, so, Taron, I will relieve you of your duties and see you tomorrow," I said with authority as I walked through the middle of him and my dad. I didn't want Taron thinking I was some needy princess who loves the fact that I'm going to have protection.

"Actually," my dad piped up, "Taron will be staying here, so when you are in the house he is in the house, but he won't be bothering you. He can use the facilities round the house, and he will be residing in the spare room on the third floor. When you leave, he leaves with you, understood?"

I stopped and spun round to face them both. Taron's eyes roaming up and down my body whilst my dad stared at me.

"Great, a full-time babysitter," I said sarcastically whilst rolling my eyes.

"Don't roll them too hard, they might get stuck back there," Taron teased at me.

Oh, he is a cocky one.

My dad laughed and patted him on the back before relieving him. I shook my head at both of them and walked upstairs to get some gym gear on. I needed to keep distracted. Yes, Taron was hot, but that was about it. He seemed like a cocky, arrogant man who knows he is good looking, and I can't stand that in a man.

I undressed quickly and pulled my black gym leggings on, then threw my black sports bra over my head and slipped my trainers on before making my way down to the basement and into the gym. I put my air pods in and turned my music on, letting upbeat dance music fill my ears. I started my work out on the cross trainer, trying to build my cardio up. I needed to keep myself busy and distract myself from the thoughts that were crossing my mind of Taron. I shouldn't even be thinking of him like that, he is an arrogant piece of shit and I am still madly in love with Josh. This was just a phase. It would pass. A silly crush.

After spending one day with him I'm sure he will make it insufferable. I shook the thoughts away and continued my work out. After fifteen minutes, I moved onto the running machine, when I saw him out the corner of my eye. Great.

I tried my hardest not to look at him, but my eyes betrayed me. His body was everything that I had imagined it would be under his tight shirt. His skin glistened as he walked under the bright gym lights, and my mouth went dry as he walked past me, not even looking in my direction.

His stomach was rock solid, his abs so defined they didn't look real. His arms were big but not over the top. I half expected him to be top heavy, but of course he wasn't.

He was proportioned perfectly, which was annoying. On the exterior he was a God, but his personality and attitude was a huge turn off.

I kept reminding myself that after tomorrow, it was just one week. One week to get through with him, then my dad would let him go. I ignored him just like he ignored me, we didn't have to talk or be friends. I upped the speed on the treadmill as I started jogging, but now feeling self-conscious that he was in here. I wasn't going to leave because he intimidated me.

I gave him the side-eye, but he was focused forward, doing his weights whilst listening to his music. After ten minutes, I called it a day, I couldn't concentrate with him being in here. I came in here to keep myself distracted, but he ended up distracting me which is not what I wanted.

He watched as I made my way to the door, I could feel his eyes on me but I didn't look back. I didn't want to fall under his spell. I didn't even know why I was thinking these thoughts. This is a business transaction, this is work to him. He must get this all the time, girls falling at his feet. His protected girls probably falling for his good looks and charm. Well, I can't say charm because he clearly hasn't got any. I felt myself getting really wound up and agitated by him. I needed to get out for a little while, for some drinks with Brooke or something.

I walked into my shower and washed the sweat off me then threw my jeans and jumper on with my converse before picking my phone up and calling Brooke. After a couple of rings she answered.

"Hey, bitch face," she said with a smile in her voice.

"Lovely, and hey to you too," I said, a bit bummed out.

"What's up?" she asked, clearly sensing my tone.

"So, the bodyguard is here. He's rude and arrogant. I don't know how I am going to stomach a week with him." I shook my head as I looked at myself in the mirror, looking at my outfit.

"Well, the good thing is you will have us. So, at least we can keep you occupied," she said.

"I suppose, it's just infuriating. I was just in the gym and he walked in. He walks around like he owns every room he walks into. I'm not sure why my dad thought he was a good fit. He is awful." I sighed. "Anyway, I was calling to see if you wanted to meet me for a couple of cocktails, I need to get out. I feel like I am going stir crazy at home."

"I'm always up for cocktails, can't have a late night though. Got a crazy busy day and don't wanna piss Ryan off at work tomorrow, otherwise I definitely won't be able to get him into my knickers." She laughed.

"You're gross," I said disgusted. "Anyway, meet me in about forty minutes. We will go to that cute cocktail bar round the corner from you."

"No worries, shall I invite the rest, or did you want

some Brookey time?" she teased.

"Just you," I said as I ran a brush through my hair.

"No worries, I'll see you soon," she replied.

"I'm just going to put a bit of makeup on then I'll be leaving, in say, ten minutes."

"Perfect, I'll leave the same time," she agreed before we said our goodbyes.

I sat down at my dressing table and put a light layer of foundation on before adding some bronzer and mascara, then finished my lips in a matte red lipstick. I rubbed my lips together, removed any excess lipstick and made my way downstairs.

I tried to sneak quietly past my dad, but it didn't happen. "Where you going?" he asked me.

"Just popping to see Brooke, I won't be long. I've got to drop something to her," I said, continuing to walk to the cloak room to get my faux fur coat.

"I don't think so, not without Taron. I have told you this. Why do you have to defy me?" he said annoyed.

"Because I don't need a babysitter to go to Brookes." I raised my voice out of frustration.

"You know the rules. Don't argue against me, Luna, or this will be a lot worse for you," he snapped. "Trust me."

I bowed my head in defeat before nibbling on my long, acrylic nails. I didn't want to look up, so stayed looking at my feet whilst my dad called for Taron. I expected to see him in a suit, but he was rocking jeans, trainers and a crew neck jumper with a black hooded parker folded over his forearm.

"David," he greeted my father, with a tone full of authority.

"Taron, please supervise my daughter with her visit to her friends in St Katherines Dock. She apparently needs to take something to her," he said with disbelief lacing his voice as he raised his eyebrows at me.

"Certainly, sir, not a problem." He nodded at my dad then stood beside me.

"Ready, Miss Luna?" he asked politely. Oh, he was good. Putting on a sweet show for daddy dearest. Where has the cocky Taron gone from earlier?

"Yes," I snapped as I opened the front door and marched out without him.

"Have fun," my dad called after me, clearly enjoying this a little too much for my liking. I didn't stop to see if Taron had caught up with me, I was too angry.

"Luna, wait up," he said as he jogged up next to me. "Stop being a brat."

I stopped in my tracks to face him. "I'm far from a brat, I just don't understand why I need a chaperone," I moaned at him.

"You don't need to understand why, just accept it," he said coolly as I started walking again.

"I have roamed these streets a plenty without a

babysitter," I huffed.

"I am sure you have, but things have changed. Your dad wants you looked after, and that's what I'm here for." He smiled down at me. I wanted to look at him, but I couldn't, I was too angry.

After a few moments of silence he started asking questions.

"Do you really need to go to Brooke's? Or did you just want to get out the house for a bit?" he asked concerned, with a soft tone.

"I don't need to drop anything to her, no, but I am meeting her for cocktails," I answered quickly. "And, yes, I wanted to get out the house," I admitted.

He nodded as if he understood before we continued our journey towards St Katherines Dock.

"You forget how beautiful London is," he muttered as we walked out of London Bridge station. "You take it for granted when you see it every day." He continued talking and I stayed silent. I felt myself relax once I saw the cocktail bar that I was meeting Brooke in.

"Just in here," I mumbled before walking in. "And try and fit in." I rolled my eyes.

The warmth of the bar hit us as soon as the door opened. It was so cosy in here, and it was one of our favourite spots to meet. I scanned the room but couldn't see her yet. Damn, I wanted her to be here before us, so I didn't have to spend my time talking to Taron.

I walked over to a little booth right near the window and sat down, taking my coat off and folding it up next to me. Taron sat opposite me, his eyes on me the whole time. We didn't speak, just sat with our eyes locked whilst we waited for the server to come over.

"Hey, can I get you two some drinks?" she asked politely, holding her gaze on Taron.

"Hey, yes, please. Can we have two cosmos, two pornstar martinis and, Taron?" I held my hand out gesturing for him to speak.

"I'll take a water please," he said politely.

"A water?" I asked a little taken back. "Do you not want a beer or anything?"

"No thank you, ma'am. I don't drink on the job," he said bluntly, a hint of a smile on his face.

"Right-eo," I replied sarcastically. The girl took that as her cue to leave.

"So, four cocktails, aye?" he asked.

"Yup, two for me, two for Brooke," I replied cockily with a shrug of my shoulders.

"Let me guess, you're the cosmopolitan," he teased.

"I am indeed," I said proudly.

"Are you and your friends like *sex and the city* wannabes?" he teased once more. "Let me guess, you're Carrie?"

"No!" I snapped at him, my eyes on the door, praying that Brooke would walk through any minute.

"Okay then," he said holding his hands up in an apologetic manner, showing that he knew he hit a nerve.

I was grateful when I saw the waitress return with our drinks. I kept my eyes on her as she placed the two cosmos down in front of me, the pornstar martinis next to mine and then handed Taron his tap water. He dazzled her with his smile before she walked away giggling. I understood her reaction, I really did, because on the surface he was most girls fantasy. Just, unfortunately, the inside of him wasn't as dreamy.

I was just about to call Brooke when I saw her gorgeous red hair through the crowds. Within seconds she was at the booth.

"Well, hello, you," she said as she took a seat next to Taron. "You're very easy on the eyes," she cooed at him. He smiled at her before turning to face me once more.

"Don't make his head and ego any bigger than it needs to be. Brooke this is Taron. Taron, Brooke." I smiled sweetly as I introduced them.

"Oh, one of them, is he?" She laughed before picking up her cocktail. We clinked our glasses before both taking a mouthful.

"Now, Taron. Am I going to be able to talk about personal stuff without you judging me and running back to my dad?" I asked seriously as I kept my eyes locked to his.

"Pinkie promise." He grinned, and my eyes

narrowed on him. "No, seriously though, I have the ability to let things I hear on the job go in one ear and out the other, so you're safe to chat away," he said before taking a sip of his water.

"Eww, what is he drinking?" Brooke asked disgusted.

"I know," I answered with an eye roll. "Anyway," I said taking our conversation away from him. "How are you? Things going well with Ryan?" I winked.

"Don't. It is so frustrating," she whined. "I really like him, and I know he likes me back, but he is just playing hard to get." I couldn't help but laugh at her.

"Why don't you tell him you like him?" I asked the simplest question that would solve her issue.

"Because, ladies don't do that. If he likes me, he will stop being a pussy about it and ask me," she said in a huff before knocking back her champagne shot that accompanied her cocktail.

"Erm, I'm pretty sure ladies do. This is a woman's world now a days, is it not?" I argued.

"It is indeed, but this world is still a man's world, baby," she said with confidence. "I am this close." She held her hand up, putting a small gap between her thumb and index finger to show just how close she was. "I'm this close to laying myself naked on his desk."

I choked on my drink as I saw Taron spit his water out of his mouth and across the table in shock at what had just come out of her mouth. Brooke faced him, disgusted by his outburst.

"What happened to, *"it goes in one ear and out the other,"* she mimicked him.

By this point I was crying of laughter. Taron was clearly embarrassed, but I don't think it was from being caught out, I think he was mortified at her outburst of what she wants to do to Ryan.

"Anyway, ears off, Taron," she hissed at him. "Anymore on Josh?"

I was getting sick of the question, but not sick enough to not answer it.

"Another three texts today. Part of me wants to block his number, but then I think I would miss the texts. I know it's sad but at least it is something I am getting from him. I would have rather a husband who didn't leave me before we were due to be married, but can't have it all, can I?" I bit my lip before flitting my eyes up to Taron who was staring out the window.

"It will get easier," Brooke assured me.

"Oh, I know. I just want it to be easier now, but I know it all takes time." I nodded. "Twenty five and left and unwanted because, *"this wasn't the life he wanted at twenty five,"* I said in a sarcastic voice before taking a mouthful of my drink.

"How could I have been so stupid?" I said quietly, hoping no one heard me.

Brooke took my hand and rubbed her thumb across

the back of my knuckles, whilst Taron turned his attention to me giving me a sympathetic look. I didn't care that he was clearly listening. I didn't care what he heard.

In that moment, I just wanted to be wrapped up in Josh's arms with him whispering in my ear how much he loved me.

Chapter FIVE

The morning was soon upon us, and I couldn't wait to get away. I had a few things to do before we left, and my new mate had to follow me around. I needed to get my eyelashes done and my waxing, then my nails re-done. I needed to get some bikinis which was going to be impossible in October, but I was hoping my friend Lena would have put some aside at her shop for me, then I had to pack. Plus I had to run to my shop to just check in, make sure everything was running okay. I knew it would be as I left Eva in charge and she is more than capable, but I find it hard to let go.

I tied my hair up into a messy ponytail and rubbed my lips together to make sure my nude lipstick was even. I gave myself one last look over in the full length mirror. I chose black skinny jeans, grey Uggs and an oversized grey jumper which had buttons down the back.

I made my way downstairs to see Taron standing at the bottom of the stairs waiting for me, standing there with his hands crossed in front of him. He was wearing black suit trousers that were tight and perfectly fitted, a tight, white shirt and tanned brogues. He looked incredible. His jet black hair was styled back with a small amount of gel. I can't deny the attraction, but his personality just puts me off of him.

"Ready?" I asked as I grabbed my tanned trench coat.

"Indeed, are you?" he asked.

"Obviously." I rolled my eyes at him. I grabbed my black Chanel shoulder bag off of the side unit then opened the front door, not waiting for him.

"You in a mood?" he asked me as he trailed behind me.

"Nope, just a lot to do." I looked back at him as I answered.

"Where first?" he asked.

"Lashes." I smiled at him as we walked towards the train station.

After a couple of stops we got off and made our way to the small beauty boutique that I use.

"You can sit out here," I said coldly as we walked into the waiting room.

"Sorry, ma'am, strict instructions that I need to be with you at *all* times." He stated the obvious.

"Fine." I sulked as I sat down.

"You're such a brat," he teased as he sat next to me.

"Be careful not to rip your overly tight suit trousers as you sit." I smirked as he sat down.

"Oh, I will," he said as a laugh left him, which made me laugh with him.

A few moments passed when Lily walked out to greet me. "Luna, ready?" she asked as she held the beauty room door open.

"Yup," I said as I stood up and marched into the room. Lily went to shut the door on Taron, when he held his hand out, stopping it from shutting.

"Sorry, I am under orders to accompany Luna at all times," he said sternly.

Lily gave me the look as if he was making it up.

"I wish he was joking, but he's not." I shook my head as I laid on the bed. Taron went to sit at my foot end when I raised myself up onto my elbows, staring straight at him.

"Uh, no. No chance. This end, buddy," I said, pointing my finger up my head end.

I saw the smile creep on his face, revealing his perfectly white teeth. Seriously, the man needed to be a model or something, not a bloody body guard. But then, if he looks after women most of the time, he probably gets enough sex. I laid myself back down as I groaned, throwing my arm over my face. I was mortified.

"Nice to see you, hun. Last time I saw you was before

your wedding…" Her voice trailed off.

"I know, feels like that was a lifetime ago already." I sighed.

"No update from him?" Lily asked.

"Nope, grovelling messages but I haven't had one today. Maybe he has finally given up? I can't bring myself to message him back," I said.

"I understand, hun. I still can't believe he did that to you, the bastard."

"I know, but he must have had his reasons, right? Anyway, I am firm believer of everything happens for a reason." I bit my lip as I said it. I felt like I could burst into tears and I couldn't do that seeing as my eyes were taped shut whilst Lily worked her magic with my lash extensions. We carried on in idle chit chat after that, not talking about Josh any more.

Two hours later, I was done. Taron sat in complete silence the whole time. Poor sod. I couldn't believe that he sat there while I had my waxing done, I was mortified. Once done with Lily, I moved into Marie's room where I sat down waiting for my nails to be done.

"Fancy getting some lunch after this?" Taron asked.

"We could do. Let me see what time we get out of here, okay?" I replied with a small smile.

"Okay, boss," he said as he sat down in the corner in silence once more.

Luckily, we were only in here for half an hour as I had red gel put on my existing acrylics. Not sure why I went for red, but inspiration hit. I was frustrated with having to go through the same chit chat with Marie as I had with Lily. I was so relieved to walk out of there. I embraced the cold, fresh air.

"So, lunch?" Taron asked as he walked beside me, his hands in his pockets.

"A quick bite, okay? I need to go shopping and pop to my shop." I smiled up at him. He was a giant.

"A quick bite is perfect, I don't want to keep you away from doing your errands." He smiled back down at me.

"Perfect," I agreed as we walked towards a small deli restaurant.

We sat down at a small table and were handed menus as soon as our arses hit the seats. I browsed the menu quickly, my belly rumbling.

"What do you fancy?" Taron asked me.

"Not sure, maybe a panini? Quick and easy." I smiled.

"Sounds good. Pesto, mozzarella and tomatoes?"

"Fab," I said quietly as I tucked a loose strand of hair behind my ear. I let out a held breath when the waitress come over to take our orders. Taron ordered for me.

"What do you want to drink?" he asked.

"Just a water please." I smiled at him, then to the

waitress.

"Two waters please," he asked her before she walked away.

"So tell me about yourself, Taron," I asked.

"Not much to tell. I have been a bodyguard for ten years, I am 35, my dad was Italian, my mum American. I grew up in California, but have lived here for fifteen years, and I don't think I would ever want to go back to America. Yeah, it's nice, but I prefer it here, I think." He smiled. "I would ask about you, but for the last two days I have heard everything I think I need to know." A small smile creeps onto his perfect face. He is annoyingly good looking.

"Is there a Mrs Sloane?" I asked before taking a bit of my panini.

"Unfortunately not. My work doesn't really allow me to date seriously," he said, his dark brown eyes flicking up to look at me. That's his way of saying he was a male slut.

"I'm sure when I meet the right girl I will give this all up, but at the moment I enjoy my job too much. The money is good, and I get to meet all sorts of people." He winked at me.

Of course you do.

"I can't work you out. You're like Jekyll and Hyde," I joked.

"I do have two sides, my work side and my actual side. Only a few people know my *real* side," he stated.

"Must be exhausting having two personalities," I

said quietly after taking a mouthful of my water.

"You do get used to it," He sighed. "Part of the job."

I felt sorry for him, putting up some pretence all for work, but then I can imagine he is getting paid the big bucks for looking after me, so being two different people for the right amount of cash probably isn't that hard.

"Come on, let me get the bill and we can go," he said as he walked towards the bar to pay. I didn't get a chance to argue with him, but I would treat him to a coffee or something later, once we are finished.

I finished my water and stood up, waiting for Taron. I felt his hand on the small of my back, butterflies fluttered in my stomach, my skin heating up from his touch.

"Ready?" he asked.

I nodded happily as we started walking towards the exit.

"Let's go bikini shopping, yay," he said sarcastically in a high-pitched voice which made me giggle.

We jumped back on the tube to get to Oxford street. I was hoping that one of my favourite little shops still had some bikinis, my friend owned it, so hopefully she had some out back. I smiled as we walked into the hustle and bustle of Oxford Street. You get all walks of life here. Taron stayed close as we made it through the busy crowds before getting to my friends' shop.

"It's manic out there," I said as I walked through the door.

"Hey, girl," I heard Lena call out. "I'll be out in a sec." I heard her bashing around. "Oh, check the specials rail, there are some bits that I know you won't be able to resist."

She was right, I could never resist her clothes. She was a goddess. She made all of them herself which was amazing, then when I wanted something that no one else had, she was my girl.

I started browsing through the rack when I saw a stunning lemon summer dress. I held it up against my petite frame, and the skirt sat halfway down my thigh. The dress was sweetheart necked, and to be honest it would make my boobs look amazing.

"I'm just going to try this on, Taron, take a seat." I held my hand out to a stunning shabby-chic chair in the corner by the changing room. He looked at me and nodded before taking a seat.

I slipped behind the curtain and took my outfit off. I checked myself out in the mirror, I have definitely lost a few pounds, luckily not from my boobs. I slipped the soft lemon dress up my thighs and pulled it up round my torso, then tucked my boobs into the tight material across my chest. I reached round to the back and pulled the zip up but could only get it halfway up. I tried numerous times before giving up.

I pulled back the curtain. “Taron, can you help me?” I asked quietly.

He looked up from his phone. “Certainly,” he said before standing up and walking towards me.

“I can’t get my zipper up,” I admitted, embarrassed.

“No problem.” He smiled as he pulled the curtain back. I turned around slowly, then pulled my long pony tail over my shoulder. I felt his breath on my neck which made goose-bumps appear all over my skin.

He gripped onto the zipper, tugging it a bit harder than he should have before pulling it up to just under my shoulder blades. He stayed behind me as I dropped my ponytail back down. I looked over my shoulder, my eyes down then slowly flitting up to him, his eyes boring into mine.

His hand came to my side before he traced his index finger up the side of my body. My breath hitched, my heart raced, the nerves were running through me and I didn’t know why. It took everything in me to pull my eyes away from him. There was a definite pull, his other hand still on the zipper.

“So sorry, I’m here, just sorting out some bits for you.” Lena appeared, a smug look all over her face when she saw me and Taron. He dropped his arm from my side.

“Am I interrupting something here?” she asked, hands still full of clothes and bikinis.

“Noooo,” I said, shaking my head, spinning round

and covering my already covered chest. Taron stepped back and sat back on his chair, his head low.

"Taron is my bodyguard." I coughed, clearing my throat.

"Oh, bodyguard." She turned around and licked her lips. "He's a beaut." She chuckled as she ushered me back into the changing room, pulling the curtain and facing me with her mouth wide open, a shocked expression on her face.

"Oh my God, he is so hot," she whispered to me.

"Shush," I scolded her, narrowing my eyes on her and looking round at the closed curtain.

"He can't hear me," she said with her eyebrows pulled. I rolled my eyes at her comment.

"No he can't hear, but I don't want to talk about it now." I shook my head. "Now, show me the bikinis." I smiled. "Plus, I am taking this dress." I winked at her.

"You can have it as a gift if you promise to take him out." She smiled sweetly at me.

"We will see. I am still trying to piece together the whole Josh situation," I said bluntly, wanting to change the subject as quickly as possible.

"Again, show me the bikinis," I snapped then blew her a kiss.

I picked up a scalloped bikini in yellow. I was worried it would wash me out even more than I already am. I slipped it on over my undies and took my bra off as I positioned the scallop top. Surprisingly the yellow made my skin pop. I tried a bandeau black bikini on and a red thong swimsuit which I would have never normally worn, but this was my failed honeymoon, so why the hell not?

We left the changing room where Taron was sitting on his phone.

"I'm done, you ready?" I asked. He nodded as he stood up and stretched his arms up above his head, showing a bit of his tanned belly and revealing a black trimmed snail trail. I ignored the fire that lit up in my belly as I walked towards the till. I handed Lena my card and took my new purchases. I kissed Lena on the cheek and said we should try and catch up when I was back next week.

Taron stayed close as we walked back onto the busy high street, and we made our way to my shop in Kensington. I loved Kensington, it was a lot quieter than most of the towns around here, plus it was stunning.

I couldn't wait to get back to my mum and dad's townhouse. I felt knackered already, but one more stop and then I could go home and pack my suitcase ready for tomorrow.

Chapter
SIX

We walked slowly up to my shop, and I smiled as I saw people entering. I had flowers all up the outside and across the sign of the shop. I wanted to make it pretty and relevant, and being a florist and a cake shop, I thought it was quite fitting.

I opened the dark green double doors and smiled as I heard the bell ring. To the right of the store was the cake and coffee area with beautiful, mismatched shabby chic tables and chairs. Then as soon as you walked in you were in the florist side of the shop.

I sought out Eva who was rushing about going through the order book. I turned back to face Taron.

"Go wait for me in there, I won't be a moment," I said as he nodded. I walked away towards my friend.

"Hey," I called out as I walked towards Eva. "All okay?"

She looked up, her cheeks flustered slightly, her brown, pixie cut hair styled.

"All fine, just going through the orders. The books opened for Christmas this week, so it's been go, go, go." She smiled at me.

"Oh, of course! Sorry I have been completely out of it," I said with an ashamed look on my face.

"Don't be silly, you've had a lot on," she said with grimace. I didn't want to bring the whole Josh situation up again. I am sick of hearing his name today.

"Anyway, I just wanted to pop in and make sure everything was running okay? Do you need help with anything before I leave for my single-moon?" I joked... Well, I tried to joke.

"Not help as such, but we can't get this arrangement right. It's out back, come see," Eva said as she pushed open the door to the back where the flowers are stored.

It was a beautiful rose and lily arrangement, and I could see what she meant. It just didn't look right. I smiled at Jane and Michelle who were sorting flowers out behind me.

"Hi, girls," I said as I stared at the arrangement, cocking my head to the side.

"Michelle, can you grab me another deep red rose please? Preferably one that is fully bloomed," I asked sweetly.

Michelle looked through the boxes on the floor, pulling out a big rose and handing it to me. I took a few thorns off then cut the stalk to the right length and pushed two of the white lilies back before slotting the big, deep red rose back into the middle. Then I pulled two smaller lilies in front of the rose and rearranged the rest of the smaller roses around the side. I took a step back and tilted my head to look at it. That looked better. I nodded at my thoughts.

"What do we think?" I asked for Eva, Michelle and Jane's opinion.

"Perfect, this is why we need you." Eva laughed.

"You don't *need* me, sometimes it just needs a fresh pair of eyes, and mine are fresh." I winked at them. "Okay, anything else?"

Eva shook her head. "We can manage. Now, go and enjoy your holiday." She smiled at me. I said my goodbyes and walked towards Taron who was looking out the window, watching the world go by.

"Hey," I said as I walked up behind him, distracting him.

"Hey." He smiled at me. "All sorted?"

"Yup. Go sit down, I'll get us a cake and coffee. Any preference?" I asked.

"Americano, no milk, and surprise me on the cake front," he said patting his belly. "I love a cake." He winked at me before sitting back down.

I couldn't help but smile, it was nice having someone who could have a laugh and actually be kind instead of an uptight, stuffy, boring bodyguard.

"Tegan." I smiled at her as she walked out from the kitchen at the back. "Can I have a black Americano and a cappuccino please?"

I stared at the selection of cakes that were sitting on display. If we had more time I would have made fresh cakes for me and Taron, but I wanted to sit down for ten and make our way home. I stared over at him. He was sitting, staring out at Kensington, my shopping bags sitting at his feet.

"Sorry, can I have two of the Victoria sponge cupcakes please" I asked Tegan as she handed me the coffees. I walked them over to our table, placing Taron's in front of him then walked back to grab our cakes. These were my favourite. Soft madeira sponge, the inside filled with rich buttercream and strawberry jam, and on top, a big swirl of buttercream, a fresh strawberry, and dusted with icing sugar. I bit my lip, trying to stop my mouth watering. These really were the best.

I sat down opposite Taron, sliding him his cake. "Enjoy." I smiled at him, showing him my straight, pure white teeth.

"You do have a lovely smile," Taron said.

"Thank you. I have been told it is one of my best features." I shrugged, flitting my eyes to the ceiling and looking through my lashes, my lips touching as I smiled.

"Thank you for the coffee and cake," he said gratefully.

"No problem, it's the least I can do seeing as you've been so patient today." I smiled again.

"It's my job, Luna, I actually had a nice day," he said before biting into the Victoria sponge cupcake, me watching him as the icing sugar left a dusting all over his lips. He let out a small moan as he enjoyed the cake.

"These are good, do you make these?" he asked me.

"I do." I nodded, choosing to break my cupcake up instead of biting into it. "But obviously not these ones. I normally get here about five thirty-six to make the cakes and sandwiches, with help from one of the other girls. I like to make sure everything for the day is made that morning, then whatever we don't sell I take to the local homeless shelter, along with a few trays of coffees, teas and hot chocolates."

I licked some buttercream off of my finger and placed my cupcake down. I touched my lip with my index finger to indicate to Taron that he still had the icing sugar on his lips. He cleared his throat as he grabbed a napkin and wiped his mouth.

"Thanks," he muttered, his eyes on mine, then looking down to his coffee. "That's a really nice thing you do by the way, with the left overs."

"It's the least I can do. Yes, I have money and have grown up wanting nothing, but I know there are people out there with nothing. I am a big charity giver, I always feel I have too much, so I like to give back where I can." I smiled at him.

"That's amazing, Luna. I've worked for a lot of big shots, none of them as kind as you, but I'm sure you have your faults," he teased before standing and picking my bags up from the floor. "You ready to go?"

I nodded and took the last mouthful of my coffee before standing up. "I am so ready to go home." I laughed. "I feel dead on my feet."

We decided on a cab home, I couldn't be bothered with the hustle and bustle of the trains this evening. After a long ride, we were finally home. I let out a deep sigh as I walked towards my mum and dad's town house. We walked through the door together, Taron nodded and placed my bags on the floor before taking his coat off and hanging it up in the cloak closet. I smiled at him as I shrugged my coat off my shoulders, hanging it up as Taron still held the door open.

"Thank you," I whispered to him.

"For what?" he asked as he shut the door behind me.

"For today, for being nice and not arrogant." I winked at him, picking my bags up and making my way towards the stairs. "Also, you're relieved for the evening," I called out as I carried on up the sweeping staircase and into my room.

I dropped my bags down and fell onto my bed. My God it was nice to be home. I checked my phone, it had been in my Chanel all day and I hadn't checked it once.

Being with Taron kept me occupied, I never once wanted to sit and stare at my phone. I had messages from all three of the girls, and no more messages from Josh.

I don't know what to feel. My heart still hurt, I felt like I would never get over him. But then spending today with Taron made me realize that maybe, one day in the future, I could find love and be happy again, mending my shattered heart. I couldn't cry anymore. I feel the lump grow but then nothing happens. It's as if my eyes are all cried out.

The evenings are the worst. I get lonely. I miss his warm skin next to mine, his tattooed chest and torso that I used to trace my fingertips up and down. I missed his scent, his eyes, his lips and his kiss. Then the burn started, and I swallowed it back down. I refused to feel like this any longer. He didn't want me, he left me and didn't really give me any real explanation why.

I deserved so much more than him. I really did.

I threw my phone down and pushed myself up off the bed, walking slowly into my bathroom in a daze. I started to run a bath as I undressed myself, then pulled my hair out of its pony tail, shaking my head to loosen the achy feeling from having my hair too tight.

I stood in my white lacey bra and matching thong as I stared into the mirror, looking at myself, trying to see all the things I loved about my body. I pulled my eyes away as I heard someone clear their throat. I twisted my head round quickly to see Taron standing there, my eyes wide like a deer in headlights before pulling a large towel sheet off of the towel rail and covering myself. I felt my skin turning crimson, burning across my face.

"Taron..." I said breathlessly.

"Luna." He smirked.

"Can I help you?" My voice was shaky.

"Your mum wanted me to let you know that we are out for dinner tonight with Chris." He nodded. I tightened the towel round my body, clinging onto the top of it. He walked closer to me, his eyes on mine, his lip between his teeth.

"Right," I whispered, trying to steady my breathing. "Thanks," I muttered after clearing my throat.

"Enjoy your bath." His voice was husky as he winked at me, stepping back. "And, I wasn't looking, so please don't flatter yourself," he said before turning on his heel and walking out the room.

I let out a deep sigh, clinging onto the sink edge. I felt humiliated from his comment. Talk about kick a girl while she's down. He was so frustrating. How could he be so sweet today, even after our moment in the changing room? I was still clutching onto my towel with my other hand, when I heard the sound of water over spilling. I moved quickly over to the bath and turned it off.

"Shit," I moaned as I stepped in the puddle of water on my tiled bathroom floor. I laid some towels down before opening the plug and letting the water run out a bit. I just wanted a bath, and that douche had to ruin it.

I put my head in my hands and shook my head. I felt pathetic. Josh, Taron, my head spun. I dropped the towel, pulled my knickers down then un-clipped my bra as I dipped my toe into the bath. I let out a sigh of relief as I sunk into the hot bubble bath, then disappeared under the water. I wanted to stay under here, but of course, I couldn't. I had to come up and breathe at some point, even though I had this crushing weight in my chest.

Rejected again, and this time by a bodyguard.

Maybe I was really just that bad? I needed my bed, and I needed a decent night's sleep before tomorrow. And I still hadn't packed.

I wasn't excited about Hawaii anymore; my stomach was in knots and full of dread.

Chapter SEVEN

We stood at Heathrow, waiting to be called to our plane. I couldn't wait to get some sunshine on my skin. I had hardly said two words to Taron since last night, I was still reeling. He didn't act like a thirty-five-year-old, he acted more like a fifteen-year-old. I rolled my eyes at my thoughts.

"You okay?" Vanessa asked me.

"Mmm hmm." I nodded whilst flicking through my magazine. I was saving my books for the beach. "I just want to get on the plane, and away from him." I nodded towards Taron. Vanessa just nodded in agreement.

"I'm sure we can lose him." She nudged me before breaking into a giggle.

Brooke arrived with a bagful of snacks and Ava was typing away on her phone. I felt a breath of relief leave me when the tannoy called our flight number. I collected my handbag, then stood up as Taron walked towards me, making him stop in his tracks. I threw him a filthy look over my shoulder before storming away towards the gate.

Me and Josh booked Upper Class suites. I offered to pay for the girls to upgrade as I didn't think it was fair that they were splurging out all this money for my failed marriage. They argued it, but I upgraded them once Ava had booked them onto our flight.

Unfortunately, my dad booked Taron into the same class as us, which was frustrating. It would have been nice to have a long flight without him.

We sat in our seats, and I smiled as I watched how excited the girls were. They placed their bags next to them and took the free champagne that was being offered around. I took my glass and took a small sip, instantly relaxing as the bubbles swam down my throat like pure silk.

I looked behind me to see Taron folding his suit jacket up and placing it on his duffle bag before sitting down, then refusing a glass of champagne. I saw his eyes on mine. I couldn't help but stare into his deep, brown eyes. It's like he wanted to say something, but he wouldn't. Or couldn't. I didn't care, I didn't want to hear his excuses for being rude yesterday about my appearance.

I know I'm no oil painting but I'm not repulsive... Well, maybe I am in his eyes? I know you can't be everyone's type, but I felt like something happened between us yesterday. If we weren't interrupted, something may have happened. I was getting ahead of myself, it was just nice having... Well, thinking someone was interested in me after Josh.

Maybe he found me repulsive as well? Maybe the thought of him spending the rest of his life with me made him feel sick to the pit of his stomach?

I just wanted to close my eyes and wake up in Hawaii. Brooke must've known what was running through my mind. Okay, not the Taron bit as no one knows what happened whilst we were shopping and after, but she knew what was going through my mind with being here, where I should have been with Josh.

I looked over at Brooke and shook my head as she went to stand. I was fine. This feeling would soon leave, and I'd be back to normal. She gave me a sympathetic smile before getting her book out of her bag, then put her earphones in. I sighed in relief. As much as I wanted to talk to her, I was glad for the peace and quiet.

I pulled my magazine and book out and started to read, being lost in the book world for the first eleven hours to Los Angeles seemed like a pretty good idea at the moment.

We were finally on our second flight from LA into Honolulu airport. I felt sticky and clammy from the long flight and short stop over. I excused myself from my seat and made my way down the aisle. As much as I felt the pull towards Taron, I wasn't letting my eyes betray me and meet his gaze.

I felt his eyes burn into mine as I walked quickly past his chair and made my way into the toilet. I shut the door quickly behind me, letting out the breath that I had been holding as soon as the door locked. I looked at myself in the mirror... I looked like hell. My blond hair was greasy and tied into a messy bun, my eyes dull. My baggy jumper and leggings felt like they were sticking to me. I felt hot and stuffy. I couldn't wait to land and have a decent shower.

I started running the cold tap and splashed my face a few times to try and cool me down. I placed my hands either side of the basin and closed my eyes, bowing my head in defeat. Defeated with myself.

Why did I agree to do this? I should have just cancelled this *honeymoon* and stayed at home, crying in my pyjamas all day, every day, whilst stuffing my face with a huge tub of ice cream. My God, I was so pathetic.

I was distracted when I heard a knock on the door. I looked back in the mirror and ran my fingers under my eyes to remove the smudged eyeliner. There was another knock, this time it was harder. I shook my head frustrated.

I slid the lock on the door across and opened it with force, catching my breath when I saw who was on the other side. Taron. My heart started racing, my adrenaline pumping through my body. He never affected me like this before yesterday. Yes, I fancied him. He was a god, who wouldn't? But this was a whole new feeling. My eyes were wide as I focused on him.

"Taron," I whispered, my knuckles white from gripping the door so tight.

"I just wanted to make sure you were okay, you looked a little pale when you walked past me." He looked concerned. My expression softened, as did my grip on the door. I let my arm drop as I relaxed. He stepped closer to me, towering over me. I felt my breath catch as I felt his stare penetrate mine.

His hand came up to my face, my throat tightening, my heart thumping in my chest. I am sure he can see it trying to escape my skin. I was frozen on the spot. I wanted to move but my feet wouldn't let me.

His fingers touched my ivory skin, sending an electrifying tingle to my core. He ran his finger slowly down my cheek before running it back up and tucking a loose strand of hair behind my ear. His warm breath was on my face, and I could tell his breathing was affected as well as mine.

He did feel something for me.

Or was he just that good at pretending?

He moved even closer, his neck craning, his lips inches away from mine. I bit my lip, trying to stop myself from lunging at him and placing my full lips onto his. I tilted my chin upwards slightly, trying to give him the green light to kiss me.

God, I wanted him to kiss me.

His hand moved up to my hip, gripping it tightly, his eyes closing as he took in my scent. His lips edged closer to mine when the plane hit a bout of turbulence and knocked me back. I grabbed onto the sink, stopping myself from hitting the floor, but Taron was hurled into me, knocking us both to the floor. My breathing fastened, his weight crushed me but in a good way.

I wanted to feel his weight on top of me, just not on the plane bathroom floor. Taron's eyes went wide as he pushed himself off of me, clearly embarrassed by what had just happened, his face full of disgust. He shook his head as he steadied himself.

"We are never going to happen," he grunted, his brows furrowed, his voice angry as he stormed out of the bathroom. Once again, I was humiliated by him. Why do I let this happen? He doesn't like me, and I don't know why I keep thinking it will change.

I pulled myself off the floor before washing my hands. I was angry. Hell, I was more than angry, I was livid. I bolted out of the bathroom and flew down the aisle before stopping at Taron's seat. I may be little, but my temper is larger than life.

"Luna," he said quietly, his eyes darting back and forth to mine, hooded and dark.

"Humiliate me once, shame on me. Humiliate me twice, shame on you," I spat before lifting my hand back and slapping his face so hard my hand instantly stung. I felt satisfied hearing the noise that came from my hand contacting his skin. His eyes went wide as he looked at me in shock. He shot up from his seat, seething, then realising where we were. He craned his neck into my ear, running his fingers slowly round my neck.

"If we weren't on a plane full of your friends, I would take you right here, right now, but not because of attraction," he whispered, standing back up, smirking, his eyes meeting mine. I didn't care about his threat. I was so done with him.

"I hate you," I hissed. "As soon as this holiday is finished, so are you."

I sat in my seat trying to calm my breathing. Brooke and Ness stared at me, trying to suss out what the hell just happened. My chest was rising so fast I was scared I was going to give myself a panic attack. I closed my eyes and took some small, deep breaths, trying to calm my breathing.

After a few minutes, I felt in control again. He knew better than to come at me again. I knew he was still sitting in his seat, but I couldn't bear to turn around and look at his face.

I called the air hostess over and ordered a bottle of champagne, I needed something to keep my mind off of what I just did. I had never reacted like that. I do have a temper, but I have never reacted that quickly.

Taron infuriates me, but I want him so bad at the same time. And it's true, I do hate him. I want this holiday over already. I roll my eyes at myself.

The air hostess was back within a few minutes with my champagne and glass. I thanked her before pouring my first glass. A few hours left and I'll be feeling the sand between my toes.

I sighed in relief as we made our way off the plane, the hot air hitting me as the door opened. The intense sun beating down on us, making our skin tingle. I breathed in a deep breath through my nose, the Hawaiian air hit my nostrils with a sweet scent. I smiled as I walked carefully down the plane steps and waited for the girls at the bottom.

I didn't care for Taron, so I left him walking behind us, where he belonged.

After an hour and a half in the airport, going through passport control and waiting for our luggage, we were finally on the transfer to the resort. I closed my eyes for most of the trip, only opening them to text my mum to let her know that we had arrived safely and were on the way to our resort.

The girls were talking quietly and, unfortunately for me, I had Sloane next to me. I couldn't deny the feelings that he made me feel, but it was quite clear that the feelings aren't mutual. I closed my eyes again and tried to ignore the pull between us and just focused on the fact that I'll be away from him soon enough.

"Luna." I heard a soft voice in the distance. "Luna," the voice whispered again.

I stirred and slowly opened my eyes. His dark brown eyes were staring into mine, my name still escaping his full lips, "Luna, we are here," he said softly, tucking a strand of loose blond hair out of my face. I pulled back, sinking into my seat.

"What are you doing?" I asked, pushing the loose bit of hair behind my ear, my large, green eyes wide in confusion.

"I was waking you up, what did you think I was doing?" he asked.

I huffed as I stood up and pulled my bag out of the overhead compartment and hopped off the bus, waiting for the driver to get our suitcases from under the coach. I snatched my suitcase off of the driver before making my way up the grand entrance of the resort. I stood at the check in, waiting for the girls to catch me up before booking us in.

"Aloha, welcome to Turtle Bay. My name is Luana." The pretty lady behind the check in desk smiled at me.

"Hey," I said quietly. "We have a reservation under the name Smith."

"No problem, let me check that for you." She beamed

as she tapped away on her keyboard. I took this moment to study her, she was beautiful. Long, black wavy hair and stunning ocean, blue eyes. I smiled at her white frangipani flower in her hair. It was a stunning flower. We only used them on special occasions at home due to the climate and expense.

I felt eyes boring into the back of my head. I turned slowly and looked over my shoulder to see Sloane staring at me, a small smirk appearing on his face. I felt myself blush before turning round to Luana.

"Okay, so I have the honeymoon suite, congratulations." She smiled at me, then her eyes darted to the girls, then finally Taron.

"We only have the booking for two... For you and your husband..." Her smile faded as her voice trailed off.

"Sorry, what?" I panicked, then laughed in hysteria. At this point Ava walked up beside me, pulling me back while she spoke to Luana.

"I'm sorry, but I called up a week or so ago and changed the reservation." Ava looked over her shoulder at me, moving closer to Luana and lowering her voice. "This was supposed to be her honeymoon, but her jackass of a fiancé didn't turn up. I called to make it a girl's week instead. Please... She needs this."

I wanted the ground to swallow me up.

I pushed my suitcase on the floor and fell onto it, sitting myself down, my legs bent as I rested my elbows on my knees, my head in my hands. I was tired and jetlagged, and once again reminded about my failed marriage. Humiliation followed me, and I was so done.

I was crazy to think that I would love again, it's wasted on someone like me.

Chapter EIGHT

“Sweetie, it’s all sorted.” Brooke came over and sat on the floor in front of me. I looked up at her and saw Ava and Vanessa standing behind her.

“There is one problem though,” Ava said with grimace. “I could only get us two ocean villas, one studio, one––”

I held my hand up to silence her, I knew where this was going. I had to share with Sloane. I couldn’t expect the girls to stay with him.

“I don’t care,” I said defeated. “I just want to go to my room.”

I stood up, pushing my hair away from my face then grabbed my suitcase and walked towards the lift, leaving them following behind me.

I opened the door to the villa, Taron standing behind me as I walked into the stunning open space. My mouth dropped open at the view, the high ceilings and chestnut floors boasted throughout the villa. The open plan kitchen was at the end of the entry way, then off of the kitchen there was an elegant bedroom, and a lounge area.

I walked slowly towards the sliding doors, catching my breath at the view in front of me. I kicked my trainers off and padded onto the soft, vibrant grass. I looked up at the hazy evening sky and felt like pinching myself.

I felt myself smiling at the banayan trees that towered over me. I still couldn't believe I was here with my friends and not Josh. My heart hurt. I placed my hand over my chest and sat myself on the grass, staring into the glistening ocean.

How could he not want me? How could he just decide to up and leave?

I bowed my head as I quietly listened to the soft waves hitting the shore. I sat like this for about half an hour before I heard footsteps behind me. I slowly turned my head to the side to see Taron flopping himself down beside me.

"Beautiful, isn't it?" he said quietly.

I sniffed and nodded before turning my view back to the ocean. I didn't really want to speak to him, but I also didn't want to be alone. He went to speak but then stopped himself, he just joined me, staring into the never-ending sea line.

We must have been sitting out here for quite some time, in pure silence, as by the time I realized, it was already dark. I pushed myself up off the floor and headed towards the bathroom. I needed to wash the plane off me. I wanted to lay in a dark room and not have anything else to think about.

As I made my way through the villa I noticed a tray with two yellow coloured drinks in tall glasses, along with a little white petaled flower with a yellow staining in the centre, another frangipani. My eyes were drawn to it. Beside it was a small note saying, "with compliments." I picked the drink up, smelling it. It smelt sweet. I couldn't smell any alcohol in it, but you couldn't smell vodka once it was laced with something else.

I put the glass up to my lips before knocking it back. It tasted like a sex on the beach. I let out a small breath through my nose, a sarcastic smile finding my lips before putting the glass back down on the tray. Without thinking I picked the second glass up, drinking that one too. I placed the empty glass next to the other one before picking up the small, white flower and bringing it to my nose, sniffing gently. I dropped my hand, still holding onto the flower and made my way into the bathroom.

I placed the flower on the side as I peeled my clothes off and walked into the glass, level-floored shower. I always wondered why they made shower trays, when you could have the shower like this. All part of the room. I looked over at the large square bath next to the shower and thought about jumping in there, but I just couldn't be bothered. I felt exhausted.

I turned the shower on and stepped in. I let the hot water burn my skin as I started to lather myself up with the complimentary shower gel, before grabbing the shampoo and making a thick lather on my long blond hair.

I felt like I needed a good scrub to help me forget everything, but how do you forget heartbreak? How do you forget the pain that someone you love has put you through? Then, what with Taron and his comments, maybe it was just a game to him? Gives me a little bit, then pulls away. Like dangling sweets in front of an innocent child, only to have them snatched away just before they take them in their grasp. I snorted and shook my head.

I rinsed my hair and body off and just stood there, letting the water cascade over my body. My skin was pink from the temperature of the water, but I didn't care. I felt relaxed. I needed to burn my feelings away. I stepped out of the shower and wrapped the white, fluffy towels around my petite frame before walking straight through the double white doors and into the bedroom.

I lifted my suitcase onto the mahogany framed bed and unzipped it quickly before rummaging through my clothes and pulling out navy-frill shorts and a navy vest top. I rough-dried my hair and brushed it away from my face before walking back into the bathroom and throwing my towels in the linen basket. I padded bare foot back through to the lounge and dining area and saw Taron standing by the room phone, chatting then putting it down, turning towards me. He was still wearing his shirt and suit trousers.

"I took the liberty of ordering room service. You didn't seem in the mood for dinner out. The girls did knock but I told them you were tired. I hope you don't mind," he said carefully, as if he knew he was on thin ice.

"That's fine. I didn't want to go out." I looked at him, my eyes boring into his. "Thank you."

I sat out on the patio area, leaning back in the rattan lounger that was facing the ocean and let out a deep sigh. I wasn't even hungry, but I knew I needed to eat. I couldn't starve myself for the week. Plus, I needed the energy to put up with Hyde.

I rolled my eyes at my thoughts. He was definitely a little Hyde, just not violent. I couldn't cope with the Jekyll and Hyde duo that he portrayed.

I often wondered what he had done before having to come and look after me, which I still didn't get to be honest, but I didn't want to upset my dad. He obviously had his concerns.

I was distracted when Taron approached to the side of me with a large glass of white wine. I smiled at him as I accepted before he walked away. The effects of the two drinks I drank earlier were starting to show, I felt fuzzy and warm. I took a big sip of the wine and let out a little moan of appreciation as the taste exploded over my taste buds, then smoothly ran down my throat. I took another big mouthful before dropping my arms slightly and closing my eyes for a moment.

There it was again, that pang that shot straight through my heart, crumbling another piece. I wanted so desperately to call Josh, to beg him to take me back, but I was too stubborn and proud. I couldn't do it to myself. He made it clear he didn't want to be with me and I had to accept that. Imagine if we actually got married and then he decided to leave me?

Before I could stop them, the tears started to fall, the tears that I thought had left. I hurt. My heart was obliterated, and I didn't know if it could ever be fixed. I loved Josh with all of me, I still do.

I placed the wine glass on the floor before bringing my knees up to my chest and wrapping my arms around them, resting my head on my knees as I let out the silent sobs that I had been holding in. I missed him, I missed being with him and feeling his warm embrace. I missed his arms around me and how he would always make me feel better by coming out with some corny joke that wasn't actually that funny, but it always worked.

He knew how to make me feel myself again. How before he kissed me, his hand would find my cheek as he cupped it gently before pulling me to his lips. He used to softly trail them along my jaw line and down to my neck before trailing them up to my nose and back down to my lips.

I licked my lips as the salty tears ran towards them. I missed those kisses. He was always so attentive to my every need, and now I felt alone. So, so alone. I tried to calm my breathing by focussing on something. I lifted my head and stretched my legs out, staring down at them. I always dreamed of long, never ending legs, but I had short, skinny legs. My thighs were thicker, and I always felt out of proportion.

I leant forward and ran my fingertips slowly up from my ankles, making my way up to my calves, then to my knees and finally up to my thighs. I traced my fingers over my silver stretch marks that I had on the side of my thighs that disappeared into my shorts. I sighed. My eyes were still brimming with tears, I was scared to blink as I knew when I did I would let them fall once more.

I felt the presence of someone behind me. Turning slowly, Taron's eyes were on mine. He came beside me and knelt down, his thumb coming under my eyes as his rough pad swept a loose tear away.

"Don't cry, he isn't worth it," he said.

"But he was." I let out a whimper. He let me sit for a few moments as I tried to compose myself.

"Come inside, dinner is on the table." He stood up and held his hand out for me to take, which I did.

He didn't let go as he led me inside before letting my hand slip from his as he pulled my chair out to sit down and pushed me in slightly. I felt like I was being looked after by my dad. I rolled my eyes when his back was turned as I didn't want to seem like a brat. I smiled appreciatively at the food in front of me, simple chicken, new potatoes and asparagus with a gravy. Not what I would have chosen but I was grateful at his choice.

We sat quietly as we ate, sipping our wine every now and again. His eyes were on me the whole time, but I didn't look up at him. I get lost in his big brown eyes every damn time.

I stepped away from the table and put my plate in the sink in the kitchen area. I wasn't sure if room service were going to come and collect the plates or whether I needed to just leave them?

I wrinkled my nose up before walking back into the lounge area and flopping onto the sofa. Taron appeared beside me with my glass of wine.

"Thank you," I muttered.

"I'm sorry for what happened with you and Josh," he said, sadness lacing his voice.

"It's okay, it is what it is." I shrugged before taking a mouthful of my, now warm, wine. I screwed my face up.

Taron let out a small chuckle before walking over to the fridge and grabbing the chilled bottle of wine and topping my glass up, then pouring himself one. I stared at him as he took a sip of it, nodding to himself at the delicious taste.

"Bloody hell, you're actually drinking," I teased,

nibbling on the inside of my cheek.

"Well, one won't hurt, will it? And I am technically off duty," he said before coming to sit next to me.

A few moments of silence passed as I felt him shuffle next to me.

"It will get easier, Luna, I promise," he said softly.

I turned my head to face him, scoffing at his comment.

"And how would you know, Mr Bodyguard?"

"I have been in love... Once," he replied.

"Oh," was all I could say. "What happened?"

"She passed away," he said, rubbing his thumb round the rim of his wine glass.

"I'm sorry," I whispered, tears pricking my eyes, sadness consuming me at his loss.

"It's okay, it was eight years ago. I haven't dated since." He shrugged. I placed my hand on my chest, I didn't know what to say. What do you say to someone who has just told you that their partner died? I took a small sip of my wine, thinking of what to say.

"I am sorry, Taron." I kept my eyes down, looking at my wine glass.

"Honestly, it's fine, I've learned to cope." He smiled as I pulled my eyes up to look at him. "One of those things that you have no control over. You just have to learn to deal with the grief."

"If you ever want to chat, you know, I'm a great

listener," I boasted, trying to lighten the mood slightly.

"Thank you, I'll keep that in mind." He ran his thumb across his bottom lip then sighed. "Now, I am proof that you can get through anything. It does get easier, the pain doesn't, but you learn to cope. Last year I couldn't even say her name without crying," he whispered.

"What was her name?" The question came out before I could stop it, I felt instantly bad.

"Emerson." He slowly nodded his head, swirling the wine in the glass.

"Beautiful name." I took my plump bottom lip in-between my teeth.

We sat in silence for a few minutes before he spoke.

"She was killed in a car accident, hit by a drunk driver." He sighed.

"Is that the reason you don't drink?" Again, speaking before I had thought about it.

"It is. I don't mind the odd one, but I try not to make a habit of it. It just brings everything back." His eyes fall down into his lap. "I thought she was going to pull through, I was told that she would recover." He sniffed. "But she didn't. They found she had internal bleeding that they hadn't picked up at first. They tried to stop it, but they couldn't."

The silence between us was heart-breaking.

Now Josh leaving me didn't seem that bad. I suppose this made sense on how he was, he was afraid to feel again.

Now I completely understood. I took his hand in mine and rubbed my thumb across the back of it.

"I am really sorry, thank you for telling me. I know that must've been hard," I muttered.

"I wanted to tell you, I wanted you to see that you can get through anything." He smiled at me, keeping his hand underneath mine.

"Why don't you get some sleep? You must be exhausted," he said gently, pulling his hand from mine. I nodded, finished my wine and walked towards the bedroom. I stopped at the white, wooden double doors before turning and facing Taron.

"You okay sleeping out here?" I asked, feeling awful for asking.

"Of course." He nodded, standing in front of the sofa. "Night, Luna." He smiled, his dark brown eyes glistening in the moonlight.

"Night, Taron, thank you again," I said before walking into the bedroom and closing the doors.

He was a broken, lost soul.

Oh, Taron.

Chapter NINE

I jumped in my sleep, waking from the muffled shouting out. I sat up in my bed, heart thumping, panicking that something or someone was in the room.

I reached over and switched my lamp on. It took me a moment to get with it and realise it was coming from where Taron was sleeping. I slid out of bed and tiptoed quietly into the living room. My mouth dropped open when I saw Taron thrashing on the sofa bed. The sounds coming from him were quiet, as if he was restraining himself from screaming, but I knew he had no control over the sound as he was asleep.

I walked quietly over to him, sitting myself on the side of the bed. He had sweat running from his brow, his eyes squinted shut, the veins in his neck were raised and looked like they were ready to pop from his skin at any minute. I leaned over, stroking my hand over his forehead.

"Taron, it's Luna. Wake up, it's okay. You're just

dreaming," I cooed quietly.

His eyes darted open, sheer panic covering his face. He leaned forward, grabbing me round the waist and pulling me into him. I didn't move.

He wrapped his arms tightly round me, nuzzling into my neck and squeezing me tight. Within minutes he was snoring lightly. I laid there, paralyzed. My brain was telling me to move but I couldn't, I wouldn't. I didn't want to. I was wide awake, a million thoughts and questions going around in my head.

I placed my small hands over his large hands and tried to quiet my mind, and my jackhammer heart.

Finally I gave into sleep, the questions still swirling round and round in my head.

-

TARON

I woke, confused and disorientated, Luna in my arms, and a morning glory poking into her back. I was mortified. I couldn't like her like that. Yes, she was attractive, very fucking attractive, but no. No. I pushed her away gently, feeling slightly disgusted with myself. I rolled out of bed and made my way to the shower. I needed to clear my mind. But as always, I couldn't. I thought back to last night, another nightmare plaguing me, it's always the same...

I watch Emerson in her car, but I can't talk to her, I can't touch her. It's as if I am floating above the situation, watching it all play out.

She is driving down the small, country lane towards our house, smiling whilst she is playing James Arthur. She loved his songs.

Out of nowhere, a rusty orange pick-up truck comes speeding down on her side of the road. My heart starts thumping, my anxiety spiking. I am screaming out, telling her to pull off the road, to pull into the farmers field, but she can't hear me.

Then, it's too late.

I watch as the pickup truck ploughs into her, head on. He hits the car with such force that her car is on its roof, in a ditch. The driver of the pickup truck is injured but gets out and walks towards her car.

Panic disguises his face before he runs to get in his car then drives away.

It then goes to the moment my phone rings, the doctors telling me that my beloved Emerson has died. Killed by a drunk driver.

Anger, grief and anxiety takes over my body. I scream out, falling to my knees but no one can hear me. I am stuck in the moment, completely paralysed until I wake.

I'm haunted, on my knees, my heart breaking and

the tears flowing.

I leave the shower, wrapping myself in the towel. I look at myself in the mirror, pushing my dark hair away from my face.

I just want to sleep, to have one night without being haunted every time my eyes are closed. This is why I can't move on. I'm not over her, I didn't want to be over her. I feel like, in some way, she is still with me, in my dreams.

I sigh before walking into the lounge area to get dressed for the day. A pang of guilt rips through me when I see Luna sitting on the edge of the sofa bed, all timid-like. She's nibbling the skin on the side of her nails, her blond hair in a bun on her head, her huge green eyes undressing me, her full lips parted slightly.

She is breathtakingly beautiful, but I can't go there. No matter how tempting it is.

"Are you okay?" she asks sweetly.

"I am, are you?" I lied.

"I'm not bad," she mumbled, her eyes pulling away from mine. I nodded and started raiding my suitcase, frowning at my creased shirts.

"You can hang them in the spare wardrobe if you want?" she offered.

"I might do that, thank you." I smiled before pulling out some tailored shorts and a tee. We didn't speak for a while, she still sat on the bed in her vest and shorts. She looked amazing, plain jane but she was beautiful. Just not for me.

I walked back into the bathroom and got dressed, then brushed my teeth and styled my hair, pushing it back away from my face. I was hot already. It was going to be a warm day.

I made my way back into the lounge and checked my phone, I had a message from David.

"Taron, I didn't hear from you when you landed. Just checking in. Josh has been in touch, still no eyes on him as of yet. Keep eyes peeled and keep my daughter safe. Anything happens to her, it's on your head. David."

Does he not realise he is paying me to look after his precious princess? He infuriated me, even more so than Josh.

I was disturbed when I heard a knock at the villa door. Luna went to answer it, but I moved in front of her and shook my head before looking through the peep hole. I let out an exasperated sigh when I saw her three minions standing there in their little bikini cover ups and massive sunglasses. I swung the door open.

"Ladies." I moved aside letting them in.

Brooke pulled her glasses down her nose, eyeing me up then winking at me before pushing her large glasses back up her nose. *No chance. Only in your dreams sweet heart.*

"Luna, come on! Get dressed. Breakfast time, then sunbathing," Ava piped up. Luna was still sitting on the bed. She wanted to talk, to ask about last night. To be honest, I wasn't sure why I dragged her into bed with me, but I wanted to. I felt like I needed her next to me. And as soon as she was, I calmed.

My mind went quiet and I felt safe. It sounded silly, but it was true. I was meant to be keeping her safe, but last night the roles were reversed.

"Give me ten, just want to freshen up and get dressed." She smiled sweetly at the girls who had now all formed on my bed. Great.

I went into the kitchen and got myself a bottle of water. I wonder what today has in store?

-

LUNA

I stood in front of the wardrobe, looking at clothes to wear. My mind wasn't with me, it was with Taron.

I wanted to know what last night was about, but then I didn't want to push for his answers. He is so unpredictable. I never know what mood he is in.

I picked an orange bandeau bikini, a white lace bikini cover-up and tanned wedges. I didn't know if it was too much, the neck line plunged down between my cleavage and was cut up at the side of my thighs. I contemplated changing but decided against it. I re-did my hair, putting it back into a messy bun and pulling a few loose strands out at the sides. I applied some light pink lip-gloss and accessorised with large silver hooped earrings. I grabbed a small over-the-shoulder bag, throwing my phone, money, sun cream and lip gloss in, then walked out to the lounge area to meet the girls.

My eyes darted to Taron, whose eyes were on mine, they continued down my body as he took in my appearance. I could feel myself blushing. I was annoyed that my body betrayed me like that in front of him. I re-composed myself, pushing my large bvlgari sunglasses on.

I walked towards the villa door. "Ready, girls? I'm starving," I chirped.

They didn't say anything, just scuttled towards the door, Taron following behind them. We walked towards the main hotel, the air sweet, the sun over bearing. I felt like my creamy skin was burning under the rays already and we had only just stepped out of the room.

I walked along with the girls in quiet chatter, Taron not far behind, but far enough for us to talk amongst ourselves.

"How was your evening?" Brooke asked.

"Not bad, spent mostly in self-wallowing and drinking alcohol," I said coolly. "What did you all get up to?”

“We ate, we drank, we missed you,” Vanessa said.

“I missed you girls too, what did you eat? Make me jealous,” I teased.

“Do you want the full shebang?” Vanessa asked.

“Obviously.” I rolled my eyes at her stupid question. I was a foodie, I wanted to know everything.

“Okay, so for starters––” She started talking before Brooke interrupted.

“Sorry but are we all going to ignore the elephant in the room?” she said harshly.

“Sorry?” I questioned her.

“Bloody hell, Luna, there was clearly some tension in that room when we walked in. We could have cut through it with a knife it was that bad.” She laughed. I looked over my shoulder, eyeing up Taron who was looking into the sea as we walked to the main hotel.

“There wasn’t any tension.” I scrunched my nose up.

“Bullshit,” Brooke shouted. My eyes went wide before looking at Taron again, who was now facing us.

“Leave her alone,” Ava stuck up for me.

“No, I want to know what happened,” Brooke protested.

“Nothing bloody happened. We ate, we had a drink, I cried, I went to bed.” I shrugged, trying to be blasé about the whole situation.

“Shall I go ask Sloane?” She stopped in her tracks,

flicking her long red hair over her shoulder then pushed her Chanel glasses onto her head. I stopped and turned to face her.

"Brooke, please just drop it. Nothing happened, and if something *did* happen, which it didn't, I wouldn't tell you about it anyway. Now, can we just go and have breakfast? I have a banging head ache and I need food and coffee," I snapped before marching towards the hotel.

"Something definitely happened," she said to Ava and Vanessa before following behind me.

Why did I think it was a good idea to come here? I should have just cancelled the holiday.

Chapter TEN

I was glad when breakfast was over. Brooke spent the whole time throwing daggers my way whilst drinking her weight in mimosas. I just wanted to lay on the beach, read my book and drink cocktails.

I dismissed myself from the table whilst Brooke, Ness and Ava finished their drinks. Taron was up like a shot, behind me, following me like a lost puppy. I was annoyed. I stormed towards the resort's beach and sat myself down in a huff on the sun lounger.

A young man walked over, his name tag saying Maui. I smiled thinking of the film Moana, yet he was nothing like Dwayne Johnson. He was skinny and tall with lovely deep, blue eyes. His smile was kind, his teeth slightly crooked.

"Ma'am, let me get you a towel. Sir, will you be joining the young lady?" Maui turned his attention to Taron.

"I will be, thank you." He nodded at Maui, Maui

nodded back, dismissing himself to get our towels.

"You okay?" Sloane asked me.

"Mmm hmm, just Brooke," I huffed. "She has the ability to just piss me off." I let out a small laugh.

"Don't let her ruin the day." He smiled at me, his eyes watching Maui as he approached us.

Maui returned with two white luxury towels, forcing me to stand as he laid them out.

"I could have done that," I said kindly.

"No, Ma'am, it's my job," he responded, making sure the towels had no creases in. He stood back and pulled out a small iPhone looking device.

"Would you like a drink?" he asked me as I laid down on the sunbed, propping the head part of the sunbed up.

"Can I have a long island iced tea please?" I replied sweetly.

"Certainly, ma'am, sir?" Maui asked.

"Just a water please, I'm working," he said, his eyes on me.

"Not a problem, I'll be back soon," Maui said as he started to walk away.

I sat up and removed my cover up, folding it neatly and placing it at the foot of the sunbed, then reached down to my bag, pulling my factor thirty sun cream. The girls would no doubt smother themselves in oil, but I was always the sensible one, wanting to make sure I looked after my skin. Plus, I didn't want to burn.

I put a large amount of the creamy solution in the palms of my hand and started rubbing myself. Once my front was covered, I looked at Taron.

"Would you do my back, please?"

He didn't respond. I turned my back to him as he started rubbing the cream in, massaging it into my skin. I couldn't deny the spark that I felt when his touch was on me. His hands moved down to my hips as he continued rubbing it deeply into my skin before working his way back up round my shoulders and neck.

I let out a slight whimper when his hands left my skin.

"All done," he muttered before he sat down on the bed next to me.

"Thank you. Do you want me to do you?" I asked him.

"Luna, I never took you for being someone who was so forward." He winked at me.

I went a crimson red. "Taron!" I shouted, shocked at his playful remark.

He placed his hands on his stomach and threw his head back as he let out a loud, deep laugh. I started laughing along with him.

"Idiot," I mumbled before continuing to laugh.

Maui returned with Taron's water and my long island iced tea. He placed it on the little table beside mine and Taron's sunbeds.

"Thank you, Maui." I smiled at him before he disappeared. I picked the drink up from the table, bringing the straw to my lips and taking a big mouthful. God, it was strong, but delicious. I licked my lips before taking another mouthful. I placed it back down and laid back on the lounger, letting the intense sun beat down onto my pale skin. I couldn't wait to get a bit of a colour.

I decided against reading my book and took this moment to enjoy being on my own. All I could hear was the sound of the waves crashing softly against the shore, the quiet chatter of people who were on the beach. I felt my eyes getting heavier as my body and mind relaxed.

I rolled my head, feeling disorientated when I realised I was still on the beach. Taron was sitting, typing on his phone. To the other side of me were the girls, Brooke was on her front, Ava was reading, Part of Me by Lindsey Powell, and Vanessa was reading, This Cruel Love by Nikki J Summers.

I must've dozed off, and I felt good for my little nap. I sat up slightly and rolled myself over onto my front before drifting back off into a sun bathing bliss snooze.

I was awoken by Taron.

"Luna, wake up. We've got to go, now! I've had a call from your father." His voice sounded urgent. I was in a sun nap haze.

I opened my eyes slightly to see Taron throwing bits

in his bag, then grabbing my arm and pulling me up. "Hey! Get off me." I scowled at him.

"I told you we need to go back to the room, and you were still laying there," he raised his voice at me. Yes, he may be a God, but he is an arrogant one at that.

"Because I wasn't with it, I was in a deep sleep," I said, pulling my arm out of his firm grip then throwing my cover up back over me.

He stood, tapping his foot, his black hair falling onto his face before he pushed it back to form his swept back look. I pushed up off the sun lounger, the girls were standing behind me, their looks batting back and forth between them. I huffed as I stormed past him.

His phone rang.

"Sloane," he snapped.

"We are on our way back to the room."

"No I won't let her in until I've scoped it."

He sounded frustrated, and now I was panicking. What the hell was going on?

I turned on my heel and stopped in front of him.

"What's going on?" I asked. "I have a right to know." I looked up at him, my brows pulled together.

"Just follow me to the room for God's sake. Can't you just follow an instruction?" he growled at me as he barged past me, grabbing my wrist and yanking me behind him.

My little legs couldn't keep up. I looked over my shoulder to see the girls whispering. Did they know what was going on? I threw them a puzzled look and they shrugged back at me.

We were finally at the room, and my heart was thumping. Taron faced me, holding his finger up to his lips for me to keep quiet. He slid the patio door open as quietly as he could as he walked into the room. I stepped back and stood next to the girls.

"What's going on?" Brooke asked.

"I haven't a clue, he won't say anything." I shook my head.

"Do you think we should be worried?" Ava muttered.

"No," I answered back confidently. "I don't think so anyway." I hesitated. Truth was, I was worried. I sighed in relief when I saw Taron walk back outside where we were waiting.

"All clear," he said firmly.

"Can you tell me what's going on now?" I asked him.

"Soon, come. Follow me," he said as he walked me through the room, the girls following me.

"Luna, we're gonna head back to the room for showers, we will message you in a bit." They didn't look back as they walked out the door.

I stood staring at Taron, waiting for some sort of explanation as to what was going on.

He paced up and down the room, his hands going to his hair in frustration. I sat on the sofa in the lounge area of the villa, he followed, stopping then standing in front of me.

“It’s not as bad as I’ve made out.” He rubbed his dark stubble. I was confused, my brows knitted together as I scrunched my nose up before running my hand through my hair.

“What do you mean?” I asked.

“Your dad called me, irate and panicked, telling me he had received a withheld call,” he said calmly, his eyes on mine the whole time.

“And?” I asked, sarcasm lacing my voice slightly, my eyebrows raised.

“They were talking about you, telling him to make sure someone has their eyes on you the whole time.” He sighed. “So, yeah, he wanted me to make sure that the room was okay, which it is. I did say to him not to worry and that everything was fine, and no doubt it’s just someone winding him up.” He shrugged coolly. “But, that being said, I will be taking extra caution with you for the rest of the holiday. The main thing is you’re okay.” He smiled slightly at me.

“Do you think we need to be worried?” I asked, now worried.

“I don’t, but we should still be cautious, just in case.” He smiled.

“Just in case what?” I questioned.

“Just in case somebody wants to take you.” He shrugged his shoulders, a big smirk gracing his smug, handsomely rugged face. "Not that they would want to keep you, but rest assured, I will keep you safe, princess." He snorted, masking a laugh as he pulled his bottom lip in-between his teeth.

"What is your problem with me?" I forced myself off the sofa and stood in front of him, looking up at him. I was pissed.

"No problem, just stating the obvious," he replied, stepping back. I moved towards him, pushing him, forcing my hands onto his steel chest. My little hands on his chest looked pathetic, my push was pathetic as well. He didn't move. Didn't even wobble.

I pushed him again, anger rising in my tiny body. I couldn't take him anymore, I couldn't take the harshness of him. He was so up and down. I couldn't cope with his moods. He didn't flinch, just kept his deep brown eyes on me.

I went to hit his chest with my palms again as he grabbed my wrists and held them against my chest. A cocky smile graced his stupid, handsome face. I went to shout at him to get off me before he pressed his lips against mine. My eyes wide, I wanted to push him away from me, but then again, I didn't.

The fire inside me alighting deep within as it rushed through my body. He pushed me back onto the sofa, kneeling between my legs. He dropped my hands from his grip and placed them on the side of my face. My hands moved into his long, black hair, grabbing it as he thrust his tongue into my mouth.

I accepted it, devouring him. He was still in his tailored shorts and tee, me in my orange bikini and lace cover up. The anger I felt for him was still there, but it had been replaced with lust. A build-up of the hot and cold between us had become too much.

A moan escaped my lips as our kiss grew deeper. I let go of his hair before bringing my hand to his T-shirt. As he pulled away, his eyes went wide as if he was a deer in headlight. He stepped back, bringing his hand up to his mouth, his fingers running over his lips before shaking his head at himself and disappearing into my bedroom, slamming the door.

I let out the breath I had been holding. I sat on the sofa, staring into oblivion. I couldn't work out what the hell had just happened.

I touched my parted plump lips with my fingertips, they were burning. My legs were still spread from where he was kneeling. I was full of mixed emotions.

I couldn't stop myself. I shot up from the sofa and walked quickly to my room, opening the door to see him sitting on the edge of the bed, biting the side of his thumb. His dark brown eyes locked on my eyes.

He dropped his hand from his mouth as I marched over to him. I didn't let my brain stop me. I couldn't stop. I climbed on top of him, straddling him. My mouth on his, our tongues crashing together as our kiss grew deeper. My hungry hands gripping the hem of his T-shirt before lifting it over his head.

I pulled away, drawing my eyes up and down his body. I smirked. He placed his large hand round the back of my head, pulling me forcefully into him. His free hand started exploring my body, his fingertips sending shivers through me. He trailed them up my bare spine which made a small moan escape my lips whilst still deep in a kiss.

He pushed his finger and thumb round the back of my neck, giving it a gentle squeeze. I broke away, tipping my head back, exposing my bare neck to his hungry mouth. His lips pressing against my slightly burnt skin.

His grip tightened as his lips traced down my collarbone, making their way in-between my chest. With his spare hand, he used his forefinger to pull my bikini top down, releasing my large breast. His lips kissed across my chest, cupping my breast before taking it into his warm, wet mouth. I moaned as his tongue flicked across my nipple.

This was wrong, but we were too far for me to pull back now. My hips started moving over him.

I wanted him. I needed him.

I lifted myself up, pressing my lips back into him as he hungrily unbuttoned his shorts.

I greedily pushed his shorts away, revealing him. He

wrapped his fingers round my bikini bottoms as he exposed me fully. Our eyes both on each other's, as if we were trying to silently give each other the agreement that this was okay.

He lifted me slightly before taking me completely, a gasp leaving my lips, my eyes closing at the pure ecstasy taking over me, consumed in lust. His thrusts were slow, but hard, hitting me in the same sweet spot again and again, building me to my impending release that I have craved from the moment I laid my eyes on him.

His moans started escaping his lips, his grip tightening around my neck, his other one round my hip, his lips pressing onto my neck. I couldn't stop this slow, sweet release that came over me. I hit my peak, Taron following as he let out a low moan.

We sat quietly, not moving. After what felt like a lifetime I lifted myself off of him, pulling my bikini bottoms back over me then walked towards the door.

He hadn't looked at me.

Mere moments ago we were full of lust, and now, he couldn't even lay eyes on me.

When I got to the door, I looked over my shoulder, hoping for his eyes to meet mine, but they didn't.

I closed the door behind me and headed to my bathroom. I stripped off completely, walking into the shower.

I felt cheap.

Used.

Dirty.

Unwanted.

And all because we got caught up in the moment.

As the hot water cascaded over my skin, I cried. Josh never made me feel cheap. He always made me feel loved. Our sex was meaningful, it meant something. He was the only person I had been with. Until Taron.

I couldn't help how I felt, a magnet pulling me towards him.

I pulled my hair out of my messy bun and let it loose as I washed away my mistake. It was a mistake. I felt humiliated and disgusted with myself.

Chapter ELEVEN

TARON

What the fuck have I done? How the hell did I give in?

I gave in to her sweet temptation. Something I vowed I wouldn't do from the moment I laid eyes on her.

I couldn't even look at her. She walked out looking disgusted with me.

How could I have been so stupid?

Fuck, I found her attractive, of course I did, but my barriers are up because of what happened with Emerson. I wanted to move on, but then again, I didn't. I didn't want to forget her.

I threw myself back on the bed, my hands flying towards my face. When my eyes closed, my mind wasn't plagued with Emerson, it had been replaced with Luna.

I had been fighting this for so long, I knew it was going to happen, but I didn't want it to. I shouldn't have just let her walk out the door, she must think I am an even bigger arsehole than I was before.

I shot up from the bed and opened the door leading to the lounge, my eyes scouting the room for her. I let out a sigh when I heard the shower running. I stood outside the door, debating whether to try the door handle or not. My hand slowly reached out to open the door when the bathroom door swung open in front of me.

Stunned, I stood with my hand still out, Luna standing in her towel, her big green eyes on me, darting back and forth. Her burnt skin more apparent than before. Something about Luna drew me in.

"Luna...I..." I stammered.

"Go away, Sloane," she snapped at me as she pushed past me, holding her towel tight round her body. Before I could tell my body to stop, I was following her. Desperate for her to hear me out. She walked into her bedroom and slammed the door in my face as I stood there on the other side. I pressed my forehead against the door and sighed. Well done, Taron.

I wanted to say sorry, I wanted to say it wouldn't happen again. It shouldn't have happened. We were both caught up in a heated moment filled with mixed emotions. I've never slept with a client, one thing I vowed I would never do, so what the hell happened when it came to Luna Smith? She's not the first attractive woman I have looked after. She isn't forbidden fruit. If anything, she is one of the most down to earth clients I've had. But there is something about her that pulls me closer to her. We've had close encounters before, but I managed to stop myself. She was a job. I was her bodyguard.

I walked back towards the lounge, angry. I didn't know what to do. I fell onto my sofa bed, staring at the ceiling.

The damage was done.

Chapter TWELVE

LUNA

I slammed the door in his face as I stormed into my bedroom. How dare he think he can speak to me after how he treated me. I was a fool for letting that happen.

Why the hell did I pursue it? He already pushed me away in the lounge, yet like an addict who was looking for her next fix, I followed him. I should have read the signs. He had already told me he didn't like me like that, that he didn't find me attractive, yet he gave in to me.

I couldn't stay away.

I sat on the edge of my bed, clinging to my towel, my cheeks burning with humiliation. I took a deep breath, I didn't want to give in to the tears that were threatening.

I was distracted from my thoughts when my phone buzzed, it was Brooke.

Hey babe, dinner soon? We are starved.

Text me back. B x

I sighed. I picked my phone up, staring at the message. I was hungry, but I didn't want Taron to have to come with us, and I knew that wasn't an option. I tapped on my phone.

Hey, yes! I've just showered so I'll get dressed. Be ready in fifteen, meet you outside the room? X

I dropped my towel to my feet and walked towards the wardrobe, pulling out a black maxi dress and tanned wedges. I put my gold hoops in and slipped a bangle onto my wrist. I dried my blond hair with the dryer, then pulled it into a low bun. I applied some highlighter onto my cheeks and sprayed my *dior bouquet* perfume.

I gave myself one look in the mirror, satisfied with how I looked. I walked out of my bedroom and stopped outside the lounge.

"I'm going for dinner," I said angrily, grabbing my bag off the sideboard in the villa's hallway then throwing my phone and key-card in there before I walked out, slamming the door behind me. I was relieved when I saw the girls all standing there.

"Am I glad to see you." I beamed.

"Everything okay?" Vanessa asked.

"It is now I'm away from him," I hissed.

"Oh dear, what's he done?" Ava asked me as we walked slowly towards the main building.

"Don't pressure her," Brooke demanded.

"Oh, stop it, she wouldn't say if she didn't want to," Ava stuck up for herself.

I shrugged and smirked before responding. "We slept together." No point beating round the bush.

"You what?" Ness asked, shocked.

"Luna!" Brooke said, not quite sure if she believed me or not. Ava linked her arm through mine.

"Tell us the details, ALL of it," she said, grinning from ear to ear. I smiled back at her, just about to tell her when I heard Taron bellowing down the hallway. I turned round quickly, sheer panic on my face.

"LUNA!" he shouted after me as he ran up behind me, pulling his T-shirt over his messy mop of black hair.

"Go away," I moaned at him as I carried on walking, dragging Ava along with me, Brooke and Ness still behind me, eyeing each other.

"Don't walk away from me," he growled.

"I'm going for dinner," I said bluntly, a smirk spreading across my face.

"Not without me you're not," he said as he grabbed the top of my arm. I was getting really sick of him and his grabbing. He tugged me towards him, spinning me to face him.

"Stop acting up," he said, his voice low.

"Who are you, my father?" I said, sarcasm lacing my voice.

"Don't," he grunted at me.

"Let go of me," I said through gritted teeth, yanking my arm from his. "I'm going for dinner."

"So am I," he replied, following me as I walked towards the main restaurant.

I let out a sigh as we walked up to the table, the girls sitting down, Taron following behind after.

I ordered two bottles of champagne, the girls exchanging looks, knowing exactly where this night was going.

"We were thinking," Vanessa piped up as she took her glass of champagne from me.

"Go on," I muttered as I downed the whole glass of champagne before topping my glass back up again. Taron's eyes narrowed, staying on mine the whole time.

"Why don't we do a day out, like an excursion?" she asked.

"Yes! I love that idea," I said excitedly finishing my glass, pouring another. I was going to get wasted tonight. I didn't care.

Taron leant towards me, his lips millimetres away from my ear. "Don't you think you've had enough?" he hissed.

I pulled my face away from his, narrowing my eyes

and pulling my brows together, giving him a disgusted look.

"No," I said through gritted teeth.

"Can we talk outside?" he asked, this time a little softer.

"I don't want to talk to you." I shrugged before taking a big sip of my champagne then turned my back on him. "So, ladies, what are we thinking for tomorrow?" I asked, a big fake smile plastered across my face, my insides falling apart.

"We were thinking horse riding or snorkelling with the sea turtles." Ava shrugged, sipping her champagne, her pinkie pointing in the air as she did. I giggled.

"Horse riding?" Brooke groaned. "God, I don't want to spend the rest of the holiday walking like John Wayne."

"Make the most of having something big between your legs," I replied, throwing my head back and letting out a hearty laugh. Ava and Vanessa were laughing too. It took me a few moments to compose myself, running my ring finger under my eyes, trying to wipe the stray tears away. I side-eyed Taron who had a small smirk on his face.

Christ, why was he so fucking handsome? I ached for him again.

"But I would like to see Taron on a horse." I laughed at my own comment.

"Not happening." He sulked, then winked, his dark brown eyes glistening.

"Oh no? Will you disobey my daddy's orders and not watch me?" I said, goading him.

He rolled his eyes, keeping his mouth shut. Good.

"I think snorkelling," Vanessa chimed.

"To be honest, we can horse ride back home. When will we get the opportunity to swim with sea turtles?" I asked.

"Yeah, I suppose that makes sense," Ava said.

"Thank God." Brooke smirked before we all clinked our glasses together, then took a mouthful of the delicious champagne.

We sat amongst light, drunken chatter for the rest of the evening, enjoying a lovely meal overlooking the resorts beach with little interference from Taron. It had gone midnight by the time we left our table and started a slow walk back to the villa.

Just as we got to the villas, Taron touched my arm softly, his grip getting firmer on the top of my arm as he tried to get me to stop.

"I want to talk to you. Girls, could you give us a minute please?" he asked, his eyes darting to my three friends.

"Luna?" Brooke asked.

"It's fine. Go inside, we will catch up in the morning." I nodded, smiling, my head feeling fuzzy from the drink. I definitely shouldn't have drunk that much.

I watched as they walked into their villa, Brooke

giving me one last concerned look. I just smiled, letting her know I was okay.

As soon as the door shut, my smile disappeared.

"What do you want?" I said raising my voice, my back up instantly towards him. I couldn't understand how one minute I liked him, the next I despised him. There was a very thin line between it.

"I want to say sorry," he mumbled, the moonlight beaming down onto his skin, giving him a glow. My face softened, my eyes penetrated through him. I wasn't expecting an apology.

"I really am. I didn't mean to react the way I did earlier..." he trailed off, stepping closer to me, putting both of his hands on the top of my arms and squeezing slightly.

"Just know I am sorry. I have felt awful all afternoon. I don't expect you to forgive me, but I just wanted to tell you. I know you were angry, but don't run from me. It's my job to protect you," he said quietly, then bowed his head over me. I felt so small, my eyes looking up at him.

"Okay," I said. "But I don't forgive you." I shook my head. He let go of my arms, stepping back from me. The tension between us so thick.

"Oh," he said surprised. He dropped his arms in defeat. The air between us cold.

A few moments passed, neither of us saying a word.

I ran my hand up and down my arm. I felt a chill, but

it wasn't cold. The air was humid.

"Taron..." My voice sounded small, trailing off. He looked up at me, his eyes wide. I could get lost in his deep, brown eyes. I didn't say anymore, I ran myself at him, jumping into him. My arms went around his neck as his held me up. My legs instantly wrapped themselves around his waist, our hungry mouths on each other.

This time it felt different.

My tongue invading his, caressing it, his matching my rhythm. We were like deprived lovers, kept from each other, when in fact, we had been together all along. We just didn't know it, our souls and bodies connecting as one once more.

He walked effortlessly into our villa, letting go of me so I was forced to put my legs on the floor.

Both of us panting, my lipstick smudged. I ran my fingertips over my sensitive lips before darting my eyes up to him.

"We shouldn't," I whispered.

"I know we shouldn't," he replied, breathless.

His large hands pushed through his long, black hair, pushing it away from his face. His teeth sinking into his bottom lip while his eyes drawled up and down my body. I felt myself light up just from his look, like a fire was set off internally inside me, burning my core.

I stepped back, keeping my eyes on him, waiting, hoping he would make the next move. I threw myself at him earlier, I know he wants this too.

He didn't move. Just kept his eyes pinned on me.

"Goodnight, Taron," I said disappointed, walking past him, not looking back as I slipped into my bedroom, closing the door behind me.

I let out the breath I had been holding, tears stinging my eyes. I rested the back of my head on the door, biting my lip, trying to distract myself from crying. I was such an idiot. I stood away from the door, peeling my dress down my petite body and folding it over the hanger before placing it back into my wardrobe, when I heard the bedroom door go. I threw my arms over my body, trying to cover myself in my underwear from Taron's hungry eyes.

"I was just coming to see if you were okay," he muttered, his hand still firmly on the door handle.

"Mmm hmm," was all I could manage whilst going a crimson red.

"Okay, cool," he said before stepping backwards and closing the door.

I kept my eyes on the door for a moment, waiting to see if he would re-appear, but he didn't. I pulled my vest and short set off the end of my bed, slipping them on. I pulled my hair into a messy bun then slipped under the covers. I just wanted to sleep. I somehow sobered myself up. Maybe it was the thought that something was going to happen with Taron again? Or maybe it was the sheer fear of being rejected? Again.

I woke with a jolt, looking around me, slightly disorientated. I needed a drink; my head was now thumping from the champagne. Even though I had sobered up, it was still running through my veins.

I threw the duvet back, then switched the air con down before padding out into the kitchen. I went to the fridge and grabbed a cold, glass bottle of water before sleepily walking through the lounge, when I saw Taron sitting on his sofa bed, his eyes fixated on the wall. I contemplated walking straight through to my bedroom, but I couldn't. I stood in his line of sight, pulling him from his daydream.

"Luna," he said exasperated.

"Taron," I replied, walking closer to him, tightening my grip on my water bottle. "Are you okay?"

"I can't stop thinking about you," he confessed, his eyes red raw where they were strained.

"Oh," was all I could muster.

"But every time I think of you, I feel guilty. Guilty on Emerson," he whispered, I could barely hear him. I felt a shiver run over me.

"I understand that," I admitted. "I feel guilty on Josh, even though he was the one that left me." I shrugged as I walked closer to him, now standing centimetres apart.

Taron's desperate eyes looked up at mine, my heart

hurt for him.

"It's okay," I said, crouching down so our eyes met. I didn't know what else to say to him. I reached out and touched his hand, I wanted to let him know that I was okay. We were okay.

"And I forgive you." I smiled softly at him. He smiled back at me. My heart warmed, as if aglow. I stood slowly from my crouched position, my legs shaky.

I walked slowly away from him before looking over my shoulder at him.

"Night, Taron," I muttered as I walked through the bedroom door, closing it on him. Separating us once more.

Chapter THIRTEEN

The door had just clicked to indicate it was secure, when it swung open, hitting the wall as it did. I jumped in my skin, wincing at the same time from the loud bang. He looked haunted, his brown eyes looked black.

"Taron, what's wrong?" I asked, concerned as he walked towards me, our lips connecting as he pushed me towards the wall. His tongue hungry in my mouth, my arms pinned above my head with one of his hands.

His free hand slowly trailed its way down my body, moans escaping my lips. He was forceful, but not in a bad way, just proving to me that he owned the room. He owned me.

His free hand gripped the back of my thigh and pulled it up round his hip before his finger hooked round my shorts and knickers, pulling them to the side before plunging a finger inside of me. His name slipped off my tongue in a moan as I pulled away from our kiss as the pleasure rippled through me.

His skilled mouth trailed kisses down my neck line, across my collar bone, all whilst his finger continued to stroke my walls. He pulled away, pushing his shorts down with his one hand, revealing himself.

I looked down, still pinned to the wall by him and admired him, my eyes hazed with lust. I licked my bottom lip before pulling it with my teeth.

"Don't bite your lip," he said in a deep, assertive tone. I blinked innocently at him, pulling my hands out of his grasp then dropping to my knees, my eyes on his as I wrapped my fingers around him, pumping him slow before pressing my lips to his tip.

He threw his head back as I took him whole into my mouth, him letting out a groan that was pure ecstasy, spurring me on. He was my drug, I craved him. Each hit from him made me want him even more.

A low growl left his throat as he grabbed a fistful of my blond hair as he harshly thrust into my mouth. I pulled him out of my mouth and continued to pump him with my hand, looking at him the whole time.

His eyes darted down to mine, his hand pushing my head back towards him, taking him gladly. I watched his pupils dilate as he came, pumping his warm arousal down my throat.

He ran his finger along my jaw line and under my chin, pushing up slightly, indicating for me to stand up. He wrapped his arms around my waist, pulling me against him, bringing his lips down to mine. He lifted me effortlessly and walked over to the bed, dropping me gently underneath him.

He stood up, looking down at me, smirking. The haunted look had left, now his eyes were full of want and need.

He wrapped his fingers around the waist band of my pyjama shorts before pulling them down effortlessly, exposing me, discarding them to the floor, then pushing my vest up.

"Take it off," he growled. I nodded, pulling it over my head and laying back down on the bed. He knelt onto the bed, pushing my legs wide before dipping his head in between my legs, licking and sucking.

I gripped onto the bedsheets as his expert tongue made me come undone. He smiled at me, holding onto my hips then flipped me over onto my front, making me gasp. He gripped onto my hips, pushing me down, then pulling my hips into the air. He ran his finger from my bum down to my core, slipping a finger in, slowly teasing me.

A sweet moan left my lips as he pulled his finger out then without warning pushed into me hard, his thrusts moving in a punishing manner. He pulled my hair tight, pulling me up onto my knees as he continued pushing deeper into me.

His hand splayed across my belly, my head tilting back, resting on his chest. His fingers slid down my belly before brushing across my sweet spot, his lips on my neck. I could feel myself tightening but I needed more from him, I needed to be owned.

"Faster," I moaned out. With that he pushed me down, releasing my hair then flipped me on my back. He pulled me to the edge of the bed before pushing into me deep and fast. This is what I needed.

He didn't let up, the sound of our skin hitting against each other was turning me on. I reached down in-between my legs before touching myself, my eyes closing.

"Look at me whilst you touch yourself," he commanded. My obeying eyes flicked up at him as he carried on with his fast, hard thrusts into me. I could feel myself tightening around him once more.

"Ah, yes," I moaned out as he hit me in the right spot again and again. I took my finger from between my legs and pushed it between his lips as he sucked, twirling his tongue around the tip.

"Fuck, Luna," he growled as he sped up, his breathing harsh and rapid.

"I'm going to come," I moaned out as I wrapped my legs tightly round him. He leant down, dipping his head into my neck, nipping my sensitive skin as I came around him hard, him following behind me.

We laid in bed, my head on his chest as his fingertips trailed lines and shapes on my bare back. I wasn't expecting him to stay with me, but I was glad he was. The silence was deafening.

"Are you okay?" he asked.

"Yeah, are you?" I lied, my heart thumping in my chest.

"Yeah, I am." His finger ran under my chin, pulling it up before pressing his lips to mine softly. As our lips parted, I giggled, suddenly embarrassed.

This was so wrong, yet it felt so right.

I woke in the morning, stretching out, turning my head to see Taron in my bed. A smile spread across my face, he was still sleeping peacefully. I got out of bed and tiptoed into the living area, flicking the switch on the coffee machine.

I ached in a good way. Taron worked me in ways I hadn't ever been worked. He was rough, and I loved it. I bit my lip, smirking as I relived last night. God, it was so much better than the first time. The first time was sensual but cold, this time was hot and wanted. Then sheer panic set through me. We hadn't used protection, we hadn't even discussed it. Shit.

I poured myself and Taron a coffee. I picked my cup up and walked out to the patio of the villa overlooking the calm ocean trying to register what had happened over the last twenty-four hours.

A few moments later I was pulled from my day dream when Taron walked over, all brooding.

"Morning," I chirped.

"Hey." He nodded, cradling his own coffee cup. "Thanks for this." He held it up, bringing it to his lips. My eyes ran up and down his body. I wanted to kiss him so bad. I patted the spare seat next to me, and he sat down, nibbling his thumb nail.

"What's wrong?" I asked sensing his emotions.

"Last night shouldn't have happened. Fuck, Luna, you're my kryptonite," he said, pushing his hand through his hair. "You're a job, my client. I don't sleep with my clients. Yet, I've slept with you twice," he said annoyed.

"Brilliant, arsehole Taron is back." I scowled standing up from the chair. He grabbed my wrist trying to pull me back down. I shook my head, pulling my arm from his grasp.

"Go fuck yourself," I shouted at him as I walked into my bedroom. How could I have been so stupid, again? He was clouding my judgement, I'm not this girl. He was poison.

I rummaged through my wardrobe and pulled out a cover-up, and my new red thong swimsuit that I bought when I went shopping with Taron. I hopped into the shower, washing myself and my hair. It was in desperate need of a wash, and I wanted Taron's scent off of me completely.

I turned the shower off, walking into my bedroom before sitting at the dresser and drying my hair, leaving it down. I dropped the towel, slipping into my red swimsuit. I smiled as I looked at my reflection in the mirror. I would never wear something like this, but I felt good. I looked good. I put my tanned wedges on and pulled my lace cover-up on. I grabbed my phone and door key and walked towards the door.

I heard the shower running from the bathroom. I quickly walked past the door and out the main villa door, making my way down to the girls' place. I knocked quietly, waiting for them to answer, getting fidgety, panicking that he would find me. I was relieved when Ava swung the door back, rubbing her sleepy eyes.

"Everything okay?" she asked confused, her eyes trying to adjust to the light.

"Just let me in." I huffed as I barged my way past her, her eyes following me as she shut the door, still looking at me, not sure what the hell was going on.

"I need to get away from Taron," I said quietly as I turned their coffee machine on.

"How are you still asleep? It's gone ten, I want to swim with the turtles." I rolled my eyes as I poured myself a coffee. "Want one?" I asked.

She just stood there, full zombie mode. It took her few minutes to respond. "We stayed up for a bit, drunk some more wine. Who are you, my mother?" she snapped.

"You're like a bear with a sore head," I said smiling, shoving the hot cup of coffee into her hands, a small smile gracing her face, her short brown hair glossy. She collapsed on the sofa in the lounge sighing.

"Christ my head," she groaned. "It was all Brooke's fault." She shook her head.

"Isn't it always?" I chuckled before sitting down next to her.

"Changing the subject, you look hot," she exclaimed, eyeing me up and down. "Like, totally hot." She winked at me.

"Why, thank you." I smiled as I fanned myself down with my hand.

"Bet Taron couldn't keep his eyes off you." She nudged me before taking a sip of her steaming coffee. I didn't say anything, praying that my body didn't betray me and make me blush from head to toe with embarrassment before bringing my cup to my lips.

"Oh my God, has something happened again?" she asked me, now turning herself to face me, tucking her leg under her other one. I held the cup up to my face, trying to hide myself.

"Luna," she squealed. "Tell me." A stupid smile on her face, that was gradually getting bigger.

"Shhh," I hushed her, I didn't need Brooke bounding in here.

"Then tell me, come on," she said patting my leg, bouncing up and down on the sofa like an excited school girl.

I rolled my eyes at her. "We had sex. Well, you knew that cos I mentioned it yesterday."

"You did." She put her coffee cup on the table by the sofa before facing me again. "Go on," she urged me.

"Well, that. We slept together." I shrugged it off. "Then we slept together again last night, well, this morning, but early hours this morning." My speech was getting faster. I was nervous spilling it out to her, telling her made it all so real. I blushed.

"Eeeek," she screamed. I swatted her arm.

"Shut up." I laughed at her. "It was just sex. He is an arsehole, like a proper arsehole." I shook my head. "I actually thought there was something between us, but nope, I was just another notch on the bed post. And he had the cheek to preach to me that he doesn't sleep with his clients. Of course he doesn't." I was arguing with myself. We were interrupted when there was a knock on the door.

"Balls. That's Sloane. Tell him I'm not here, please, I beg you," I said panicked, my eyes darting round the room for somewhere to hide. My only option was to escape. Ava hopped up off the sofa, putting the chain on the door before opening it slightly.

"Let me in," Taron growled.

"Why?" Ava asked, pretending like she didn't have a clue.

"I need to get to Luna." His hand was reaching round

the door. "Ava, let me in, please." His voice sounded desperate. That was my cue to go. I slipped out the patio doors that led to the grass area, running towards the beach. The sun was intense already, burning on my creamy skin. I leant down, taking my wedges off then discarding them on the sand. I dropped my arms to my side, throwing my head back and letting the sun burn everything away.

I needed this break. I shouldn't have got myself caught up with Taron. I'm a relationship kind of girl, not a hook up.

I tilted my head forward, my green eyes focusing on the calm sea, the mix of greens and blues glistening from the sun beams. I walked towards the shore line, smiling as the tide covered my feet, the sea crystal clear. I pulled my cover-up off and threw it over to my shoes, along with my bag.

I couldn't care less if someone took it, I just didn't care anymore.

I tucked my hair behind my ears before walking into the warm ocean. I instantly felt relaxed before diving into the sea, letting the water wash everything away.

I swam further out, rolling onto my back, staring into the clear blue skies. All I could think about was Taron. The way his expert tongue bought me back to life last night.

The sex was rough, but it wasn't just sex.

It was more.

My feelings growing intensely for him.
I didn't want to fall for him, but I couldn't stop.
I had fallen, so hard.

Chapter FOURTEEN

TARON

My heart was racing. I can't believe she ran out on me, again. She had tried, and I caught her. This time she ran while I was showering. I went to the girls' villa, Ava was adamant she wasn't there. If she was, she was fucking good at hiding. She let me in, searching the rooms, but I couldn't find her. She must've slipped out the back doors.

I was just about to give up when I got to the beach, scouting along the strip. My heart calmed when I saw her shoes, cover-up and bag. Seriously, she's just left her bag in the middle of the beach for anyone to take. Rage was brewing deep inside me.

I knew I had pissed her off, I shouldn't have treated her the way I did, but she was pulling me in. I was catching feelings for her, but I couldn't tell her.

I vowed to Emerson I would never love another. I couldn't break my vow.

I walked onto the beach, picking her bag up and checking it, sighing in relief when her phone, money and key card was still in there. I looked into the sea to see her swimming towards the shore before standing up, the water round her waist.

She looked fucking incredible. Her tiny hips sashaying out of the water, her blond hair wet and pushed back, emphasizing her facial features. Her green eyes on me, glistening from the reflection of the water, her full lips parted slightly.

She was wearing a tiny red swimsuit, the material plunging down in-between her large breasts. The lower part of her swim suit rising high up her thighs. Then I remembered our shopping trip, this was the red thong swimsuit. Fuck.

I felt like she was walking in slow motion and I was living in a real life Baywatch. I walked towards her. God, I wanted to pick her up, kiss her all over and apologise for being such a dick, but I couldn't. I couldn't let this happen again. I can't deny that there isn't a pull there, we are like two magnets, attracted to each other, but I need to stay away. Keep a safe distance.

I met her on the shore line, her hands up in her hair, pulling it over her shoulder and wringing it out. I watched the water run down her breasts. I automatically bit my lip before realising what I had done.

"You ran," I scolded, my sunglasses still on.

"I did." She shrugged as she went to walk past me.

"Aha," a laugh left me. "I don't think so." I grabbed her tiny waist, pulling her towards me before throwing her over my shoulder. She started screaming and kicking as I held her firmly in place. I had to take two deep breaths, having her perfect, peachy arse literally next to my face was proving difficult. I was already hard from her walk out the water, I ached for her.

Before I could tell my brain to stop I turned my head to the side, nipping her bare arse cheek before kissing it softly.

A cocky smirk spread across my face as she continued to kick and scream for me to put her down.

I can't do that, princess.

I'm your bodyguard.

Your protection.

Chapter FIFTEEN

LUNA

I screamed, slapping his bare back and kicking my legs into his stomach. I was livid.

"Put me down," I shouted out, protesting. He ignored me, just throwing me over his shoulder even more as he tightened his grip around my bum and legs. People were staring. I had never felt so humiliated in all my twenty-five years of life.

After five minutes of screaming I gave up, it was pointless. I wasn't going to win this battle, so best to just keep quiet about it. I let out a sigh of relief when he placed me on the floor outside the villa, then pushed me inside as he opened the front door, locking it behind him.

"Just in case you think about running again," he said, his eyes dark, his voice booming in anger. I stomped over to the sofa, plopping myself down then crossed my arms across my chest before looking out at the calm sea.

"You're such a child sometimes," he said as he placed a cup of water on the table in front of me. "Drink," he ordered.

"I'm not thirsty," I protested.

"Just drink the bloody drink, Luna. Can you just do one thing that I ask?" he asked me, defeated. I rolled my eyes before picking the glass up and taking a mouthful. I wasn't going to admit it to him, but I was gasping. As lovely as the sea was, the sun was hot, so I needed this drink more than I wanted to admit.

"Once you're finished, we're going out for the day," he said as he got himself a drink.

"Oh yeah, where we going?" I asked with attitude.

"Out," he said bluntly. He was infuriating me.

"Just tell me," I pleaded.

"No," he said as he walked into his bedroom, closing the door behind him. I heard my phone beep, I slowly got off the sofa and walked over to my bag that was sitting on the side in the kitchen, smiling when I saw it was my mum.

Hi my baby, how is Hawaii? I hope you are having a lovely time, we miss you so much. Daddy hasn't stopped worrying about you, even with the bodyguard there. Facetime me tonight, darling. Love you loads. Mummy X

Mummy. She made me laugh. I made a mental note to facetime them later, once we were back from our day out. I opened up my messages and clicked on our group chat.

"Ladies. Any idea where happy bollocks is taking me?" I tapped, relieved when I saw the three dots on the screen.

"Not a clue, hun. He told us to stay away and that you would catch up with us later. We have decided to go to the manoa falls, spoke to one of the reps and they suggested that, so grabbing a coach from downstairs in five. Fancy cocktails tonight?" *Vanessa replied.*

"Yeah, okay, cocktails sounds good." *I typed.* ***"Have fun, sounds... interesting."***

"We will, you too. See you in the reception at eight Xx" Brooke replied this time. ***"Oh, and I think we need a chat, don't you?"*** she typed.

I bit my lip before throwing my phone in my bag,

now feeling frustrated that I didn't know where I was going.

I walked into my bedroom, grabbing the sun lotion and rubbing a generous amount over my face, arms and legs. I just needed my back done, but like hell was I going to ask Taron. I didn't want him touching me again. Even though with each touch he set my skin alight, he made me feel things I only ever read about in romance novels.

My mind drifted back to the night before, the way his kisses trailed down my neck and to my collar bone, his dominance in the bedroom. The way he made me come so hard that my insides shattered completely. I jumped out my skin when I heard the bathroom door slam.

"Luna," he shouted. I could hear his footsteps hitting the tiled floor.

"Luna," he called again.

"I'm here." I sighed as I appeared in my bedroom door way, his brown eyes taking in every inch of me.

"So, can I know where we are going?" I asked.

"No," he said, this time with a small smile gracing his handsomely rugged face. He rubbed his stubble as he packed his rucksack with water, our phones and key cards.

"Come," he said firmly as he walked towards the door, holding his arm out for me to walk by him. As I passed him, our bodies close and nearly touching, his scent filled my nose. I was hypnotized.

I stood outside the villa as he closed the door behind

me, checking if it was locked before standing beside me. "Ready?" he asked.

"I suppose," I said apprehensively.

"Don't say it like that." His brows furrowed, eyes narrowing on mine.

"Well, how can I be ready for something when I don't know what I'm doing?"

"Okay, fair point." He shrugged. "Still not telling you though." He laughed as we walked back towards the beach. We didn't speak, just walked quietly, taking in the surroundings, the sweet air intoxicating.

I loved it here, I could quite easily close up shop and move here on my own. Well, actually, I would have to bring my mum and dad, and of course Chris. Couldn't be without them.

We made it to the end of the beach before coming to some rocks. I watched as Taron effortlessly started climbing up.

"Did you not think it would have been wise to tell me to change my shoes?" I said sarcastically, raising my perfectly shaped eyebrow.

"Why would I want to do that?" he said, poking his tongue out slightly then sinking his teeth into it. Just seeing his tongue made me melt, the thought of his tongue in-between my legs made my breath hitch. I shook away the thoughts as his voice shook through me.

"Okay there, princess?" he asked me.

"Brilliant," I said sarcastically. "Can you help me?" I asked, as much as I didn't want his help.

"Of course." He softened his expression, jumping back down from the low rock and onto the sand, my eyes drawing up and down his body. He really was hot. Too hot.

He stepped towards me, holding out his hand. As I took it, a surge of electric ran through me, startling me. His gorgeous grin faded.

"What's wrong?" he asked.

"Oh, nothing," I lied.

I gripped onto his hand as he dragged me towards him, sweeping me up into a cradled carry as he effortlessly climbed over the few rocks, letting me down gently once we were at the top.

As I peered over, I saw a secluded cove, the clear water crashing softly against the sand. I could see a man standing there with a diving suit up to his waist, the arms hanging down beside him, along with three oxygen tanks. My heart thumped.

"Oh my God," I said in barely a whisper.

"Surprise." He beamed, holding both his arms out towards the beach.

"We're swimming with the turtles?" I said, my face breaking into a huge smile baring my white teeth.

"Yeah, we are, baby," he said as he started walking towards the cove.

Baby.

I played the sound of his voice over and over in my head. I needed to calm down, he wasn't calling me baby. I followed him, still in shock at his surprise. I thought I was going to be doing this with the girls, not Taron.

"Hello there," the young, handsome man called out as we approached him, my wedges in my hand. There was no way I could walk down the hill on the other side of the rocks in them, and the way I was feeling I couldn't have Taron close to me as I wouldn't be able to control myself.

The instructor must've been late twenties, a golden brown tan, his black hair short and cropped. His eyes caramel with a smile that would melt anyone. His body was toned, more toned than Taron's. He had the famous 'V' lines disappearing into his pulled down diving suit that made my mouth dry. I quickly looked at Taron, trying to hide my blush.

"I'm Kona," he said as he held his large hand out, firmly gripping Taron's hand, then placing his free hand over the top, extending his arm to me as he gripped mine, this time not as tight.

"Okay, have either of you scuba dived before?" he asked, rocking back on his heels, his hands clasped together.

"Never." I shook my head.

"A few times yes, had to do it as part of my training in the marines," Taron said, his voice full of authority.

"Fab, okay, so I won't go through the set up with you

as such, but…" He stopped, realising he didn't know my name.

"Luna," I said sweetly, Taron rolling his eyes at my manner.

"Luna, come over here. I'll get you set up." His eyes were smiling at me. I walked over to him, standing next to him, my eyes on Taron the whole time. Taron's eyes were hooded, he didn't like it. Good. I relished in the fact that I made him jealous.

I felt Kona's body close to mine, his hands touching my hips gently.

"Hands off of her," Taron scolded, his eyes narrowing on Kona. "No one touches her but me."

I was shocked at his outburst.

"I'm sorry, dude, I didn't realise you were a couple," Kona said apologetically, dropping his hands from my hips.

"We're not boyfriend and girlfriend. He works for me, it's fine," I stated, I wanted a reaction from Taron, I wanted to rile him up.

"Oh, okay, cool," Kona said, his frown turning into a smile. "Where were we?"

Taron's eyes burned into mine, I had pissed him off big time. Shit.

We were ready and set up. I was grateful that I didn't have to wear a diving suit, we literally had black straps around our waist with our tanks on the back along with goggles and our mouth pieces. I got the giggles when I saw Taron walking in his flippers, yet he still made it look hot.

I pulled my phone out of my waterproof phone bag that was round my neck and snapped a photo of him without him realising, smiling internally at how handsome he looked. I slipped my phone back into the bag around my neck before walking into the warm water. Taron looked at me.

"You okay?" he asked.

"I'm wonderful." I beamed back.

"I'm glad." He winked, taking my hand as we walked further into the water, following Kona. My heart thumped, I was scared but excited at the same time.

"Okay, guys, listen to me," Kona said loudly as we stood waist deep in the water. "We have around an hour of oxygen in the tanks." His accent was thick in his voice. "Stay close to me. When we get to the clearing you are free to explore, but please keep an eye out for my signal when it's time to head back." His face was serious.

"Got it." I nodded a bit too excitedly.

"Okay, let's go diving," he said, grinning from ear to ear.

I swam anxiously, my eyes taking everything in. I couldn't get over how stunning it was, like a completely different world.

I looked to my side to see Taron's eyes as wide as mine as he took it all in, then placed his index finger and thumb tips together to form an okay sign. I did it back. I looked ahead and saw Kona calling us closer by curling his hand. We swam towards an edge, knowing full well it was safe, but when you're in that situation the nerves take over.

I gasped when I saw Kona dive deeper down past the cliff edge, me and Taron apprehensively following him. The breath felt like it was knocked out of my lungs, literally. The view was breath taking, then there in front of me, swimming freely were the sea turtles. If I wasn't in the water, I would have been crying tears of happiness. I couldn't believe I was seeing these beautiful creatures so free.

At that moment in time I just wanted to be free with them. I swam slowly, floating towards them, in absolute awe. I looked behind me, Taron was treading water, just staring at me. I felt my heart glow, I couldn't have wished for a more perfect moment then this.

I turned to face the turtles, one swimming so close I could have touched them, but I was scared too. Not that I was frightened, but because I didn't want to hurt them.

I felt his presence behind me, turning my head slightly to see him with his phone in his water bag, snapping photos. Normally I would've hit the phone away, but I wanted to remember every single moment from today.

After we took our tanks off, I wrung my hair out, watching Taron fall down onto the sand. I instantly felt irritated, I couldn't think of anything worse than being covered in sand. Kona walked towards me.

"So, Luna, was it everything you thought it would be?" he said, his cheesy smile beaming at me, his eyes glistening.

"Everything and more." I smiled back at him.

"So, I'm sorry if this is crossing the line, but could we get a drink sometime?" he asked brazenly.

"Yeah, that would be nice," I said, looking over my shoulder to see Taron's eyes brooding. "But I can't, I'm here with my friends," I declined as politely as I could. His eyes went sad, no glisten to them this time, and I instantly felt awful.

Taron was behind me in a shot, his hand wrapping itself round my waist, pulling me into him. The confusion flooded me, this guy was hot and cold. Jekyll and Hyde. It was infuriating.

I grabbed his hand and removed it from my hip, my temper rising.

"Thank you so much for today, Kona, and do you know what? I'm going for cocktails with my friends tonight in the hotel bar if you wanted that drink?" I asked.

"Fantastic, eight pm?" he asked.

"Eight is perfect." I winked before grabbing my

wedges and cover-up and walking out of the cove. Take that Taron.

Chapter SIXTEEN

I was glad to be back at the villa, Taron was furious, but I left him to it. I wasn't getting into anything with him again. I unlocked my phone to message the girls.

Still okay for cocktails tonight? Eight in the lounge bar, I'm bringing a man, & no, it's not Sloane.

I smiled as I sent it, seeing the three dots straight away.

Ooo, who you bringing? & why not Sloane? How were the turtles? A x

I tapped a reply.

Don't worry nosey, you'll see at eight.

Fuck Sloane. Turtles were amazing, everything and more. Manoa falls? X

I put my phone down and headed for the main bathroom, I wanted to have a bath. I shut the door, shutting myself away from him.

I peeled my red swim suit off and dropped it to the floor. I looked at myself in the big mirror, smiling at the slight kiss from the sun on my skin. I turned the water on in the giant bath putting way too much bubble bath into the running water. The smell filled the room.

I dipped my toe in before sinking down into the bubbles, it felt so good. I felt the tension from the last half hour wash away. Taron sulked the whole way home, not saying anything to me, but to be honest, that suited me. I didn't want to talk to him. He can't use me when he feels threatened.

Each time we've had sex it's been meaningless to him, he can't even look at me after.

I sunk under the water, washing the hard salt water out of my hair. My skin felt dry from the sun.

I washed my hair, then washed the suds off of me and smothered my hair in conditioner. I rinsed it off then jumped out the bath, wrapping the fluffy towel around my body and brushing my wet hair. I opened the door checking for Sloane and sighed in relief when he wasn't there. I walked towards my bedroom opening the door, when I saw Taron sitting on my bed. I gripped onto the handle of the door, my knuckles going white.

"Get out," I said bluntly.

"No," he said sternly.

"Please," I pleaded.

"No." He shook his head. I rolled my eyes walking towards my wardrobe, scouring my rail. I decided on the little yellow summer dress I bought the day I went shopping with Sloane. I grabbed it off the hanger, laying it on the bed. I went to step back when Taron grabbed the towel, pulling me close to him, his desperate eyes looking up at me, pleading with me.

I gripped onto the top of my towel, worried it was going to fall down.

"That's not going to stop me," he purred.

"Taron, no. I can't keep doing this. You can't keep wanting me when it suits you." I shook my head, pulling myself back away from him, as much as my body wanted me to pull towards him, I had to be strong.

"Don't?" Taron asked. His big brown eyes burned into mine as he wrapped his long fingers round the seam of the towel and pulled it open. His bottom lip going in-between his teeth as he placed his large hands on my hips, then ran his hands up and down my side in a tantalizing manner, his eyes following his hands as if he was mesmerizing every inch of my body. My senses tingled, my soul was on fire. I needed to stop him, I needed to push him away, but I didn't want too. That was the difference. I didn't want too.

He sat forwards, on the edge of the bed, opening his legs and pulling me even closer, his eyes back on mine.

"Did you invite Kona just to make me jealous?" he asked.

"Nope." I shook my head, smirking down at him.

"I don't want you having drinks with him," he said sternly.

"Why? You only want me when it suits you, and I'm not about that. You either want me and only me, or this stops." I pulled away from him, and tried to walk a couple of steps away, but I couldn't. He wrapped his arms around me, pulling me down onto him.

"I do want you," he whispered, his mouth covering my lips, a whimper leaving me as the contact that I have craved is finally given to me.

I climbed onto his lap, him pulling the towel completely away as I sat on him naked, aching for his touch. His kiss was fierce, his tongue invading my mouth. He ran his hand round the back of my neck, squeezing it tightly as his kiss grew hungrier.

I felt him harden underneath me, a little moan left my lips. I smoothed my hands down his torso before hungrily pulling him free from his swim shorts. He was still sandy, but I wasn't letting that stop this happening.

I pulled away from him. "Stop," I whispered, completely intoxicated in lust.

"No chance," he said, pulling me back to him.

"No, Taron, stop, please." I pulled away once more, this time he listened. "We can't keep going on like this, you're a head fuck." I bit my lip. "Also, we haven't used protection." I blushed.

“I’m clean,” he said, his eyes on mine. “Are you?” he asked.

“I’ve only been with Josh... Well... And you,” I admitted, slightly embarrassed at my inexperience.

“Really?” he asked.

“Mmm.” I dropped my head, my chin to my chest. His index finger ran under my chin, pulling me up to look at him.

“Hey, don’t be ashamed, there is nothing to be ashamed of.” His eyes dipped down to mine. “And I’m not a head fuck,” he defended himself as he laid back on the bed, pulling me with him.

I was suddenly very aware that I was naked. I grabbed the towel that he discarded to the bed and wrapped it round me before laying on top of him, my chin resting on my hands that were placed over his chest.

“You are.” I smirked.

“Luna, I haven’t been with anyone since Emerson.” His eyes hazed over. “This is all new to me. I didn’t want to like you, but I did. From the moment I saw you in your home in London, I wanted to get to know you. But I have demons and ghosts that I am constantly fighting, that’s why I push you away. I want to get close to you, but when I do, I get this almighty fear that something will happen to you,” he admitted, his eyes on mine the whole time.

“You can’t worry about things like that,” I said quietly. “We have no control over those things.” I tried to give him a small smile, he didn't return one.

"This has been such a whirlwind, but I just can't gauge you. One minute you're lovely, warm and attentive. The next you're cold, vicious and a jerk." I shrugged. "I call you Jekyll and Hyde, because that's who you remind me of."

"Jekyll and Hyde… Seriously? The dude was a monster." He laughed before raising his eyebrows.

"Yup." I laughed with him, I was glad to see him laughing. He doesn't do it enough.

"Can you cancel cocktails tonight? Let's just stay home," he begged.

"I can't, I haven't seen the girls. This is meant to be a friend's holiday," I said, about to sit up before he wrapped his toned arms around me, pulling me back down so our chests were together.

"At least cancel Kona then," he said, his eyes soft. I could lose myself in his deep, dark brown eyes.

"Okay, fine." I rolled my eyes then scrunched my nose up.

"Perfect," he muttered before ripping the towel from me again and throwing it to the floor, then leaning up and kissing me softly, igniting the fire deep within once more.

A burn so intense brewed in my belly that needed extinguishing. I pushed myself up off his chest, feeling brazen, lust hypnotizing me. His eyes glared at my naked body, slowly working their way from my face to the apex in-between my thighs. I bit my lip as I fisted my hand down the front of his shorts, desperate to release him and feel the contact I was so desperately craving.

He lifted me up from him, then lifted his hips, pulling his shorts down to his ankles before pulling me down to him. I leant down, pressing my full lips onto his. A delicious groan left him as we made contact.

I slowly grinded my hips into him, his hands tightening their grip round my small waist. I pulled away from him, sitting myself up as I lifted myself ever so slightly to position him exactly where I needed him. I slowly slid back down onto him, taking every inch of him, a deep sigh escaping my lips of the exotic feel of him filling me completely, a moan coming from deep within me.

He sat himself up, our eyes connected on each other's as he slowly thrust up into me, matching my slow hip movements. I wrapped my arms around his neck, supporting myself as I let him take control. He dipped his head down, his hungry mouth taking my nipple into his mouth, his teasing tongue flicking and licking before sucking hard, making me whimper.

He removed a hand from my hip and glided his hand between my soaked legs before rubbing my sensitive spot. I instantly clamped around him, the feelings getting too much, his mouth and his fingers taking me to heaven.

I threw my head back, my hips moving with him so I could get him as deep as I could. He opened his legs slightly, making me drop, but his thrusts became so much deeper as he hit me right where he needed too.

He moved his mouth from my pert nipple and pressed his

full, hot lips at the base of my exposed throat, planting a soft kiss before sucking. I came, having no control, moaning his name as he picked up his speed, the sound of our skin clapping together was too much.

His thumb still firmly on my nub as I came hard once more, this time he followed, shouting my name out, his forehead on my chest, his hand squeezing my waist hard causing pain, but a good pain.

He fell back onto the bed, taking me with him. We were both consumed in a complete sex state, my head on his chest, his heart thumping in my ear. I had never felt so safe in all my life. His arms wrapped tightly round me, us both waiting for our breathing to still.

Chapter SEVENTEEN

I slipped into my lemon sun dress, pulling the thick straps up my shoulders and arranging my large boobs into it, before stepping into my faithful wedges. I sprayed my perfume, then applied a light layer of nude lipstick.

I styled my blond hair into waves before putting my gold-hooped earrings in. I grabbed my phone and walked into the lounge, waiting for Taron to get ready. I tapped a message out to the girls telling me to meet us in the lounge at eight, then I realised that I hadn't messaged Kona. Balls.

I scrolled through my phone, looking for his number, so I could cancel. I felt bad, but I did say to Taron I would. I heard his bathroom door go, pulling my eyes from my phone I looked up to him, my mouth going dry at his appearance. I could've pooled on the floor at his feet. His one smouldering look could floor me, making me melt into nothing. I licked my lips before smiling at him

"Hey," I cooed as I walked towards him. He was

wearing a white linen short sleeved, fitted shirt, tanned chino shorts and suede loafers. His long, black hair pushed back and styled.

"Hey." He smiled as he walked towards me, linking his arms around me, pulling me in for a small peck on my lips. "Ready?" he asked.

"Yup." My eyes lit up.

We walked out the front door, our fingertips brushing each other's before we pulled them away. We weren't quite ready for public displays of affection.

We walked past the girls' villa, deciding not to knock as it was only seven thirty.

"Would you mind when we get to the bar, if I called my mum? I said I would video call her, and well, I've been a little pre-occupied." I blushed before a silly grin spread across my face, and I looked down at my manicured toes.

"Of course not," he said softly, his hand touching the base of my back, then realising what he had done he pulled his hand quickly away. We walked through the communal gardens of the hotel, stretching towards the stunning beach and sea. The sights were truly breath taking. We didn't say much more, enjoying the silence before walking into the main bar.

It was busy, but not overly. We found a small booth in the corner, where the lights were dimmed. I scooted into the cosy booth, the tanned leather sofa smelt amazing. I sat for a moment, taking in my surroundings.

The dark oak tables with the glass jar hanging lights that were lowly lit. The dark oak bar going round in a complete circle. In the middle of the bar was bottles upon bottles of alcohol.

I felt hungry, realising we hadn't eaten all day, and I screwed my face up.

"What's wrong?" Taron asked.

"I'm hungry, we haven't eaten." I sighed grabbing the bar menu off the middle of the table, my eyes hungrily scanning the menu.

"Well, let me know what you want, I'll order us some food and drinks before your friends get here. Then, I was thinking I'll leave you to it. I have some bits to catch up on." He smiled sweetly, his hand coming to my face, cupping it. I tentatively laid my face into it, smiling back at him, completely drunk off the sight of him. His thumb rubbed my cheek before he stood out the booth, then straightened his shirt.

"What do you fancy?" he asked.

"Cheese burger, chips and a cosmo," I said, pushing the menu away from me.

"Sounds good, won't be a minute," he said before walking to the bar.

I took this moment to pull my phone out and video call my mum. After waiting a few seconds it connected.

"Hello, my darling Luna," she cooed.

"Hey, Mama, you okay?" I asked, waving and smiling at her.

She blew kisses at me through the phone. "Oh, my angel, I have missed you." She pouted.

"I've missed you too, Mum, but I am having such a wonderful time. It has been so needed." I nodded, my eyes wandering from the screen over to Taron, drinking his sight in once more. God I was love drunk from him. My feelings so raw and deep for him.

"What you been doing?" she asked.

"Not a lot to be honest, done a bit of reading, sun bathing and me and Taron went scuba diving with the sea turtles today, and oh my God, Mum, it was one of the best things I have ever done." I beamed like an excited school girl.

"Is that my princess?" I heard my dad bellow in the background.

"Hi, Daddy," I said.

"You look lovely, my darling, Hawaii has been kind to you." He smiled, but his face looked aged, covered in worry.

"What's wrong, Daddy?" I asked, suddenly concerned. "Has something happened? Is Chris okay?"

"I'm fine, princess, and yes, Chris is fine. I just worry about you, that's all," he admitted, his brows pulling together, his eyes narrowing down the screen.

"I'm fine, Daddy, I promise. Taron is doing a

wonderful job of keeping me safe, even though I didn't want him here originally." I laughed.

"Well, good, I'm paying him enough to do his job." My father's tone is abrupt and clipped. I roll my eyes. Instantly putting me in a bad mood.

"Darling, go away, you've dampened her mood," my mum said, snatching the phone off of him before shooing him away with her hand.

"Sorry, honey," she cooed in a motherly tone.

"That's okay," I said quietly, nibbling the skin on my thumb.

"Just ignore him, you know what he is like," she said shaking her head.

"Yeah, I know…" I trailed off, looking up at Taron, my heart thumping when I saw his eyes lock on mine. I could lose myself in his deep, brown eyes.

"Luna," my mum called through the phone.

"Yea, sorry, Mum, I've got to go. Dinner is here," I said. Lying.

"Okay, sweetie, stay safe. Check in tomorrow please. Love you always," she said waving at her phone.

"Bye, Mama, I love you too," I said, waving back at her then cutting her off.

I fell back against the sofa in the booth feeling utterly exasperated from that conversation. My dad was such a killjoy sometimes. Taron appeared in front of the table, placing my Cosmo down, along with his beer before scooting in the booth.

"What's wrong?" he asked.

"Oh, nothing, just my dad. He annoys me, but that's just Daddy," I said shaking my head, my hands in my lap.

"Is everything okay?" he asked concerned. I couldn't tell him that the reason I was annoyed was because of his comment about Taron.

"Yeah, fine, I'll be okay. Thank you for the drink," I said, leaning across and grabbing my glass, pulling Taron's beer towards him. He placed his arm on the top of the leather sofa before drinking a mouthful of beer and nodding in appreciation. I took my first sip, my taste buds exploding.

"Oh, this is so good," I said before taking another mouthful. Taron's eyes on me, I faced him. "What?" I giggled.

"Am I right in thinking this is the dress you needed help doing up?" His eyes dark and stormy as they focussed on my chest that was combusting out of my dress.

With his other hand he ran his index finger from the middle of my collar bone, slowly down towards my breast. My breath hitched, my face blushed. I was grateful for the low lighting.

He moved closer, his mouth near my ear. "If we weren't here, I would take you home, tie your hands behind your back, then take this pretty fucking dress off before taking every inch of you and make you scream my name over and over again," he said in a low, sexy voice before sliding away from me and taking another mouthful of his beer.

I couldn't say anything, I couldn't get the thoughts out of my head, my knickers damp from his dirty words. My mouth opened slightly as I held onto the stem of my cocktail glass a little too hard, my eyes staring into my pink cocktail. It took a lot for me to pull my big green eyes and focus on him, my cheeks flushed, my breathing fast. He sat there, facing forward as he brought his beer up to his full lips, a stupid grin spread across his face.

Just as I was about to say something, my friends turned up.

"Luna," Vanessa shouted, pulling me from my hypnotic state.

"Oh, hey," I said a little too enthusiastically, waving fast at them.

"That's my cue to go," he muttered, his hand gripping my bare thigh, squeezing it before he scooted himself out the booth. "I'll be just over there." He smiled at me, picking up his beer and walking towards the second table across.

God, I wanted him more than ever now, the constant ache deep inside me was distracting, and he knew exactly what he was doing. Bastard.

"So what's the deal, do they come over to take your

order or do you go to the bar?" Brooke asked.

"Bar." I said, finishing my drink in one, swift mouthful then holding it up, shaking it in front of her face. "Another, please." I smiled innocently.

They looked amazing, their skin was sun kissed, all three of them were wearing similar tight, bodycon dresses that emphasized their curves.

"You all look hot." I winked at them.

"You drunk?" Brooke asked, flicking her long, red hair over her shoulder then looking to Vanessa.

"No I'm bloody not," I defended myself.

"You sure?" Vanessa said, her honey eyes on mine.

"Yes!" I exclaimed, my eyes wandering over to Taron who was smirking on his phone. "Can you just go order drinks, please?" I smiled.

"Fine, same again?" she asked.

"Surprise me." I winked as I watched Brooke sashay off towards the bar, gaining the attention of the room. She was beautiful, so I couldn't blame them.

Vanessa and Ava sat next to me, my eyes lighting up when I saw my dinner coming over.

"You ordered without us?" Ava asked.

"Yup, not even sorry. I haven't eaten today, and I couldn't wait." I shrugged.

"It's okay." Ava nudged me.

"Good." I giggled as I accepted the burger and chips off the waiter. "Can I have some mayo and ketchup, please?" I asked sweetly, batting my eyelids.

Within minutes they were back with the sauces, I couldn't help licking my lips.

Brooke whistled for Ava and Ness' attention to help her with the drinks. What the hell had she ordered, I thought as I ate a mouthful of burger. Oh, it was good. My stomach growled in appreciation. Ness and Ava walked out the booth towards Brooke. I felt Taron's eyes on me. I turned slightly to look at him, when our eyes met he winked before turning back to his phone, snorting a laugh.

Brooke, Ness and Ava came walking over with two trays of drinks. Cocktails filled one, tequila shots filling the other. Christ.

"Thirsty?" Brooke smirked as she placed the tray down, followed by Ava.

She handed me a tequila shot, before passing one to Ava and Ness, holding them out in front of her. "Ladies, cheers." She smiled.

"Cheers," I said before knocking it back, licking the salt and sucking the lemon, wincing as the sour hit my tongue.

After only getting through half my burger and a quarter of my chips I pushed the plate away. "Want some?" I asked the girls, they shook their heads.

"Why is hottie sitting over there?" Ava asked me, her brown hair up in a ponytail, her dark brown eyes on mine.

"He said he wanted to give us some space." I

shrugged, wanting to get off the conversation sooner rather than later.

"Why is that?" Brooke pressed.

"I don't bloody know, why don't you go ask him?" I said abruptly, shaking my head before taking a mouthful of the long island tea she bought.

"Oi, Taron," she shouted over the booth, his brown beautiful eyes looked up, first looking at me then Brooke. "Why you sitting over there?"

"Not that I have to explain myself to you," he said sarcastically, "But I wanted to give you all some girly time." He smiled a big smile at her.

"Fair enough." she shrugged, dropping the subject.

"Luna, didn't you say you were bringing someone?" Ava asked, twirling her ponytail round her index finger.

"I did, but he cancelled," I lied.

"Oh, that's a shame, was he hot?" Ness asked.

"Yeah, he was." I felt guilty, knowing Taron was in ear shot. "But he wasn't my type."

Brooke rolled her eyes. "Anyway, you never got back to me, either of you. How was manoa falls?" I asked finishing my cocktail and having another shot before moving onto a pornstar martini.

"It was breath taking," Ava said dreamily. "Wish you could've come, but I know you were pre-occupied." She poked her tongue out.

"I know, I wish I came too, but the sea turtles were

amazing. I couldn't miss out on them." I sighed. "And Sloane was nice enough to take me." I nodded before taking a mouthful of my drink.

"To be honest, it did sound amazing," Ness piped up after downing her blue lagoon. "And you got to see hottie in his speedos." She laughed out loud.

"He doesn't wear speedos!" I scrunched my nose up, my mind drifting back to earlier today, my heart racing.

"What does he wear?" Brooke probed.

"Trunks," I said bluntly, rolling my eyes.

"Did he leave much to the imagination?" Brooke teased.

"Pipe down." I laughed, bringing my drink to my lips. My eyes roaming to Taron.

"Can we actually spend the day together tomorrow?" Ava pouted, tucking a strand of loose hair behind her ears.

"Of course," I said loudly.

"Yeah, because you've been more occupied with hottie than us," Ness said, playing with her hair whilst drinking her coke and rum through a straw.

"I know, I'm sorry," I admitted, feeling like a shitty friend. "Things just got in the way, and to be honest, Taron has been a good distraction. Not a constant reminder," I said quietly pushing my pornstar into the middle of the table. "Not that you three are reminders," I explained myself suddenly feeling awful.

"We get it, Luna," Brooke said. "We really do, but

this was your idea to come on a girl's holiday, then you bought the baggage with you," she said bluntly.

"I was left on my wedding day Brooke," I hissed. "It's not something you can just forget about, but since being here, with Sloane, he has made me forget." I slammed my glass down on the table with force. Taron was up over by the booth, standing at the seat entrance.

"You okay, Luna?" he asked, his eyes darting between me and Brooke who was sitting there, wrapping her tongue round an olive from her martini. She was so vicious sometimes.

"Fine," I said bitterly, tears springing in my eyes.

"No need for that Brooke." Ness shook her head, pulling me into her hugging me tightly.

"Well, one of us had to say it, I couldn't take another minute of you two whining about it in the villa." She rolled her eyes, dropping her cocktail stick before emptying her glass of martini straight down her throat. Her eyes cold, no remorse in her voice.

I pushed myself off of Vanessa and stood, sliding past her to get out.

"Luna," Vanessa called out. I turned around, tears now flowing down my face.

"What?" I shouted.

"Don't go," she begged.

I looked at Ava, praying that she would stick up for me, but she didn't. She sunk down into the sofa keeping her eyes on the floor.

"Do one. I don't do two-faced people, especially ones who are meant to be my best friends," I said pointing my finger at her before turning my hand slightly and sticking my middle finger up at all three of them. Shaking my head and wiping my eyes, I turned on my heel and ran out the restaurant, Taron behind me.

Chapter EIGHTEEN

TARON

I was hot on Luna's heels, there was no way I was letting her out of my sight after what just happened. I didn't hear the full conversation, but from what was said when I stood up, I kind of got the gist. What I couldn't get my head around is that these girls are meant to be her friends, they should be happy that she is smiling, but instead they're bringing her down because she spent the day with me. Women. I could never understand them.

I didn't dwell on it too much as no doubt they would be laughing and talking tomorrow as if tonight didn't happen. I didn't say anything to her, just stayed close so she knew I was there. I was grateful when I saw our villa, jogging slightly to get ahead of her.

"Let me go first," I said as I held my arm out stopping her. "Just in case." I smiled weakly as I held the key card on the contactless door fob.

I opened the door, switching the lights on before walking down the hallway, scoping the room. I felt uneasy. I checked the kitchen and lounge area before walking into her bedroom, Luna pacing behind me.

"Go back," I said sternly.

I looked round her room, her wardrobe and suitcase open, her clothes pulled out.

"Luna, did you leave your wardrobe and suitcase open?" I shouted out.

"I could've done, I'm not sure." I heard her unsure voice, and not convinced I walked back into the lounge, when I noticed the patio door was unlocked and slightly ajar.

"I definitely locked this," I mumbled, now locking the door again.

"Oh my god, is someone in here?" she asked panicked, looking white as a sheet.

"No, baby, no one is in here. Maybe I left it unlocked?" I said trying to calm her. I knew I hadn't left it unlocked.

She stayed close to me as I had one further look round, feeling tense. I hadn't been told what had happened to David to make him want to hire me, nor did I care, normally. But with her, I did care. I cared a fucking lot.

It doesn't make sense, I am normally fully briefed, but when David took me on, I was told that she needed protection. He got a tip from an outside source, that outside source being Josh. I pinched the top of my nose and closed my eyes tightly.

I walked over to the front door of the villa, locking it and putting the catch on before walking into Luna's bedroom. I wanted to make sure she was okay after the shit storm of tonight. She was sat on the edge of her queen sized bed, rubbing her thumb over her phone screen, her white teeth sinking into her full-bodied lips. I held onto the door frame to her room before knocking on the door.

"May I?" I asked.

"Of course, you don't need to ask." She smiled, throwing her phone down on the bed then patted the spot next to her. I walked in, cautious smiling at her before sitting down next to her.

"Heard from them?" I asked as I looked over my shoulder at her phone.

"Nope." She sighed, her eyes on mine. "Brooke, I'm used to it. That's what she is like, believe it or not, she acts that way because she cares. But Vanessa and Ava? They've never acted like this. It's not like I've spent the entire two days we've been here talking about it. I've pushed it so far down that I don't think it will ever surface again. I'm trying to get over it and process all of this as well as I can. I just don't get why they're being like it? Maybe I have been a shitty friend?" She shrugged before sighing deeply, her gorgeous emerald eyes dull.

I reached up and tucked a loose wave of hair behind her ear, then ran my finger down her jaw, moving down to her neck, wrapping my finger under her thick yellow sundress strap and pulling it down her shoulder slightly.

"Let me help you out of this, then we will get into bed with hotel television, how does that sound?" I said softly, my finger still firmly curled under her strap.

Her eyes flicked up to mine, her breathing fastened at my touch. I glided my finger across her shoulder before trailing it down her spine as I gripped onto the zip on the back of her dress, then slowly pulled it down, exposing her bare back, putting small circles on her skin in a tantalizing manner.

Her breath hitched, her skin covered in goose-bumps. I knew nothing was going to happen, I wanted it too, but it wasn't the right moment. And I wasn't a complete arsehole who was only out to get his own.

I moved behind her, putting my legs either side of her tiny body before pushing both of her straps down off of her shoulders and pressing my lips along the top of her shoulder, trailing soft kisses along the top of her back, moving along to the base of her neck before finishing on her other shoulder.

Her head rolled back in appreciation. My hands stayed on her shoulders the whole time, then delicately pulled her straps down to her wrists where she pulled them out. She stepped off the bed, shimmying out of her dress, her head twisting over her shoulder, her eyes batting down before bringing them up to me, her cute button nose crinkling before her beautiful smile appeared on her face.

There it was, the most beautiful thing about her.

Her arms cuddled round her bare chest before she turned to face me, just standing there in her white lace thong. I moved myself back towards the head board, pulling the quilt back for her to climb under, the air con nipping the air, making the room comfortable. She hopped in before covering her glorious, milky skin with the thick white duvet.

I lifted my arm up ready for her to nestle under my arm, laughing when she took in a big sniff of my scent.

"Mmm, you smell like a man." She giggled before getting comfortable. I picked her phone up, giving it a quick glance to see she had messages from Ava and Vanessa. I turned the phone upside down, placing it face down on the side table. She didn't need to read the messages just yet. I grabbed the television remote, turning it off of standby.

"Anything you fancy watching?" I asked her, her fingertips twirling in my light dusting of chest hair.

"Gossip girl," she said sleepily. I quickly searched and found the complete box set on there. I looked down at her, her sweet smile on her face, her eyes lighting up with happiness. I leant down and placed a delicate kiss on the top of her head, taking in her scent, filling my lungs with her.

She was intoxicating.

Chapter NINETEEN

LUNA

I woke after an amazing sleep, having Taron's arms round me all night made me feel safe and comforted. I stretched up, turning to face him, studying his beautiful face. His dark stubble longer then when we first met, his lips full and blush red, his olive skin tanned with gold undertones, like honey.

I never understood why they called it olive-skinned; when I was younger I used to literally think of a green olive. I snorted a laugh before running the top of my finger down his throat and onto his chest, entwining my fingers in his light dusting of dark chest hair. I didn't want to move from this spot, but I needed to go and speak to the girls.

"Morning, you beauty," he said sleepily in a husky voice.

"Good morning." I beamed. I watched as he

stretched out in bed, my eyes flitting up and down his body. He was a God.

"I'm gonna go shower," he said before rolling out of the bed and walking towards the door. I felt a little sour that he hadn't given me a morning kiss. I was needy for him. I had never been the needy type.

I watched as he stopped when he got to the door, turning and striding back over to me, placing his hands either side of my face and pulling me in for a gentle kiss. Pulling away and smiling at me before he made his way to the shower.

I flopped back down in bed, in my holiday bliss. We had two days left here, I didn't want to leave.

Back to the real world. What would happen to me and Taron? Was this just a holiday romance full of sex? Or was there something more there?

I grabbed my phone from Taron's side and noticed the messages from the girls last night. I opened Vanessa's first.

Luna, I'm sorry. It's just been brewing, and we missed you. Ignore Brooke, you know what she's like. Sorry again, we love you x

I rolled my eyes, then I opened Ava's.

I'm sorry, baby girl x

I locked my phone and rolled out of bed, padding my way into the bathroom. I stood in the doorway admiring Taron's toned physique in the shower, biting my lip, crossing my legs, trying to dull the ache.

I slid the shower door back before stepping in and pressing my body up against him, running my hands to his belly then up to his chest, kissing in-between his shoulder blades, feeling a spark course through me. I pulled my lips from him, feeling him sigh as I did, and I pressed my forehead on his back, closing my eyes. I didn't want this to end, I wasn't ready for it to end. I needed to speak to him about it.

He turned around, his hair dripping water down his face as he wrapped his arms around me, pushing me up against the wall, his mouth over mine. His hand slid down my wet, soapy body before reaching down between my legs, pushing them open before gliding his fingers in-between my thighs, pushing his finger into my soaked opening. Moaning against his mouth as he slowly pushed in and out of me.

His other hand wrapped in my wet hair, tugging my head back, kissing and sucking my neck. When he pulled away from me, a whimper left my mouth at the loss of contact. He pushed the door back on the shower, grabbing the white fluffy towel and wrapped it around his waist as he marched out the bathroom, leaving me under the running shower with an ache so dull my insides were burning. I needed my release. I wasn't the reason he ran out like that, I know it wasn't me. We were past that stage. I hoped.

I washed my hair and washed the suds off my silky skin before leaving the shower and wrapping myself in a towel, walking out to the lounge area.

I jumped out my skin as I saw Brooke, Ness and Ava sitting on the sofa with Taron standing up, still in his towel. I went a crimson red as they've just seen me walk out of the same bathroom he came from.

"Busy, were we?" Brooke said, her tongue slowly licking her top lip while twirling her hair round her finger. Vanessa was staring at Taron and Ava was flushed, most likely because the hunk with the perfect teeth was standing half naked in front of her.

"What do you want?" I said bitterly, standing behind Taron.

Brooke rolled her eyes at me before uncrossing her legs and dropping her hand into her lap. "To say sorry," she said, sincerity in her voice before darting her eyes to Ness and Ava. "Don't you two need to apologise?" Her eyes narrowed on them.

"We did text," Ness piped up, Ava nodding her head next to her.

"Oh, so it's just me in the dog house then," Brooke

snapped.

"That's my cue to leave," Taron said quietly, turning and squeezing my shoulder before he walked into the bedroom, closing the door behind him.

"That was a dick move last night," I said to Brooke, my eyes not leaving hers.

"It was, yeah, but it was also the truth." She shrugged, no guilt on her face at all.

"Brooke," Vanessa hissed. Brooke rolled her eyes so far back in her head I thought they would get stuck back there.

"Yes, I'm sorry," she said, standing up and wrapping her arms around me. "Can we just have our day now?" She smirked before sitting back down on the sofa.

"Give me ten," I said quietly. "And I'm sorry too." Smiling, I slipped into my bedroom, relieved when I saw him sitting on my bed. His dark brown eyes devouring me.

"All okay?" he asked as I sauntered over to him.

"Yeah, all fine, sorted. I think, anyway. You never know with Brooke. She could throw it back in my face again any minute." I shrugged.

"I'm glad it's sorted. Don't let her talk to you like that again though," he said, his lips twitched as he rubbed his thumb into the palm of his hand. My eyes fell to the floor before looking back up at him.

I could tell he was agitated from the situation. I dropped my towel, swaying my hips as I stood in front of him, linking my arms around his neck before climbing onto his lap, kissing him.

"Thank you for looking out for me." I smiled at him before kissing him back on his lips again. Taron's arms wrapped around my body tightly, pulling me closer into him. A smile so wide graced my face, my teeth showing as our kiss turned playful. A giggle left me as he pulled me down, squealing as he rolled over on top of me.

"Stop," I screamed out while still laughing. "I need to get dressed, the girls are waiting."

"Fuck the girls," he said, his eyes on mine.

"Taron," I scolded before he kissed me. "Fine, as much as I want to keep you here with me, exactly as you are, you're right." Leaning down and pecking me once more on the lips. "Let's get ready," he said before pushing himself up. "Meet you outside in five." He winked.

I hesitantly pulled myself off the bed, grabbing an orange bikini, slipping it on and tucking my boobs away, then grabbed my lace cover-up before putting my hair into a messy bun, pulling a couple of strands of hair down in front of my ears. I put my gold hoops in as I walked out the bedroom, smiling at the girls.

"Finally," they said in unison, all standing from the sofa.

"Ready?" I teased before winking and poking my tongue out, Taron stepping out behind me.

We walked onto the beach of the hotel, looking

around at the hustle and bustle. We found a quiet spot, kicking our shoes off when Maui walked over. "Luna," he said cheerily. "Aloha."

"Aloha, Maui, how are you?"

"Glorious, thank you for asking. What can I get you?" he asked.

"Do you have any sunbeds?" Brooke asked, looking down her nose at him.

"Let me see what I can do, we're really busy today." He shrugged before walking back towards the hotel.

"Fancy a walk along the shore?" Taron asked, creeping up behind me.

"Yes," I said, a little too excitedly. Maybe this could be our chance to talk about what will be when we get home?

"Girls, we're just going for a walk, if Maui returns, can you grab me a sex on the beach?" I asked.

"You sure you're not going to be getting that in a minute?" Brooke jibed getting an eyeroll from me as a reaction. I turned to face Taron as we started our walk towards the sea.

"So, why did you want a walk? The girls too much?" I joked.

He sighed heavily. "A little, it's just Brooke. I saw a completely different side to her yesterday, and I didn't like it."

"I know, but that's just Brooke. You do sort of get

used to it." I shrugged my shoulders in a small motion. He laced his fingers through mine, gripping tightly before bringing my hand to his lips and kissing the back of it

"I like you," I cooed, my eyes staring up at him.

"I like you too." He smirked, turning his head to face me as we continued our slow walk along the sea front.

"What's going to happen when we go home?" I asked, nerves riddling me. I slowed my breathing, anxious as to what he was going to say. He went to answer when we heard a man shout out.

"Taron!"

I saw Taron's eyes dart across the beach, trying to work out where the sound was coming from. "Taron, over here mate," we heard again, Taron's eyes locking on a guy, waving.

"Come," he said before pulling me towards this stranger.

I watched his handsome face break into a smile when he realised who this familiar stranger was.

"Carter," he said, his voice slightly high pitched and happy as he shook Carter's hand. He then extended his hand to, I'm assuming, Carter's wife. I stood and studied them.

Carter's mousy hair was tousled, his eyes were the most stunning sage green, slight freckles specked across his nose. He was handsome, I felt guilty for thinking it when I had Taron next to me.

My eyes wandered to the lady by his side, her long auburn hair was styled in beach waves, her eyes were crystal grey, focussed on her husband. As my eyes carried on looking at her, her little pot-belly was apparent in her coral bikini, which made me smile.

"Carter, this is Luna. Luna, this is Carter and his wife Freya," Taron said, his arm snaking round my waist, pulling me close.

"Nice to meet you, Luna," Carter smiled, a slight twang to his voice which made me wonder where he was from.

"Nice to meet you too, Carter, Freya," I said, extending my hand out to both of them.

"You too." Freya smiled a warm smile at me.

"Mummy, Mummy, sandy castle." This strawberry blond little boy came from behind her tapping her leg. "Mummy, Mummy," he carried on.

"Okay, Parker, darling," she said. "Excuse me." She turned her back on us and wandered over to her son's sandcastle.

"How's it going? Busy with work?" Carter asked, taking his glasses off of his head then pushing them up his nose.

"Yeah, man, really busy. I'm actually working now," Taron said, nodding his head down to me.

"Oh, like that, aye?" Carter let out a deep chuckle.

"Yeah, we didn't plan this. Just happened." Taron

shrugged.

"Sorry, we couldn't find a spot for you in our security department, mate," Carter said softly. "But, I can see things worked out." He looked at me and smiled. "Luna, what do you do? It must be high profile to have Taron look after you."

"Aha, no. I own a florist and coffee shop. My dad made me bring Taron with me for reasons I'm unsure of, and Taron hasn't said anything." I shrugged at him.

"A florist and coffee shop?" he asked, his eyebrows raising as he asked his question.

"Yup, in Kensington." I nodded. "It's called *Cake & Roses*, so unoriginal I know." I laughed

"I know the place. Stunning little shop, that's where I bought my now wife's flowers from when we first started dating. A dozen white roses." He smiled at the memory.

"Well, I'm glad we could help. You chose well." I beamed.

"What, the wife or the flowers?" he joked, his deep chuckle coming out again.

"Both," I said.

"I see Freya is expecting, congratulations my friend," Taron said, stepping forward and patting him on the back just as Freya came and stood next to her husband, Parker attached to her hip.

"Yup." He beamed proudly, pulling his wife close to him then kissing her. "We're expecting a daughter, three months until the big day," he cooed, the look of love plastered all over his face.

"How wonderful," Taron said, "Little boy and a girl. How old is Parker now?"

"Just over two."

"He speaks well for two," Taron said as I admired the little boy. He had his mum's skin tone and his dad's beautiful sage eyes. He was going to be a heartbreaker. His parents were stunning.

"That he does, don't you, buddy?" he said taking him from Freya's hip and cuddling him and kissing him in his mop of strawberry blond hair, before kissing his wife.

"Anyway, we will leave you be," Taron said, lacing his fingers back through mine

"Yeah, no worries, mate, when do you fly home?" Carter asked.

"Two days' time."

"Ah, that's a shame, we are here for another week, belated birthday present for the wife," he said smoothly.

"Enjoy." Taron chuckled.

Carter pulled his wallet out of his shorts pocket and handed Taron a card. "Give me a call when you get home, I might have a job available. Get you off this bodyguard gig," he jeered, pulling his glasses down his nose and winking, Freya shaking her head at her husband.

"Ah, thanks, mate, I will do. To be honest, I think its time to give up this gig anyway, especially now," Taron muttered before kissing the side of my head, butterflies fluttering deep in my tummy. *Did this mean that he did want more when we got home?*

"Enjoy the rest of your holiday, safe flight," Carter said as we started to walk away.

"You too, good luck both of you with the baby. I'll definitely call," Taron called out.

"Take care, mate." He waved. "Bye, Luna."

"Bye, Carter, Freya." I waved, Freya smiling and waving back. What a couple.

We strolled back along the beach towards the girls, seeing them in the distance Taron pulled me back, spinning me into a cuddle before craning his neck down and kissing me softly on my lips. The sun beating down on our skin, I felt the electric running through my body. I didn't want to leave his arms, I could've stayed here forever.

He pulled away, a silly smile on his face, him pulling his bottom lip between his teeth.

"So, what were you saying before we saw Carter?" he asked, scooping my hands into his and rubbing his thumbs across the back of my knuckles.

"Oh, erm..." I stuttered, embarrassed to be bringing it up with him. It took a lot for me to get it out the first time. I took a deep breath before speaking.

"What is this?" I asked.

A confused look crossed his face, his eyes on mine,

pushing me for an explanation.

"This being, us," I said, motioning my index finger between me and him.

"Well, do we need to label it?" he asked abruptly.

"Er, well, no, but I just want to know, is this going to be some Hawaiian fling or are we going to try and make a go of it when we get home?"

"Luna, I'm thirty-five and a widow. I'm not in a 'fling' territory." He smirked. "I want you."

I didn't say anything, I threw my arms around his neck before his arms wrapped around my waist, then lifted me off the floor, kissing me as he spun me around on the shoreline.

"You've made me the happiest girl alive." I beamed before kissing him again as he dropped me down onto the wet sand. "Come on, better get back to the girls." I groaned before grabbing his hand and pulling him towards them. I was on cloud nine.

"Hey, girls." I waved as I sat on the free sunbed.

"Hey, baby," Ness said. "We did order you a sex on the beach, but it was getting warm, so I drank it." She shrugged before laying back down on her bed.

"No worries, we bumped into one of Taron's friends and got chatting." I sat on the sunbed, pulling my cover-up over my head and throwing it onto the sand. I needed the sun on my skin, a cocktail in my hand and Taron next to me.

I looked over at him, laying on the sunbed watching his muscles ripple under his skin. God, I wanted him more than ever.

We walked back towards the girls' villa, my skin sizzling from the sun, but in a good way. Taron stayed close, his eyes always darting around when we were out of the villas. We got to the girls' villa, standing outside the front door.

"You want to come in for drinks?" Brooke asked.

"Yeah, I do," I said quietly before looking at Taron, his eyes hungry. "Taron, do you mind?"

"You can come as well, Taron," Ava piped up, Brooke shooting her a look.

"What? He is her bodyguard after all," Ness backed Ava up.

"No, it's fine, go. I'll be up soon. I don't have to worry about you when you're with your friends, especially when you're with Brooke," he teased before walking towards the villa.

I felt lost without him suddenly, I felt like he had been in my life forever, but he had only been with me a few days. I closed the door behind me before falling onto their sofa as Ava served me up with a vodka and soda out the mini bar.

"So, are you feeling better since being here?" Ava said as she slumped down next to me, handing me my drink.

"I really am, I feel so free. What happened at home feels like a distant memory here." I sighed. "But, I know when we land back in London in two days, it's going to hit me like a ten tonne lorry. I can't cry, I sometimes want to, because my heart hurts. I don't ever think I will get over the pain he put me through, my heart will never be whole again. It will always be tarnished by Josh." I bit my lip, like clockwork, tears springing to my eyes.

"Oh, Luna, please don't cry." Ava wrapped her arms around me, Ness and Brooke walking over to me.

"I'm sorry. I'm fine, honestly, I'm fine," I protested as I dabbed my eyes with the tissue that Brooke grabbed out of the box on the coffee table.

"It's okay to cry, babe," Brooke said, showing her softer side.

"I know, I'm just sick of feeling like shit. When I'm with Taron, I am free, I feel alive. As soon as I'm alone without him, I have a gaping hole in my heart that I don't think will ever close again."

"But it will," Vanessa said. "I promise, and if you do have something with Taron, and he makes you feel that strongly, then this is good. Because he gives you hope to love again." She smiled, pulling me in for a cuddle.

And just like that, yesterday was all forgotten.

Chapter TWENTY

TARON

I waited until the door was closed before I walked towards mine and Luna's villa. I pulled my key-card out to unlock the door when I saw it was ajar slightly. My heart was racing.

I pushed the door open, my eyes searching the hallway, hoping to get to the sofa bed to retrieve my gun, just in-case anyone was in here. I made it to the bed, reaching under the sofa mattress and grabbing my hand gun, shoving it down the back of my shorts and running back out of the room when I saw a figure run out the front door.

"Fuck," I cursed as I ran towards him, getting into the hallway, not seeing another person in sight. "Shit."

Do I chase a dead end, or do I hope they come back?

I dropped my hands, my head falling back. My mind started racing. *What if Luna was in the room, were they there for her? Had I imagined it? No, I definitely didn't imagine it.*

God, I can't leave her on her own. I need to be near her.

My anxiety spiking, my chest tight. I walked up to her friend's door, banging on it. Brooke swung the door open.

"Taron," she said surprised as I barged past her, my eyes seeking out Luna. There she was, my beautiful Luna sitting on the sofa. As I got closer I could see her green eyes shimmering from her tears.

"Baby." I sighed before dropping to my knees and cupping her face with my hands. "Why are you crying?"

"Just my reality." She sniffed but dazzled me with her beautiful fucking smile. God, she was beautiful. My heart swelled in my chest, restraining against its steel casing that was so tightly bound.

"I'm here now," I soothed her, pulling her into an embrace, kissing the side of her head. My anxiety slowing, her instantly making everything better in that moment.

"Why are you here?" she asked, pulling back from me, confusion on her face.

"I missed you." I let out a sigh, it wasn't all a lie. I did miss her, but I needed to know she was safe. I wanted to call David, then I would tell her about what just happened. I wanted to check in with him first.

"I've just got to make a call," I said, standing from

the floor, Brooke side-eyeing me as I walked towards the sliding door.

As I closed it behind me I let out a deep sigh, I couldn't stop thinking how things could have been different if she walked in without me. Not that I would have let her out of my sight, but this is how my anxiety works. Complete over thinking about scenarios that are so out of reach they seem ridiculous, but how can you calm an anxious mind?

I pulled my phone out my back pocket, walking down towards the beach as I clicked on David's name. After a few international rings, his gruff voice answered.

"Taron," he said abruptly.

"David," I said exasperated, I despised the man. "We've had a small issue."

"What?" he shouted down the phone. I pulled it away from my ear and winced. "What do you mean you've had a *small* issue?" He emphasized on the small. I could picture his chubby, red face as he bellowed down the phone at me.

"Luna is fine before you think that it's something to do with her," I said calmly even though he was making my blood boil. "She went into the girls' villa, I said I would give her an hour or so without me because they had a falling out last night––" I was cut off.

"Get to the fucking point, Sloane," he snapped. I put my fist in my mouth, biting down on it to stop my anger.

"Anyway, as I was saying," I rolled my eyes, "Luna is fine. I went to our villa and the main door was ajar. This isn't the first time I have noticed something––" Again, I was cut off.

"Why haven't I been told about this? Fucking hell, Taron. Spit it the fuck out before I fly out to you and ring your fucking neck," he threatened down the phone.

"David, let me finish, please. You're jumping down my throat before giving me a chance to tell you the full story. I have told you the most important thing twice; Luna is fine." He was annoying me that he wasn't listening to me.

"Anyway, when I got to the villa the door was ajar, I scoped the hallway before walking to my room to retrieve my gun, then moved into Luna's bedroom. As I walked back out, I saw a tall figure running for the door. I chased after him but lost him. I haven't said anything to Luna just yet, but I will because I don't want to keep anything from her."

"Taron," he said in a low voice, I heard a door shut before he started speaking again. "You will not tell Luna about this, she doesn't need to know any of this on top of what she is going through. Just do your fucking job and keep her safe. Keep me posted if there are any developments," he said before cutting the phone off.

He was such a prick. I was in two minds about calling back to tell him about the feelings I had developed for

Luna, the feelings that were slowly turning into love. A word that scared me terribly.

I smiled as I thought about her, before opening a new text message screen, clicking his name and typing.

Oh, David, I didn't get a chance to tell you, because you cut me off, but me and your daughter are together now. Have a nice day. See you in two days, Dad.

I sent it, waiting for the noise to indicate that the message had sent. The message turned green to show it had been read, I nibbled the inside of my mouth as I saw my phone light up with him calling me. I cut it off, then turning my phone off.

Stew on that.

Arsehole.

I walked back into the lounge, my beautiful Luna's face lighting up the room. "Ready to head home?" I asked as I walked over to her.

"Yup," she said. "Girls, I'll see you later for dinner, yeah?" She grinned at them.

"Can't wait, we will see you later, eight o'clock?" Brooke asked.

"Perfect," Luna cooed.

We walked towards the door, closing it behind us as I scooped Luna up, her legs wrapping around my waist, her arms clinging round my neck as I carried her into our villa, a stupid grin on my face as she kissed me. She was my favourite way to spend my afternoon.

My new beginning, my saviour, my Luna.

Chapter
TWENTY ONE

LUNA

A rush of anxiety swept over me as I dropped my suitcase to the floor in my hallway, Taron close behind me, his hand resting on my belly. I knew what was coming. My dad was about to hit the roof. Taron filled me in on their conversation, telling me why he originally called him. We didn't see anyone else in the villa again, Taron still wasn't sure if he was imagining it or not.

"Luna," I heard my mum's voice echoing down the hall way as she ran towards me, looking as perfect as ever. Not a single hair out of place or wrinkle in sight.

"Mum," I said excitedly as she crashed into me, hugging tightly. God, I had missed her.

"Oh, my darling, you look wonderful. You're simply glowing," she said as she pulled away, rubbing her hands up and down my sleeved covered arms. Her eyes then darted towards Taron. "Tut, tut," she said, shaking her head with a smirk on her face. “David isn’t happy with you.” Just as she said it, my dad came walking down the hallway.

“Is that my princess?” he bellowed, holding his arms out. I moved Mum out the way and ran towards him, hugging his big frame. He kissed the top of my head.

“Oh, look, and she’s bought the pauper along with her,” he jeered. I looked back at Taron, my eyes wide, feeling protective. I ran from my dad’s side, standing next to Taron as I linked my fingers through his, then clasped my other hand over the top, looking down at my feet before batting my big doe eyes up at my father.

“What is this? Shack up with my daughter for her money? Can you not find anyone your own age? You have to settle on my daughter who is ten years younger than you?” He laughed, his eyes boring into Taron.

“Daddy,” I shouted. “Stop,” I pleaded. “This is happening, just leave it, will you? Would you rather me be single and heartbroken?” I clung onto Taron’s hands so tight, worried I would fall if I let go. My legs were already like jelly.

He narrowed his eyes on me, then moved them up to Taron’s. He turned on his heel and marched down the hall way into the kitchen, my mum following like a puppy dog. I let out my breath I had been holding.

“I’m sorry,” I muttered, kissing the top of his arm.

“It’s fine, I’m fine,” he assured me.

"Let's go upstairs," I said dragging his hand to follow me.

Walking on the soft carpet of my bedroom was something I had missed while in Hawaii, it was something so simple, yet so satisfying. I sat on my bed pulling Taron onto it with me.

"Are you sure you're okay?" I asked, worried that my father had upset him.

"Honestly, Luna, I am fine. I've had much worse, trust me." He smiled at me, but his eyes were dull. I didn't believe him.

I shuffled up the bed, resting against my pillows as I flicked Netflix on. Taron stayed sitting at the bottom of the bed, his eyes on me the whole time. I put *Gossip Girl* on, reminding me of the night we spent together in Hawaii.

My eyes left the television for a moment, just to focus on how handsome he was, a soft smile gracing my face, just for him. He crawled up the bed, pushing my legs apart then laying his head on my chest. I ran my fingers through his hair, twirling it round my fingers. Having his body close to me stirred my insides, making me hungry for him. He wrapped his arms around my back, nestling in-between my boobs.

"I like being here," he teased.

"I like you being there," I said, my voice silky.

He turned his head to look up at me, so his chin was

now resting in-between my boobs. He pulled his arms out from behind me, propping himself up, his arms resting on my thighs, pushing my legs further apart.

His fingertips softly brushed along my boobs, through my long sleeved tee and bra, but still arousing me. His eyes drifted from mine, slowly making their way down my body, his hungry hands following. He stopped at the hem of my top before pushing it up, revealing my milky complexion that had been sun-kissed by the Hawaiian sun.

He trailed soft, long kisses from the waistband of my leggings, dipping his tongue into my belly-button before following up the line and kissing my breast bone. His eyes flitted up to mine as he ran his hand over my bra, giving my boob a gentle squeeze then running his free hand round my back and unclipping my bra in one, swift movement.

I sat up slightly, pulling my tee over my head, then slid my bra straps down my arms before discarding it on the floor. A wicked smile graced his face before taking my nipple into his mouth, sucking and licking, a little moan escaping.

He sucked harder, puckering it before moving onto my other breast and doing the same. He nipped across my boobs before placing kisses down my body, running his fingers on the inside of my leggings then tugging them down before positioning himself in-between my thighs, tucking his fingers under my black knickers, slowly pulling them down.

His eyes alighting with lust, he placed his index finger at my soaked opening, the tip teasing at my entrance. I whimpered at the little contact that I so desperately craved from him. He continued his kissing, starting from my hip bone, trailing across my stomach before going towards my other hip.

My breathing was harsh and fast, and he hadn't even started with his pleasure. He nipped my hip before his kisses moved back across my stomach then kissed down my pubic bone before his hungry mouth covered me, his experienced tongue flicking and licking over my sensitive bud as he pushed his finger into me at the same time, causing my back to arch and a whimper to leave my lips.

I felt more aroused that I was completely naked, and he was still fully dressed. I propped myself up on my elbows to watch his expert tongue stroke the most intimate part of my body, building me up, then ready to make me fall apart under him.

His deep, brown pools were on mine as he watched me watch him devour me. He gripped the top of my thigh with his free hand as his tongue caressed me, his finger stretching and hitting my sweet spot.

I felt the delicious build up deep in my belly, my legs began to tremble as he sucked my bud, inserting another finger into me as I came hard and fast around him, crying out his name. I felt exposed but in the best possible way. I loved being under his spell, under his control.

I laid in his arms, engrossed in the television and cuddles. I didn't want him to leave. After spending the week with him, day and night, I didn't know how I was going to cope without him. I propped myself up on his chest, my hands resting over the top of the other.

"Stay with me tonight" I asked.

"I shouldn't," he said, his eyes hazy.

"Why?"

"Because I can't leave you alone, and I need to be able to leave you alone." He smirked, his eyes flitting back and forth to mine.

"Then don't." I playfully shrugged at him.

"Let's make a deal," he said.

"What's that?"

"I'll stay tonight, then we can sort some sort of routine out, so we see each other as much as we can." He leant forward and kissed my nose.

"Okay." I smiled at him, jet lag kicking in as our eyes fell heavy, succumbing to sleep.

I woke, reaching over for my phone, groaning at the time. Three am. I felt all over the place and disorientated. Taron was still snoozing, he looked so peaceful. I was besotted with him, completely and hopelessly in love with him.

I snuck out of bed, tiptoeing down the sweeping staircase and making my way into the kitchen to grab a glass of water and a snack, I was starving. I opened the fridge, eyeing up my options when I saw a bowl of pasta in the fridge. I grabbed the bowl and opened the drawer to get a spoon, and I stood at the kitchen island shovelling the pasta into my mouth, groaning in appreciation.

After eating half of it, I covered it back up and put it in the fridge before throwing my spoon in the sink. I filled my glass with water and walked back down the hallway when I noticed my father's study door was ajar, the light on. I walked past, ignoring it when I heard his voice and curiosity got the better of me. I stopped in my tracks and tiptoed back to earwig, I couldn't help myself.

"Yes. I told you I would deal with it, I'll make sure of it." He was sitting slumped over his desk, in his dressing gown and slippers. He rubbed his hand over his face in frustration.

"Of course I want her happy, that's all I care about." He dropped his hands, tapping his large fingers on the desk top. I saw him push his chair back, getting ready to say goodbye when I scarpered down the hall way and up the stairs, moving as quickly as I could back into my bedroom. I sat on my bed, my heart racing, my head spinning.

Who the hell was he talking to?

He was probably talking to Chris about me and

Taron. Chris was probably telling him to leave us be, I deserved to be happy after everything. I instantly relaxed, I just wanted to forget about it. I turned the tele on, watching my favourite *Gossip Girl*, turning the volume down. I needed to quiet my mind. I felt too wired to fall asleep. I took a couple of mouthfuls of my water, then snuggled back into Taron.

I was woken by Taron getting out of bed. "Sorry, baby," he cooed, a small smile on his face.

"That's okay." I stretched up. I felt cold in my tee and short PJ's, so I pulled the duvet up round my chin.

"Am I okay to have a shower?" he asked, just standing in his boxers.

"Of course," I mumbled. I drank him in, his toned body, his thick legs. His face chiselled at his jaw, covered in stubble. His dark brown eyes enticed me in to his soul, falling faster and deeper for him. Our souls like magnets, pulling us towards each other.

He walked into my life when I wasn't searching, but it was like he had always been here. My heart belonging to him, his heart belonging to me. I knew he had demons, but I was hoping in time, my light would shine stronger than the darkness within him.

After all, I was named after the moon, and sometimes in the darkness, the moon is your only form of light, guiding you home. I was his home. He was my mine.

He was my protector. I was his saviour.

And in that moment, he leant down, kissing me softly, his lips brushing mine delicately. He lingered a little longer, breathing in deeply as he did, before pressing harder into me as if he was trying to leave his mark.

"I love you," I said under my breath, the words slipping out in my post-kiss-haze before I could stop it. My eyes shot open at my remark, his eyes steadied on mine, soft and full of lust.

"I love you, Luna," he said before kneeling on the bed towards me, his hand cupping my face before his lips crashed into mine, the world surrounding us blurring from our sight.

I melted into him, his hand moving round the back of my head, holding onto my neck and tipping it back, his eyes burning into mine, leaving an imprint.

His mouth trailed along my jaw line, nipping and kissing before he got to my chin, then continued his sensual trail of kisses down my neck and along my collar bone. My tight bedtime tee betraying me, my nipples hard from his kisses.

He grabbed the hem of my tee hungrily as he bunched it up around my neck and sucked on my nipple, biting and licking. The sting and pleasure combined was enough to make me come.

"Taron," I whispered before he wrapped his fingers round the leg of my shorts and tugged them to the side, pulling me up by my tee so I was sitting on the edge of the bed as he pushed my legs apart and slid a finger into me.

"Watch me," he growled. My hungry eyes watched his finger slowly pushing in and out of me before his tongue flicked across my bud, my head tipped back before he pulled my tee again, forcing me to look.

The bubbles of pleasure were boiling over deep inside me, my insides clenching as the build was climbing, my breathing slow and shallow, matching his finger inside me. He pushed into me so slow, it was torturous. My legs began the tremble, my full lips parted as I tried to control myself.

Just as he was about to tip me into oblivion, he stopped, grabbing my blond hair as he stood up. He pushed his tight, restricting boxers down with his free hand and forced himself into my mouth. I didn't reject him, I sucked him hard as he thrust his hips into my hungry mouth.

"I own you," he said in a low growl as his thrusts got deeper into my mouth, taking him as far as I could.

I placed my fingers around him, moving my fist fast up his thickness before he pulled out of me. He picked me up, putting me down in front of my dressing table, bending down onto his knees and pulling my pyjama shorts down, then running his hands up the back of my thighs, pushing me forward slightly so I stepped out of my shorts before pushing me back onto my dressing table, running his hands around to my bare bum and lifting me onto the edge before pressing his hands in-between my thighs and pushing them open before standing his tall, lean body in-between them.

He slid into me, fast and hard as he squeezed my bum before pulling my hips forward, closer to him. His teeth gritted as he hit into me, whimpers leaving my mouth. My insides were burning, yearning to combust from all of him.

I crashed my lips into his, biting his bottom lip as the moment took over me before pushing my tongue into his mouth, our tongues dancing together. He moved one of his hands to my neck, wrapping his fingers and thumb round it, not overly tight, but enough to know he was there as he sped his thrusts up, hitting my sweet spot again and again, our lips still locked before he took my bottom lip in-between his teeth, sucking it.

That was it, the moment I hit my high, crying out as he continued to spear into me, coming with me before collapsing his head onto my chest. Both unable to speak, both too lost in lust.

Chapter TWENTY TWO

Evening was soon upon us, and I felt empty now that Taron had left. I couldn't wait to see him tomorrow. He promised to pop into work and see me.

I was lying in bed, I hadn't showered since Taron left. I didn't want to wash his scent off of me. We had spent the afternoon watching tele, eating and having sex. It was the perfect afternoon.

I reluctantly pulled myself out of bed and stomped to the shower, letting the water wash away my mood. I threw my towels and dirty washing in the basket in the corner of the bathroom, then grabbed a clean tee and shorts and slipped them on before falling into my bed.

I had a missed video call from the girls. I ran downstairs to grab a bottle of white wine out of the fridge and a glass, then headed back to my bedroom, pouring myself a glass of wine then popping the bottle on the side table.

Picking up my phone and unlocking it I called the

girls back, after a few rings they answered.

Me: "Hey, ladies, sorry I was in the shower."

Brooke: "No worries, we thought we would just have a catch up, how you doing?

Me: "Yeah, all good thanks, just having a glass of wine." I smiled, holding the glass up for them to see.

Ava: "Very nice, I'm with you on that," she said, swinging a champagne flute side to side.

Vanessa: "I've got a cuppa; the jet lag is doing me in." She laughed.

Me: "Tell me about it, I'm struggling."

Brooke: "Can't sleep?" she asked.

Me: "Yeah, just feel unsettled. I've spent the last week with Taron and all of a sudden, I'm without him, I just feel lost," I admitted.

Ava: "Yeah, I can understand that, hun. Must be weird. How were things left with you?" she asked.

Me: "Yeah, good, he is coming to see me at work tomorrow. I'll tell you what's weird though, I heard my dad last night talking to someone on the phone, saying that he just wanted me happy, I think it was Chris. I have messaged him, he has told me it's not him, but I know he wouldn't admit it if he thought I had cottoned onto him. Oh, I don't know." I shrugged, biting the inside of my cheek.

Brooke: "Who else could it have been, if not Chris?" she asked, taking a massive mouthful of red wine.

Me: "Honestly, Brooke, I haven't a clue."

Vanessa shrugged.

Me: "Just a bit weird. I know he isn't happy with me and Taron, but he is going to have to be. I love him." Only then I realised I hadn't told the three of them just how deep I was into him.

Brooke: "Love?!" She nearly spat her red wine out all over her expensive white carpet, Vanessa shooting her a look.

Me: "Yeah," I said anxiously, my eyes looking down at my swirling wine in my glass.

Brooke: "How can you love him? You hardly know him."

Me: "Actually," I said in my defence, "I know him a lot better than you would think. Don't forget I have been with him, every second of every day for a week."

Ava: "That's true." She nodded a little too enthusiastically.

Me: "Anyway, yes, I do love him. He loves me. Daddy will just have to accept it."

Brooke: "Luna, babes, this is your father." She laughed, her laughter full of menace. "If he doesn't want you with someone, you won't be with them, simple." She pointed out a pretty good fact to be honest.

Me: "I know that, I was just hoping that with everything going on, and what happened with Josh, he would want me to be happy. And Taron makes me so incredibly happy. Honestly, I never felt this happiness with Josh. Yes, I loved him, more than I could ever explain, but it's over. He didn't want this anymore. We grew apart. I didn't realise how stagnant our relationship was until Taron."

Brooke: "Just be careful," she warned. "Last thing I would want is for you to be hurt. Again."

Me: "I know."

Ava: "We just love you, honey, we don't want to see you sad anymore."

Me: "I know, and I love you all too, but I won't be sad," I said, shaking my head while smiling. "Taron took all the sadness from me," I said like a silly schoolgirl with her first crush. "Anyway, ladies, I feel beat. I'm going to watch some tele and give Taron a call. I hope work goes well tomorrow, miss you all already," I said, waving at the screen.

Brooke & Ness: "Bye." They waved.

Ava: "Bye, hun." She waved with them before I cut them off.

I text Taron good night, he replied night and said he was out running a couple of errands. I sighed as I wanted to talk to him, but he promised he would see me tomorrow. With that, I snuggled myself into bed, wine glass still in hand, eyes heavy and I was gone.

-

DAVID

I sat in the busy bar in Mayfair, waiting for him, sipping my whiskey. I didn't want to be having to do this, but I knew I had to. For her sake. For her future.

The rain was hammering down outside, November was just around the corner, the air turning bitter. I felt a cold breeze blow through me as the door to the warm bar opened.

I felt his eyes on me, burning into the back of my head. He wasn't someone I wanted to get on the wrong side of, but, yet, I wasn't scared of him. He didn't know what I was capable of, and if he knew what was good for him, he would leave.

I pulled the white envelope out of my pocket, placing it on the table, patting my hand over it as he sat down in front of me.

"Thank you for coming," I said, bringing the whiskey to my lips, wincing as it burned down my throat.

"Didn't really have a choice, did I?" Taron hissed at me, his eyes black.

I slid him the envelope with his cash in, as agreed. His hand shot forward across the table, opening the envelope and looking in it before folding it back down and putting it in the inside pocket of his Barbour jacket.

"Was that all?" he asked, raising his black eyebrow.

"Unfortunately not." I shook my head.

"How did I know that was going to be your answer?" he said.

"Inside the envelope is a note for you. Do me a favour, read it and listen." My eyes were burning into him now.

"Can you give me an idea of what it is? Or do I have to guess?" he said cockily, pushing his tongue on the inside of his cheek, his eyes on mine.

"Have a guess," I said in a provoking manner.

"Stay away from Luna." He shrugged.

"Bingo." I smiled. "Got it in one."

"And why would I do that?" he asked back, confidence in his voice.

"Because if you don't then bad things will happen, and we wouldn't be wanting that now, would we?" I said.

"Nah, sorry, won't happen. I love your daughter, she loves me," he said as he went to stand.

I softened, knowing full well this was going to break my daughter's heart all over again. "You don't understand. I need you to stay away." My eyes showing the seriousness in my voice.

"Are you in trouble, David?" His voice now also softer. "I can help you," he offered.

"I know you can, but I can't. I just need you to stay away, understand?" I couldn't be the bad guy anymore. I was in trouble, being threatened by an unknown source. They asked me to ditch the bodyguard, her protector, which is what I was doing.

"Is Luna in trouble?" he asked, his face cracking under the strain, his eyes glazed over.

I looked over my shoulder to make sure no one was in earshot of our conversation, then letting out a deep sigh, I said, "She will be if you don't leave. We all will." Bowing my head, I continued, "Please, Taron, leave."

"David, I can't bear to be away from her for five seconds, how am I supposed to just walk away?" I watched as he crumbled in front of me, like I had just taken his whole world from him.

"I need you too," I begged.

"Tell her I love her," Taron said, broken. "Please." He got up and walked out the door.

-

LUNA

I woke early, getting dressed in black skinny jeans, a cream jumper and my black Ugg boots. I pulled my hair into a high, messy pony-tail, pulling a few strands out. I sat in front of my dressing table, glowing, thinking back to mine and Taron's sex yesterday morning.

My fingertip trailed down my neck, towards the collar bone, my breath hitched. I had to stop. My face flustered.

I brushed some bronzer across my cheek bones

before applying a nude lipstick then grabbed my Mulberry bag as I headed downstairs. I dropped my bag and phone by the front door as I walked into our kitchen.

"Morning, Mum, Daddy." I smiled, kissing my daddy on the cheek as he ate his cereal with his morning paper and coffee.

"Morning, princess," he said. "Looking forward to getting back in the shop?"

"I am. I'm meeting Taron at the shop this afternoon which I'm excited about," I said cheerily, pouring myself a coffee.

"Toast, avocado and eggs, darling?" Mum asked as she turned around, hair immaculate.

"Please, I'm starving." I licked my lips before sitting next to my father at the dining room table, taking a mouthful of coffee, moaning in appreciation at how good it tasted.

"There we go, darling," my mum said sweetly as she placed the plate down in front of me, handing me a knife and fork.

"Thank you," I said before adding some salt, pepper and chilli flakes on the crushed avocado.

Once I had finished breakfast, I made another cup of coffee for the journey.

"See you at dinner," I said as I walked down the hall way.

"Bye, darling," my mum called out, standing at the

doorway in the kitchen, waving her arm.

I grabbed my bag, keys and tan trench coat before shrugging it on and closing the door behind me. I put my earphones in and played, Lewis Capaldi, as I started my short journey to work.

I was grateful that it wasn't raining, but it was bitter. I wrapped my arms round myself, wishing I was back in Hawaii under the intense sunshine, laying on a beach, sipping cocktails with Taron and the girls.

My heart hurt, I missed him so much and it had literally been one evening.

I walked up towards my shop. The flower arch looked amazing as I walked through the dark green double doors, smiling as the smell of freshly ground coffee, sweet flowers and delicious cakes filled the room.

"Morning," I called out as I walked into the coffee area, my eyes lighting up when I saw Tegan. Her chocolate brown hair bobbed on her shoulders, her blue eyes going down the list of cakes that still needed to be made. "Tegan." I smiled and hugged her behind the counter "How's it going?" I asked her.

"It's been busy, especially with all the Christmas flavours, which are to die for by the way. Good choice," she said, her eyes looking behind me. "No hot bodyguard today?"

"He is meant to be coming in at some point today," I said, looking at my phone, a bit gutted that I hadn't heard from him yet.

"Oh, love a bit of eye candy." She laughed before going out back. "Fancy making the cakes today?" she called out from the kitchen.

"Yeah, I'll be there in five, let me just check in with the others," I said before walking into the florist.

I walked out the back to see Eva, who was busy arranging the flowers before the shop opened.

"Hello," I said as I walked round the door, Eva jumping out of her skin as she ran over to me.

"Oh, I am so glad to see you." She smiled, rubbing her hands up my arms. I took in her appearance, she looked exhausted. Apart from Valentine's day, Christmas was our second busiest holiday. Her hair was messy already, swept into a low bun. Her honey eyes tired but still glistening.

"Been busy?" I said, asking a rhetorical question. She answered with a roll of her eyes before she turned her attention back to the flowers that had been delivered at five am this morning.

"I'm just going to whip the cakes up, Jane and Michelle should be in soon, shouldn't they?" I asked re-tying my hair into a pony tail.

"Yeah." She nodded as she concentrated checking the stock. I left her to it, walking towards the coffee shop, grabbing my apron from the hook and tying it up around my back.

“What’s on the list” I said as I entered the kitchen area.

Tegan was drying her hands. “Erm, red velvet cupcakes, Victoria sponge, chocolate cupcakes and blueberry muffins,” she said.

“Lovely, okay, I’ll start the Victoria sponge, you okay to start the muffins?” I asked her.

“Yeah, course. Glad to have you back,” she said patting me on the back as she walked over to her station.

“Me too,” I said, getting the ingredients I needed from the cream Smeg fridge that was in the corner of the room before walking towards the mixer, adding the eggs, butter, flour and caster sugar.

“Was Hawaii amazing?” Tegan asked.

“Oh, Teags, it was amazing. Honestly, I wish I could go back,” I said, smiling at the memories

“I bet, how was the brooding bodyguard?” she asked, her eyes on mine as she started mixing the muffin mix.

“Broody as ever.” I winked over at her before giggling. “Nah, he was lovely, was nice to actually get to know him.”

“I’m glad,” she said genuinely. “Sorry to ask, but have you heard from Josh?”

“Not a word.” I shrugged “But, do you know what, as much as I loved him, because I did, I’m glad all this happened, because I would never have had the chance to meet Taron. I know this sounds like some cheesy corny line, but he is my soulmate, we are destined to be with each other. I have never felt as strongly as I do now, with him."

"Oh, Luna, you've got it bad," she said, singing, '*Usher, U Got It Bad,*' before breaking into a full bout of laughter as I joined her.

Two hours later, thirty minutes before opening time, the cakes were made and put on display. I smiled, admiring our work. I took my apron off, hanging it back up before walking out back to see Eva.

"How we doing, all okay?" I asked.

"Yeah, good to go, hun," she said, finishing her flower arrangement.

"How many we got going out today?" I asked Michelle.

"Fifty," she said, rushing the bouquets into the back of the truck.

"Are you delivering?" I asked.

"Yup. Jane and Eva are going to be starting the Christmas orders."

"Perfect," I said. "Do you need me to do anything?"

"Nope, we've got it sorted, thanks, boss." She smiled before I walked out to get lost in the accounts. It was the worse job in the world, but someone had to do it, and the thought of seeing Taron made it so much more bearable.

My phone buzzed pulling my eyes from the computer, smiling when I realised it was Taron. It had already gone two pm, I was so engrossed in paperwork that the morning just flew. I put my pen down, pushing the paperwork to the side as I unlocked my phone, my smile disappearing as I read his message.

Hey Luna, baby. I can't do this. I'm sorry for hurting you, sorry for leading you on. Taron.

I dropped my phone, my mouth falling open.

I don't get it. How could he have been so sure last night, yet this afternoon he was done with me?

As I blinked down at my phone, my tears began to fall. I pushed myself away from my desk, snatching my phone and my bag as I walked out into the main part of my shop. The coffee area was heaving, the florists rushed off their feet. I didn't want to say anything, so I just pushed the doors open, getting out as quickly as I could.

I didn't know where to go, the girls were all at work. I couldn't burden them with more of my shitty love life. I jumped in a taxi and headed home.

I ran up the stairs to my front door, unlocking it and running into my dad's office. My mum wasn't in my line of sight, that I was grateful for otherwise she would be up my arse then straight on the phone to my dad.

I sat at his desk, trying to open the drawers, but they were locked. Of course they were. I banged my fist on the table in anger, the sadness leaving my body. I looked around the room when I noticed his filing cabinets with the keys still in it.

I needed his address.

I jumped up from my dad's chair and pulled the filing cabinet open, flicking through the numerous files with my fingertips when I saw his name, *Sloane, Taron.*

I pulled it out, slamming it shut before sitting back down at my dad's desk. I opened the brown file before pushing the pages, trying to find something. Anything.

Everything Sloane had told me was here. Emerson. Marine. Widow. I knew it all, he would've never opened up to me if he didn't feel something for me. Something has happened to push him away.

I grabbed his front sheet, my eyes scanning it for his address. I pulled my phone out and snapped a photo before shoving it all back in the brown folder, putting it back into the filing cabinet then shutting it, and running out the office.

I got to the front door when I heard my mum.

"Luna, darling. Is that you?" she called out as I slammed the front door.

I felt bad ignoring her, but my head was all over the place. I looked at the address on my phone and I saw he lived in Kensington, frustrated that he was near my work.

I hailed down a taxi telling him where to go. I don't even know if he would be there, but I wanted to try.

After a short taxi ride, my anxiety peaking as we pulled up outside a beautiful, white terraced house with a black iron gate in-between two white concrete posts. I tapped my card on the driver's card reader before leaving the car and letting myself in his gate, clutching to my phone as I banged on his door, nibbling the side of my index finger as I waited.

I knocked again this time screaming his name as I did. My heart thumped when the front door opened, but it wasn't Taron. It was an older lady, grey hair pinned up with what looked like a knitting needle, and crystal blue eyes. She was wearing a floor length skirt, white loose shirt and a pinny. She reminded me of my nan, my heart swelling in my chest as I looked at her.

She pushed her glasses up her nose, looking me up and down. "Can I help you?" she asked curtly, keeping the door partially closed, her voice tone not matching her sweet appearance.

"I'm looking for Taron, Taron Sloane," I said, my eyes trying to look behind her.

"I know who Taron is. But he's not home, he has gone away," she said boldly.

"Gone away?" I asked, my heart crumbling in my chest as I sat down on the floor slowly.

"Yes, dear," she said a lot softer this time, my eyes

looking up at her in a desperate plea to tell me where he was.

"He has taken some time to think, I take it you're Luna?" she asked as she sat down on the door step next to me.

"Mmm hmm," I said, nibbling the inside of my lip, trying to stop the tears from falling.

"He has your best interests at heart," she said, rubbing my back.

"That doesn't make it any easier. His message was vague, I have no clue what the hell has happened from last night to this afternoon." I shook my head.

"I don't know the details, dear," she said smoothly, cupping my hands. "But you need to let go."

My eyes flitted up at her, sheer panic coursing through my body, my heart hammering in my chest.

"Let go," I managed in a whisper, my throat tight from the solid lump that had formed there. She just nodded, held my hand a little longer then stood up, walking back into the house and closing the door. I sat there, numb, my phone still tightly in my grip.

"Let go," I mumbled to myself again before pulling myself up and walking away.

Chapter TWENTY THREE

TARON

I stood at my bedroom window, only slightly peeping round to see her walking away. Completely dishevelled.

I rolled back against the wall, my heart racing in my hollow chest. I wish I could tell her that I loved her, but I needed to do this for her. To keep her and her family safe.

My eyes darted up to the door when I saw Gloria walking towards me.

"How was she?" I asked, bunching my tee at my chest. Gloria was like my adoptive mum, after losing both my parents at a young age, Gloria was our housekeeper, and for some reason, my parents gave her full custody. Back then, I was angry. Today, I am grateful.

"Broken," she said grimly. "But, just keep thinking of the long run. You will get her back, Taron." She smiled sweetly.

"I know. It just doesn't help the here and now, does

it? I need to get looking into who's blackmailing him. It must be the same people who threatened Luna," I said, thinking out loud.

"Taron," she said with a warning tone. "Don't get too deep into this. Ride it out, bide your time."

"Gloria, I can't." I shook my head, her small frame walking over to me before putting her hands either side of my face.

"You need to, my dear boy." Her blue eyes looked deep into mine.

I relaxed, closing my eyes and dropping my head in defeat. She was right. I needed to wait, wait for the right moment to get her back.

And I would get her back.

Chapter TWENTY FOUR

LUNA

I spent an hour wandering the streets of Kensington and Chelsea before making my way home. I just wanted to go to my bed and switch off from the world.

I opened the door quietly, hoping and praying that I didn't gain the attention of my parents. I needed to call Eva, explain why I just ran out. But how can I explain another relationship fail? I couldn't. Pride wouldn't let me. I didn't even want to call the girls, I definitely wasn't in the mood for Brooke's blunt opinions, which I knew she would quite happily air to me.

I put my coat on the long bench in the lobby area of my parent's house before tiptoeing up the stairs, wincing when I heard her voice.

"Luna, darling," my mum called out, arms opened ready to embrace me as she reached me on the small landing between stair cases.

"How was work?" she asked as she let go of me.

"Yeah, busy, I'm completely whacked, Mum," I said, eyes darting to the floor.

"Okay, honey, dinner will be done at seven. Chris is coming over tonight as well, so please make sure you join us. I can't remember the last time we had a family dinner. Make sure you freshen up and re-do your makeup." She smiled, rubbing her thumb over my cheek before walking down the stairs, disappearing out of sight.

Great, just what I wanted, to get dressed up for dinner in the dining room. Don't get me wrong, I loved family dinners, and I'm so glad Chris is coming home for the evening, but I could just do without it tonight. I just wanted to lose myself in a film and forget about my shitty day.

I looked at the time on my phone, it was five pm. I was grateful I had a couple of hours to chill before I had to make myself up for dinner. I walked into my bedroom, falling on the bed, burying my face in my pillow and letting out my held in sobs.

All the emotion from the past month had become too much for me. I wasn't a crier, I was annoyed that I had cried so much over the last two months over men.

The thing was, I wasn't crying over Josh anymore, I wasn't even remotely sad about him. It was only Taron.

I sat in front of my dressing table, trying not to let my mind drift to what happened here with Taron. I brushed my knotty pony tail out before clicking my straighteners on then curling my hair with them, brushing the tight curls out to give me a more wavy hairstyle. I was grateful that I had my lashes on, only having to add some concealer to my bags before coating my cheeks in a brush of bronzer, then applying a red lipstick.

I walked to my wardrobe, pulling my jeans and jumper off before grabbing a black skater dress that I paired with tights. My mother would expect me to wear shoes, but I wasn't. I slipped my black Ugg slippers on before making my way downstairs and into the kitchen to grab a glass of champagne.

My mother's disapproving eyes focused on my feet, tutting at my slippers. "Luna." She sighed as she shook her head before turning her attention back to the oven. I walked into the lounge to see Chris sitting on the sofa with my dad, deep in conversation.

"Chris," I squealed, running over to him. He stood from the sofa, grabbing me and swinging me around.

"Luna." He smiled as he put me down. "How was Hawaii?"

"Oh, it was amazing," I said as we both sat down on the plush cream sofas, my daddy sitting in the corner in his sherlock chair, rubbing his finger round the edge of his brandy glass.

"Yeah?" he asked, not convinced.

"Honestly, Chris, it was so good. I would go back in

a heartbeat." I nodded.

"That's amazing, Luna. How was it with the bodyguard, was it weird?" he asked.

"Bit annoying at first, but I got used to it. We got to know each other quite well, decided to make a go of it before he text me this afternoon and told me he couldn't do it." I shrugged at Chris, firing my eyes up to daddy dearest.

"You joking? What a jerk." Chris scoffed before laughing, standing up to pour himself a whiskey from my dad's crystal decanter. "Want one?"

"Please, ice for me though," I said smiling sweetly, crossing my legs. My dad stood, excusing himself, my eyes followed him until he was out the room.

"What is this dinner about? Do you know? The only time we dress up for family dinner is when something serious is going down," I said accepting my glass from Chris before he sat down, bringing his glass to his lips, wincing slightly as the brown, potent liquor ran down his throat like silk. I mirrored him. I didn't even like whiskey.

"Oh, stop it, it's a family dinner. You've been away, I have been swamped with work. It's just a family get together." He shrugged.

"Bullshit. I'm telling you something is going down. I'll bet you, I'm that confident." I smirked.

"How much?" He smirked, holding his hand out.

"£5K," I said bluntly, holding my hand out to him.

"Okay, deal," he said as he took my hand and shook it firmly. "God, I can't wait to have that £5k." He laughed before Mum called us in for food. He stood up, me following as we giggled into the dining room.

I sat down at the table next to my brother, the smell of roast chicken filling my nostrils. My God, I didn't realise how hungry I was. I loved a roast dinner, it was my favourite.

My dad always sat at the head of the table. He stood from his seat, pouring an expensive bottle of Dom Perignon champagne into our glasses, before holding his up.

"To my wonderful family and new beginnings," he said as he held his glass out into the middle of the table. We all clinked our glasses just when we heard the front door close. My heart thumped in my chest, hoping, praying it was Taron.

My eyes on the dining room door, my dad's grin spreading across his face when I saw Josh striding through the dining room double doors. My jaw hitting the floor, Chris' smile disappeared when he saw him, his face turning to anger as he got up from his seat, grabbing him on his suit collar and smashing him hard up against the wall.

"What the fuck are you doing here?" he said, his blond hair flopping down his forehead as he smashed him back into the wall, his perfect white teeth gritted.

"Chris," my dad shouted angrily. "Put him down. Now." Chris dropped him, pushing his hair back before straightening out his own jacket.

"Want to explain?" Chris snapped holding his arm out, facing Josh, before throwing his arm down to his side.

"I invited him," my dad said, fidgeting on the spot, his eyes shooting to me, then my mum. I followed his sight, looking at my mum who looked genuinely shocked.

"What do you mean you invited him?" I spat, I was livid.

"He has something he wants to say," my dad said.

I turned in my chair, champagne in hand, staring up at Josh, crossing my legs over themselves.

"Come on then," I hissed. "I'm listening, the stage is yours." My eyes shooting daggers into him.

"Luna, please," my dad said, coming up close to me before standing with Josh.

"Please what, Dad? Or are you forgetting this arsehole left me before we were due to get married?" I said agitated, raising my eyebrows. "Now, come on, Josh, we are *all* waiting."

"I had to leave you on our wedding day," he said, bowing his head. "I didn't have a choice," he said sighing. "As you know, I work for the police, but, I am an undercover cop. I have been working on a case for the last two years." His eyes burned into mine now.

"The guy we had been after for the last two years got wind of it somehow, we are assuming through a rogue colleague." He shrugged. "That's when they threatened me with you. I called your dad, begging him for a bodyguard until I knew we had him, until I knew you were safe." A small smile graced his face.

"And that time is now. We got him, baby. We can be together again." He stepped towards me. I stood up holding my hand up for him to stop.

"Excuse me?" I shook my head. "Don't think because you explained your little story you can come waltzing back into my life, looking to pick up where we left off. You're deluded." I laughed before looking towards my dad.

"And you were in on this? Is this why Taron had to just leave and tell me he didn't want me anymore?" I shouted at him. "Was this all part of your little plan? Oh, let's invite Josh for dinner, let him be the knight in shining armour who swoops poor, broken, unwanted Luna up? Well, you can both go fuck yourselves. I'm out," I shouted before downing my glass of champagne and walking towards the double doors before turning on my heel.

"Oh, and, Chris, you owe my 5K," I said before sticking my middle finger up and storming to my room.

I grabbed my Louis Vuitton holdall before shoving a handful of clothes, pyjamas and underwear in a bag, shoving my Ugg boots on, then running down the stairs. My dad, Josh and Mum were standing in the lobby when

I got there.

"Where do you think you are going?" my dad asked.

"Anywhere but here," I snapped back at him, pushing my arms through my trench coat.

"She's coming with me," Chris said as he stormed down the hallway into the lobby, barging his way through Josh and my dad and opening the door, grabbing my holdall and walking out onto the street.

I looked between my dad and Josh, at my mum crying, I felt awful that she had to see this, but I couldn't ignore that she was most likely involved in this as well. I walked out the door, shutting it behind me as I followed Chris to his Porsche. He popped the boot, then threw my holdall in the back before opening my door.

I fell into the bucket seats as Chris shut the door and walked round to his side, turning the key and listening to the engine roar. We didn't speak on the short journey home, Chris was festering just as much as I was.

He pulled into the underground car park, then grabbed my bag as we walked towards the lift to his penthouse.

"You sure you don't mind your little sister crashing at yours?" I asked.

"Of course not." His frowning face softening into a smile.

"Just warn me if you're going to be bringing any lady friends home," I joked as I elbowed him.

"Gotcha." He winked as he gestured for me to walk into the penthouse before him. I loved his apartment, it was modern and sleek decor, but it still felt cosy.

"Drink?" he asked as he dropped my bag outside the guest room.

"Please," I said before falling into his sofa.

"What an evening, aye?" he said handing me a glass of iced vodka and a slice of lemon.

"Thanks," I muttered before taking it. "And, yeah, tell me about it." I rolled my eyes. "I knew Dad was up to something when Taron said he couldn't see me anymore." I shook my head.

"Were you two serious then?" Chris asked, joining me on the sofa with a brandy.

"Not serious as such, but feelings were definitely there. I fell in love with him." I sigh before bringing the glass up to my lips and taking a small mouthful.

"Ah, shit, Luna." Chris rubbed my shoulder. "It'll sort itself out. Ignore Dad."

"It's hard to, you know what he's like. If he wants something he'll get it." I put my drink into my lap, cradling it.

"May just be best to ride the wave, babe," he said, taking a mouthful of his brandy.

"Mmm." I made a noise in my throat whilst nibbling the inside of my lip. "Anyway, enough about me. What's been going on with you?" I smiled a fake smile. I needed to quiet my brain. I needed to stop the talk of Taron, Josh and my dad.

It was gone midnight by the time we had stopped talking, copious amounts of alcohol had been consumed.

"I need to go to bed," I slurred, standing up, glass still in hand. Chris jumped up, taking it off me and guiding me to my bedroom for the night. My head was fuzzy, I felt my hangover starting already.

He ushered me into the guest room. The walls were a light grey, the bed was a lavish queen sized frame with a soft material and a buttoned headboard. The duvet and pillows crisp white and mirrored wardrobes running along the back wall.

"You going to be okay?" he asked, concerned.

"Yup. Absolutely fab," I said laughing as I fell onto the bed.

"Night, sis," he said before closing the door. After ten minutes of the room spinning I pulled myself up, walking over to my holdall and rummaging for my phone. I got back into bed, fully dressed and squinted at my bright phone screen, trying to find Taron's number. I wanted to call him.

After fifteen minutes of tapping and calling random people in my phone, I got to his name. I hesitated for a moment before clicking his number and then put him on loud speaker. After the sixth ring, just when I was getting ready to hang up, he answered.

"Hello," he said, sleepily and grumpily. My heart smiled at the sound of his voice.

"Hey," I said softly.

"Luna," he said in a desperate whisper. Tears stung my eyes as I let them fall, my shaky voice betraying me when I replied, "Taron, I miss you."

The phone line fell silent, and I could hear his breathing before he said, "Goodbye, Luna," then he cut the phone off.

I dropped my phone on the bed, falling back and crying myself to sleep. It was really over.

I woke the next morning with a thumping headache. I rolled over trying to focus my eyes on my surroundings, when I noticed a glass of water and two paracetamols that Chris must've left for me before leaving for work.

I checked my phone, checking the time then groaned. Shit, I needed to get to work.

I climbed out of bed, grabbing the glass of water and throwing the tablets to the back of my mouth before swallowing. I took a moment, sitting there, thinking about what was going to happen next, and the uncertainty was crippling.

I shook away the thoughts and moped towards the bathroom, I needed a shower. I was still sitting in my clothes from last night and I reeked of alcohol.

After my shower I shuffled into my black skinny

jeans and threw my white tee and cardigan on. I rough dried my hair before leaving it down. I applied a small amount of makeup, more so to cover my eye-bags, then smothered my lips in a red lipstick. I grabbed my phone off charge and threw my bits in my bag before leaving my room.

I was starving but decided to wait until I got to work. The journey was a bit longer from Chris', but it gave me a chance to try and clear my head. When in the taxi, I put my earphones in and clicked my music playlist, closing my eyes trying to forget everything that was currently going on in my life.

Chapter TWENTY FIVE

I was glad to walk into the shop, a little bit of normality for me. I walked through to the coffee shop, smiling when I saw Tegan. Her eyes darted to the seating area, and I rolled my eyes when I saw my dad sitting there. I stayed up at the counter with Tegan.

"You okay starting the cakes? I just want to grab myself some breakfast."

"Of course, Luna, anything you need." She smiled before disappearing out back after me. I raided the fridge and whipped myself up some pancakes, drizzling with syrup then stopping at the coffee machine and making myself a black americano. I needed something to wake me up and prepare me for my dad.

I walked confidently over to him, knowing full well he was going to blow his top at me for embarrassing him, no doubt, at dinner yesterday.

"Dad," I said abruptly as I sat down opposite him on my favourite table by the window, the table that me and

Taron sat on.

"Luna," he replied just as abruptly whilst sipping his tea.

"What do you want?" I asked, spooning a large mouthful of pancakes into my mouth.

"Your behaviour last night was unacceptable," he said, his eyes burning into me as I looked down at my plate.

"So was yours," I batted my eyes up at him then shrugged.

"Luna," he warned in a threatening tone. "Don't push me."

"Hardly pushing, Father." My tone was vindictive.

"Now, here is what is going to happen. This has been on the cards since you were born. You and Josh will be getting married," he said, his eyes dark and hooded. I went to protest but he held his hand up. "Don't. I'm not finished."

I took a big mouthful of my coffee, pushing my plate away from me, suddenly no longer hungry.

"You are going to marry Josh. Me, and his father planned this from the moment you were born. We know why Josh did what he did. I was angry, Luna, of course I was. But, he has explained, you will forgive, and you will both move on with your life. I have already been on the phone to his father this morning, discussing this. You will go over to Josh's and apologise for your despicable behaviour last night and I will hear no more of Taron, do you understand me?" His face now going red as his temper rose. I looked down at my lap, biting my lip.

"Do you understand me, Luna?" His voice was loud and clipped.

"Yes," I whispered, instantly feeling my freedom leave me.

"Good, then that's settled. This is best for the family, best for the business." He nodded.

Once I found my voice I looked up at him, my eyes glassy. "Dad, can I ask one thing seeing as you have forced my hand in this?"

He nodded.

"Did you have anything to do with Taron leaving?" I asked.

"No, Luna. I didn't. But he obviously knew he didn't stand a chance in this family," he said, standing up and pushing himself away, then throwing ten pounds on the table. "I will see you at home tonight, Luna," he said, bending down to kiss my cheek as he walked out of my shop.

Once I heard the door go, I let out my breath before throwing my head in my arms and crying. My life was officially over. Being kept in a loveless marriage all for business and the family name.

I felt a hand on my arm, my weepy eyes looking up to see Tegan.

"It'll be okay, Luna," she said before sitting opposite me. "I'm sorry."

I smiled at her before breaking out into tears again. I didn't say anything else, but she still stayed with me, so I wasn't alone. And I was so grateful.

An hour had passed, I wasn't sure at what point Tegan left. I had no tears left to cry, my eyes were dry, my throat hoarse and my heart obliterated. I pulled myself out of my pity party trance and walked into the kitchen.

"Need a hand?" I sniffed, looking over at Tegan who was covered in flour and icing sugar.

"Only if you don't mind?" she asked.

"Of course not, I'm okay now. I just needed a moment." I let out a little laugh, trying to hide the fact that I was dying inside. I grabbed my apron, putting it over my head and tying it round my waist before looking down the list of cakes.

"Sorry for putting us behind," I said with a small smile.

"That's okay, boss, we have a few out already from this morning." She smiled back at me. This is what I needed, I needed to lose myself in something for a couple of hours.

Once I had finished my cakes, I was going to arrange some flowers. My mind needed to be kept busy until tonight.

On the way home from work I stopped off at Chris' apartment, grabbing my bag before heading back downstairs to my waiting taxi.

"Thank you," I muttered as I climbed back into the car, my heart racing when we pulled away. Normally I am relieved to be home, but tonight, under Daddy's orders, I had to go and get changed and then go back out again, to Josh's. I didn't want to see him, any bit of love I did have for him had been replaced with hate. I felt nothing for him.

I had a quick shower, wrapping my towel round myself then looked in my wardrobe for something to wear. I decided on a pair of blue jeans, a white tee with see-through long chiffon sleeves and my white converse.

I straightened my hair then slipped some gold hoops through my ears. I applied a soft layer of bronzer and a clear lip gloss, then sprayed my perfume before making my way downstairs into the kitchen.

I walked into where my mum and dad were sitting.

"You look nice, darling," my mum cooed as she served my dad's dinner up. My belly rumbled. "Would you like a plate?"

"Please." No tone, no emotion to my voice. I sat opposite my dad at the island, I didn't want to be near him. My belly groaned in appreciation when my mum served up a chicken stew with loads of vegetables and dumplings. I grabbed the spoon and ate in silence, ignoring my parents. My mum was in on this, and I was disappointed that she chose my father's side instead of her daughter's, but that was a conversation for another day. I didn't have the energy to discuss it now.

Once finished, I placed my bowl and spoon in the dishwasher and walked out of the kitchen towards the front door, slamming it behind me.

I decided to walk to Josh's, it wasn't that far, and I needed the fresh air.

I still couldn't believe this was happening.

I was being forced into a marriage I didn't want.

I started to question everything about our relationship previously. Had he ever really loved me? Or was it just because he did what his father said?

I was, well, I thought I was so head over heels in love with him, but it was all a lie, he was a fraud. It doesn't even matter, I couldn't escape now. This was my fate.

After a thirty minute walk I was outside his parent's luxurious town house.

Taking a deep breath, I walked up the steps towards the black front door. I reached out for the ugly, gold lion knocker before banging it down a little harder than I anticipated. I stepped back, nibbling on my false nail. I had waves of mixed emotions swimming round inside of me that I couldn't put a lid on.

My eyes pulled from the floor and up to the door as

Josh opened it, a warm smile appearing on his face, holding his hand out for me. I stepped forward, refusing his hand and walking into the lobby area of his home.

"Oh, look, my doting fiancé," I snarled at him.

"Luna, don't be like that, come on. You know what we had was special, we are made for each other," he said reaching out for me.

I slapped his hand away. "Don't touch me." My eyes narrowed on him. "We didn't love each other, we had nothing special."

His whole demeanour changed in that moment.

A stupid, vicious grin spread across his face.

"Your father said you would co-operate, I believe you owe me an apology for your, what was it he said? Oh, yeah, *despicable behaviour,"* he spat out at me. "Now, come on, be a good fiancée and apologise to me."

He stepped closer, running his hand round the back of my head and pulling my face so our noses were nearly touching. "Say it," he said through gritted teeth.

"I'm sorry," I said in barely a whisper, ashamed that I had caved.

"There's a good wife. Now, let's go discuss this in the study, shall we?" he said, licking his lips then grabbing my arm and walking me into his father's study, slamming and locking the door behind us. I jumped as the door banged into the frame.

"Sit," he demanded as he sat down in his father's

chair on the other side of the desk.

He unlocked his father's drawer then pulled out a black velvet box and threw it towards me across the table. "This is for you," he barked.

I didn't touch it, I didn't want to because then this makes this real, this nightmare will actually be coming true.

"Open the box, Luna, you don't want me telling Daddy that you didn't co-operate, do you?" he said in a chilling, slow voice, his eyebrows raising. I leant forward and snatched the box, opening it to a huge oval diamond ring set on a platinum band.

"It's five carat," he boasted.

"You could've just got me a fake one, then it would truly reflect our relationship and marriage," I hissed at him, sliding it onto my finger.

"Doesn't that look pretty?" He smiled. "Now, I'm thinking a spring wedding next year, spring good for you?" he asked.

"Oh, so I do have a say in this then?" Sarcasm laced my voice.

"Of course you do." His face softened. "So, spring?"

"I suppose." I sighed.

"Outside or inside?"

"Inside," I said, spitting it out at him.

"Okay, inside. Obviously, everyone will be there, it has to be a big wedding because of our family names.

Everyone wants to see the Smiths and Cameron's join together. You'll be Luna Cameron." A sickening grin was on his face.

"Great," I said under my breath.

"Now, get up and come and sit on my lap. We have lots of lost time to make up for, and I want to claim you as mine. Brand you for everyone to see that you are mine, more so, to make you not forget who you belong to," he snarled at me as he pulled me onto him.

His scent filled my nostrils, making me nauseous. I didn't have the connection with him like I did with Taron, but there was nothing I could do.

Taron left me, and I was being forced to marry this man, my husband to be, so I had to oblige.

The morning after I woke in Josh's bed, I ached, but not in a good way. He was rough and forceful, claiming every inch of me. I felt battered and bruised, humiliated and belittled.

Josh wasn't in bed, and I rubbed my eyes before finding my clothes on the floor, scurrying over and rushing to put them on.

I wanted out.

I wanted my freedom while I still had it.

I grabbed my bag and tied my hair in a messy ponytail before leaving the bedroom, running down the stairs to get to the front door. My hand reached for the handle when I heard his cold, callus voice.

"And where do you think you're going?" he asked, and I spun round to look at him.

"I'm going home, Josh, I have work," I muttered.

"You not going to kiss me goodbye?" he said, walking towards me, his body wrapped in a silk gown. He looked ridiculous.

He grabbed me round the waist, pulling me into him and kissing me hard. My already sensitive lips were bruising by the minute. His tongue pushed its way into my mouth, darting all over the place.

I pushed him away. "Enough, I haven't brushed my teeth," I said, trying to make out that was the reason why I couldn't have his lips on mine anymore.

"Oh, don't be embarrassed about that," he said, swooping in for another kiss, but I managed to turn my face, so he kissed my cheek.

"I've got to go," I said, my voice small and quiet.

"See you tonight," he said, chipper.

"Mmm." I nodded and opened the door.

"I love you," he said as I stepped into the bitter November air.

"Ditto."

As soon as the door shut, I cried.

I couldn't say the words back to a man I didn't love.

My thoughts trailed back to last night and the events that unfolded. My breasts had bite marks all over them, I had a hicky on my collar bone that I was afraid no make-up would cover. In-between my legs felt bruised and heavy where he pushed his way in, harsh and fast.

I felt like my soul had turned black, the purity completely gone.

When I saw a taxi drive down Josh's road, I held my hand out for it to stop. I hopped in before putting my ear phones in, trying to quieten my thoughts. I just wanted to get home.

I took my phone out my bag and texted Eva. I wasn't going into work today. I needed a day at home, in my bed.

After a short taxi ride I was relieved to see my house approaching. I tapped my card against the card reader and wished the driver a good day before hopping out and walking towards my door. I unlocked it quickly, kicking my shoes off and running up the stairs and straight into my bathroom.

I raided my bathroom cupboard for something to take the sting and the achy feeling away. I found some tea tree oil that I shook into the empty bath before turning the hot tap on and letting the bath fill with boiling water.

I stripped my clothes off, throwing them straight into my bin, I didn't want to be reminded of last night.

I stepped into the boiling bath, wincing as the burn imbedded itself into my skin, but I didn't care, I just wanted to sink in and feel better.

Once I was completely covered by the water, I felt my

achy muscles relax. I sunk under the water, letting it wash over me as I took my hair from its pony tail, sliding back up the bath.

"Luna, was that you?" I heard my mum's voice. Bollocks.

"In here, Mum," I muttered, trying to cover my body with my arms.

"Sweetie, how was last night" she asked.

"Fine," I said, refusing to turn my head to face her as she walked into the bathroom.

She was next to me, looking down at me, her mouth dropping open before she threw her hand up to her mouth. She fell down onto her knees, grabbing my arms away from my chest.

"Oh my Christ, Luna," she said loudly, her concerned voice echoing around my bathroom as she looked down at the bite marks across both of my boobs. My big eyes were on her, her expression bringing it all back as I sobbed, completely breaking down in front of her.

"Did he do this to you?" she said in a whisper. I couldn't talk, I just nodded as my tears continued to fall. She leant into the bath, hugging my wet body and kissing my cheek.

"He's a monster," she said.

"A monster that Daddy has forced me to marry. This isn't the Josh I loved and was going to marry a few months ago. He didn't care. I'm in pain. Emotionally and physically, and now I am trapped in this loveless relationship because Daddy said so. It's nothing more than a business deal," I said through choked sobs, I just couldn't stop.

"Luna, I had no idea. I don't know what your father has set up with Carlisle." She shook her head as she dropped her arms into the burning water before grabbing a flannel and washing my back softly, her motherly instincts taking over.

She reached for the shampoo and washed my hair for me, before rinsing it with the shower head. She smothered my hair in conditioner, leaving it a few moments as she just sat there, staring at me. She knelt back up, rinsing my hair again and wringing it out for me.

I never needed my mother like this, but today, I was grateful.

She knelt back, sitting on the bath mat next to me, not saying a word, but knowing she was there with me made everything better.

Well, as better as it could be.

Chapter TWENTY SIX

After my bath, my mum grabbed the clothes I threw in the bin and took them downstairs to discard, agreeing to my request to throw them out. When she returned to my room, she dried my hair for me, then French-plaited it before disappearing into her bedroom and returning with some arnica cream. She handed it to me, a small smile gracing her face, but her eyes were red from her silent tears.

"Rub some of that into the bite marks, darling, it'll help with the healing. I will go downstairs and grab you some paracetamol," she said in a caring tone as she stood in the doorway. "Do you want some food?"

"No, thank you," I said as she walked out the room. "Oh, Mum," I called out, her little head popping back round the door.

"Yes?" she asked.

"Thank you." I smiled at her.

"Anything for you, Luna," she said, a big smile on her

face too. Her smile soon faded when she heard the front door shut and my dad's voice boomed down the hallway.

"I'm home, darling."

Her botoxed face tried it's hardest to form a frown, her eyes angry. "I'll be back shortly," she said as she stormed out the bedroom.

I snuggled down into bed, flicking the tele on in my room and putting *Gossip Girl* on, then grabbing my phone to text Eva and Tegan to see how today went. They replied instantly, telling me that all was okay and wanted to know if I was okay. I text them back saying I was fine, I just needed a day off.

I placed my phone on my lap as I grabbed the arnica cream, putting a large blob on my finger, pulling my pyjama top up and rubbing the cream into my bites, wincing as they stung for a moment.

I put my top back down, putting the cream on the side and getting myself back under the duvet.

Half an hour had passed, and my mum still wasn't back.

I hopped out of bed and made my way down the hallway to the stairs.

I got halfway down when I heard my mum shouting at my dad. Sitting on the stairs, I took this moment to listen in. I knew I shouldn't, but I wanted to hear what my dad had to say for himself.

"You should see what he has done to our daughter. I

have been trying to stop myself from going over there and giving him a piece of my mind," she screamed at him.

"Tabitha," he bellowed back at her. "What are you going on about? You sound like a mad woman."

"Don't you raise your voice at me, you bastard."

I heard the sound of a kitchen utensil hitting the worktop. I winced, throwing my hand to my mouth at the shock of the loud noise making me jump.

"Don't play dumb," she snapped.

"I don't know what you are going on about," he said in defence.

"Josh," she screamed, I could hear the sadness in her angry voice.

"What about him?" My dad's voice, now quieter, calmer.

"He took advantage of our daughter last night." My mums tone matched his. "I know you don't want to think about this, David, but you need to know. She has numerous bite marks across her chest. She was bathing in tea tree oil because of the pain she was in..." Her voice trailed off, I could only imagine she was pointing to the area she was trying to tell him about.

"He did what?" he screamed, the chair screeching across the marbled floor as he pushed off, it smashing to the floor. He ran down the hallway, grabbing his coat off the stand.

"I won't be long," he shouted back at my mum, her

tiny legs running down the hallway after him.

"David," she called out. "Don't do anything stupid," she pleaded.

He turned around to look at her, yet his eyes found my big, green ones looking down at him from the stairs.

He didn't say anything, but his eyes said it all. He was sorry.

I climbed back up the stairs and to my bed. I had just covered myself up when my mum walked into my room with a bowl of tomato soup and warm, crusty bread, smothered in butter with a glass of water and paracetamol.

"Thanks, Mum," I said as I took the tray off of her, placing it on my lap. She sat on my bed, close to me as she pushed my loose bit of hair behind my ear.

"It'll be okay," she said.

"I know," I muttered before taking a mouthful of the soup. "Mmm."

"Daddy will sort it," she said confidently.

"I know he will, but, Mum," I said, putting my spoon down for a moment. "I am still going to marry him. I'm worried that some deal has been struck, from the way Josh was talking about our names merging as one, I don't want Daddy in trouble." I sighed.

"Luna, darling, Daddy won't care about a stupid deal, if one has even been made. Your happiness and safety are more important," she said, shaking her head at my comment as she tucked a piece of her blond hair back into her clip.

"It's happening, Mum. He won't lay a finger on me like this again after Dad's finished with him," I said, picking my spoon back up. "Besides, the man I truly love has left. He doesn't love me anymore."

"You never know, Luna."

"I do, Mum, and what me and Taron had is over. I need to do what's expected of me, and that is to marry into the Cameron family." I furrowed my brow then pulled my eyes from my mum to my soup.

My mum stood, then leant across me, kissing the top of my head before she walked out of the room. I know I had upset her, but I knew in my heart what I needed to do to make it right.

-

As I waited in the Ritz for the girls, I sat back and reflected over the last couple of months and everything that had happened.

My father came back that night, after going to Josh's to confront him. I knew my father had laid a hand on him, and Carlisle let him after harsh words were exchanged. Carlisle and my father butted heads but ironed it out over a whiskey. Josh apologised profoundly and promised me the world and more and said he would never lay a finger on me again if I didn't want him to.

Our relationship improved. There still wasn't any

love and we both now treated it as a business transaction.

I hadn't heard from Taron. His phone had been disconnected and the one other time I did go to his home, the old lady that lived with him told me he had moved away and wouldn't be returning. He had moved on with his life and got a new job with Carter, who he bumped into in Hawaii, and he wanted to leave his old life behind.

I would be lying if I said it didn't hurt, it fucking did. The last remaining bit of my heart that was still together finally shattered on his doorstep.

Josh would never be able to put it together again, and in my heart, I feel that me and Taron will be reunited, maybe not in this life, but definitely in another.

I saw Brooke, Vanessa and Ava arrive, walking towards me, smiling.

"Hey, doll," Ava called out as they got to me in the waiting room.

I stood up, embracing all three of them. God, I had missed them. It had only been a couple of weeks, but that felt like a lifetime for us.

We sat down at our table, waiting for our annual New Year afternoon tea to be served. "What a year it's been," I muttered as I drank a mouthful of cold champagne.

"Hasn't it just?" Brooke chirped.

We always came for afternoon tea on New Year's

Eve. It started when our mums used to bring us all together from a young age, and it's just something that stuck.

"Doesn't Hawaii seem like a distant memory?" Ava sighed.

"It does indeed," Vanessa replied.

"God, I would do anything to be back there now," I whined, swirling my champagne round in my glass, focussing on the gold fizz swishing.

"Maybe you could do another honeymoon there, with Josh?" Ava asked, raising her eyebrows, a small smirk spreading on her red lips, exposing her perfect white teeth.

"Aha, no. That place holds a special memory for me. I don't want to tarnish it." I shrugged, trying to swallow the small lump that was bobbing in my throat.

"I can understand that." Brooke nodded. "So, I have something to tell you three."

"Oh my God, what?" I said excitedly.

"Ryan has asked me to move in with him," she squealed as she wiggled her petite frame in her chair then held her champagne glass up in the air.

"Brooke, that is amazing," Vanessa said. "But, I am going to miss you." She dropped her bottom lip out.

"And I am going to miss you too, but things are going so well with Ryan, and things are moving in the right direction. I would be a fool to turn him down." She sighed.

"You would," Ava piped up. "He is such a hunk." She blushed. "Talking of news..." Her eyes flicked to mine. "I am dating someone."

"Ooo, who?" I chimed, getting overly excited.

"Do we know him?" Ness asked.

"Yup." She nodded. I suddenly started to rack my brains thinking of someone we all knew.

"Who?" I asked.

"Chris," she said, her eyes on mine, waiting for my reaction.

"That's awesome." I clapped, jiggling in my seat, kicking my legs out.

"Yeah? You're happy?" she said, letting out a relieved sigh and touching her chest. "I thought you would be angry."

"Angry?" I shook my head, smiling. "God, why would I be angry? My brother and my best friend." I stood up and wrapped my arms around Ava. "God, I am so happy." I choked back happy tears.

I moved back to my seat when I saw our afternoon tea tower being walked over.

"Thank God, I am starving." I laughed as the waiter placed the two sandwich and cake towers down.

"More champagne, ladies?" he asked.

"Yes, please," I chimed. "And keep them coming, we are celebrating."

"Certainly, ma'am." He bowed his head and walked

towards the bar.

I helped myself to a couple of sandwiches and a cake before Vanessa blew out her cheeks.

"Okay, seeing as we are sharing as such, well, mine isn't so much a share but an ask," she said before her eyes were on mine. "Can I bring a date with me to the wedding?"

"Of course you can, hun, you haven't got to ask." I smiled.

"Thank you." Her smile small as she took a bite of her salmon and cream cheese sandwich.

"What's his name so I can add it to the table plan?"

"Erm, Blake," she blurted out before having a mouthful of champagne.

"Okay, last name?"

"Spencer."

"Cool, Blake Spencer," I muttered to myself as I made a note in my phone. "So, is it serious?" I asked after I put my phone back in my bag.

"No, not really. Only recently dating, but I really like him," she gushed.

"That's great, Vanessa," Ava said. "Really happy for you." She pulled Ness in for a cuddle.

"Ah, look at us, I'm soon to be married, Brooke is moving in with her sexy boss, Ava is dating my brother and Vanessa is seeing someone." I clapped my hands together out of happiness, and the waiter appeared with another two bottles of champagne. He popped the cork and we all cheered before holding our glasses up.

What a way to see out the year.

Chapter TWENTY SEVEN

I sat in the lounge area of my parent's home, taking every little thing in.

This was my last night here before I was married to Josh. Before my life of an arranged marriage begun.

Vanessa had been amazing once again, planning mine and Josh's second wedding. I'm so glad she offered to work for us again.

I had boxed up all my stuff, ready for our own home that we would be moving into tomorrow. Carlisle had gifted us a stunning townhouse in Kensington, so we were still close to our families. I was grateful, but I was miserable. My heart still beat for Taron.

Josh was kind now, we were friends, but nothing more than that. I couldn't give a rat's arse if he was putting it about every night with another woman. We didn't sleep together. We haven't slept together since that night when we were first reunited.

I was pulled from my thoughts when Josh walked

into the room.

"How you doing?" he asked, planting a kiss on my cheek before sitting down next to me on the sofa.

"Not bad, how about you?" I asked.

"Yeah, okay. What you doing in here?"

"Just taking everything in. I can't imagine not living here," I confessed, running my fingers up the arm of the sofa.

"I can imagine." He took my left hand in his, running his thumb over the back of my knuckles. I turned my head, smiling, tipping my head back slightly and resting it on the back of the sofa.

"I'm going to shoot, get some sleep," he muttered before kissing me on the side of the head. "I'll see you tomorrow."

"Bye," I mumbled as he walked out the door.

I was lost in thought at how different this wedding was going to be to the one in the Plaza last year. Yes, all the same people were coming, maybe even more now, but it wasn't going to be as lavish as such.

We were having a church wedding in a little village, then moving it back to the Cameron's manor house in Surrey, then having a sit down meal in their grand dining room. Once evening rolls in, we will be having a barbeque out on the lawn. I had been checking the weather all week, and luckily it was going to be bright and warm.

I always loved May weather. It wasn't too hot, but the

weather was always nice in May.

I pulled myself up off the sofa and decided to get an early night. Hair and makeup would be here at seven am, we were getting married at two pm.

Brooke, Ava and Vanessa were going to stay, but I decided last minute that I just wanted a night on my own and they could come over in the morning.

When I got to my bedroom, I sighed at all the boxes. Twenty five years of life in no more than ten boxes.

I walked into the bathroom and hopped into the shower, I needed to wash my hair ready for the morning. Once out the shower and dry, I slipped my pyjamas on then sat down at my dressing table, drying my hair with the hairdryer. I plugged my phone in, putting it on charge. I knew Taron's phone was disconnected, but that didn't stop me from texting him every night before bed, even though I knew he wasn't even getting them. I opened up his name, clicking on the message icon.

Hey, I can't believe it's the night before my wedding. The only wedding I thought I was going to be attending again was mine and yours. Yet, that didn't happen. Josh has been kind. I miss you more every day. I hope you are keeping safe. I love you Taron, always. Love, your Luna X

I took a deep breath, waiting for the automated message telling me that it hadn't been delivered before locking my phone. I pulled back my quilt and snuggled down under it, then switched *Gossip Girl* on.

"Luna." I heard a distant voice.

"Luna, darling, it's time to get up." I heard my mums soft voice. I groaned, I felt like I had been asleep for five minutes.

"I'll go get you a cup of tea and some breakfast," she chirped before leaving my bedroom. I rolled over, checking my phone. I rubbed my eyes, thinking I was dreaming when I saw the two ticks showing my messages had delivered to Taron. I felt my heartbeat stop before it raced in my chest. I tapped a message to him.

Taron?

I sat, waiting anxiously, watching the screen, waiting for the two ticks to appear, but nothing. Just the single tick.

I threw myself back in bed, then threw the phone across my bedroom in temper just as my mum walked through the door. Her eyes followed my phone as it hit the wall.

"Well," she said, not phased as she gave me a cup of tea and some honey on toast. My tummy rumbled as the smell of the toast hit my nostrils. My mum sat on the end of bed, watching me eat my toast.

"Are you excited?" she asked, rubbing my leg under the duvet.

"Mmm, I wouldn't say excited." I shrugged, biting another mouthful of my toast. "It's a loveless marriage, isn't it? Nothing more than a business transaction. But Daddy can kiss goodbye to grandchildren. There is no way I am having kids with a man I don't love."

"Oh…" her voice trailed off.

I finished my last mouthful of toast, putting the tray down on the floor beside me then wrapped my hands round my mug of tea.

There was a ring on the doorbell, my mum shot up.

"That'll be hair and make-up," she sang before leaving my bedroom and making her way to the front door. I threw back my duvet and slipped out of bed before pulling back my curtains. The sun was shining already, birds chirping. It was going to be a lovely day for a wedding.

Ava, Brooke and Vanessa all came rushing through the door, the hair and make-up stylist behind them.

"Morning," Ava said loudly, dropping her bags then brushing down some fluff on her lounge suit.

"Morning." I smiled at them. I was glad to have them by my side again.

Tanya placed her stool down on my carpet, Lorraine

following suit. Lorraine huffed as she dropped her heavy shoulder bag to the ground. Tanya's assistant popped her head round the door with her bags, trying to place them delicately on the floor.

"Okay," Tanya called. "Luna, let's start your hair, then we will move onto the rest of the party. Mum, would you like to sit down, and we can start your makeup?" She smiled.

I sat down on Tanya's stool, letting out a deep sigh.

"Nervous, honey?" she asked as she ran her fingers through my blond hair.

"Aha, no. Not that." I smiled at her in the mirror. "I'm fine."

"Chignon bun, was it?" she asked.

"Please, then the girls low, loose buns."

"Yup." She nodded as she started separating my hair. I looked over at my mum smiling, she was so beautiful.

I decided on neutral make up, didn't want to overdo it. My mum was wearing a fitted, blush dress and the girls were wearing blush pink chiffon dresses. Loose and flowy. Yes, it was a big wedding, but hopefully it would be more relaxed than The Plaza.

Three hours later and we were all done. I had drank two bottles of champagne already and was starting to feel the effects. I downed two big glasses of water and took some paracetamol, just to be on the safe side. The girls were in their dresses and looked beautiful. I was so lucky to have such amazing friends.

My mum walked back into my room with my wedding gown, my heart fluttered slightly at the thought of wearing another wedding dress, imagining to myself that I was about to marry Taron.

She hung it up on the back of my door before pulling the zip down and revealing my ivory gown. I clasped my hands together, the look of love as I stared at the stunning gown. I decided for a chignon bun, styled with fake flowers as the back of the dress was open.

My mum carefully removed the dress from the bag, pooling it on the floor for me to step in. My seamstress managed to sew a bra into each breast of the dress for some support. I slipped my Jimmy Choos on before holding onto Brooke's hand, stepping into my gown, my mum slowly standing as she pulled the dress up my body.

I smiled as I felt the satin against my skin, then I ran my hands softly over the dress as my mum did the one button where the back met again. It had a 'V' neckline and narrow straps that tapered into a thinner strap behind my shoulders, revealing my bare back which scalloped where the buttons met.

I loved that the gown fitted my petite curves before flowing out slightly from my knees and creating a stunning, scalloped train. I decided against a veil, the dress was simple but stunning and I didn't want to ruin it.

"Absolutely beautiful, darling," my mum cooed just as my dad walked into the room, his eyes brimming with tears. He was donning a black tuxedo with a black bow tie.

"Oh, Luna," he said, walking towards me and taking my hands in his. "You are breath-taking," he whispered before kissing me on the cheek.

"Thank you, Daddy, let's just hope the groom stays around for this one." I giggled, Tanya and Lorraine looked awkwardly at each other. My dad ignored my comment before walking towards the door.

"We are leaving in five," he said smiling before walking out.

Our bouquets were downstairs. I was tempted to go with the frangipani's, but I felt I couldn't. If it was Taron, I would have.

I settled for white roses.

I walked out of my bedroom towards our staircase, holding onto the bannister as I carefully walked down the stairs, one step at a time. My mum grabbed my bouquet, handing it to me.

"Thank you," I mumbled before walking towards the waiting Rolls Royce outside. *Typical Cameron's.*

My dad opened the door for me, letting me climb in before he climbed in and sat next to me. Brooke, Ness, Ava and Mum would follow behind in another Royce.

I took a deep breath as we pulled away, watching my home shrink smaller and smaller into the distance before turning my head back around and facing the road.

My father took my hand, squeezing it tightly before bringing it to his lips and kissing it, then placed his other hand over the top, cradling my small hand. I wanted to rip it away, but I couldn't. My heart wouldn't allow me.

Things hadn't been right since the night my mum told my dad about Josh. I know it wasn't his fault completely, but if he hadn't made me go over there then it wouldn't have happened.

I pulled my eyes from him, looking out the window as we started driving through the rolling countryside to the church.

I let out bated breath as we pulled up to the idyllic church.

This was it. The moment I became a married woman.

I had such a rush of mixed emotions surge through me. I closed my eyes for a moment, trying not to cry. Not to let the sadness show. I couldn't be weak at this moment. I wasn't a weak person, but these last few months had been torturous.

"Darling, we need to go," my father said as he opened the door, stepping out to the flashing lights of the camera. He held his hand out, clasping mine as he helped me step out of the car.

As I stood, I looked behind me, pulling the back of my dress out. The sound of the tyres on the gravel of the church car park distracted me. I smiled when I saw my mum and my friends. Vanessa walked over, pulling my train out completely.

"I'll meet you inside, need the loo," Vanessa said quietly before slipping away and into the church.

Chris walked out, looking at Vanessa rushing past him. "Is she okay?" he asked.

I shrugged. "Think so, said she needed toilet."

Chris took me into a brotherly embrace, kissing me on the cheek. "You look breath-taking, Luna. Josh is a lucky guy, but he already knows that." He smiled. His eyes darted over to Ava, taking her in his grasp and kissing her on her lips passionately. My heart swelled for them. I wanted that love again.

"Ready?" Brooke said as we stood at the bottom of the stairs that led to the church.

"Ready as I'll ever be," I said, taking a deep breath as I clutched my bouquet of roses tightly. I walked up the steps slowly moving towards the church door, stepping over the threshold of the lobby area before stopping at the big, oak doors that lead to the aisle.

"How long have we got until I have to walk the aisle?" I asked, nerves now setting in. Fear crushing my chest. I felt like I couldn't breathe.

"We could hold them off for about ten minutes," Vanessa said. "How comes?"

"I just need five minutes." I gasped. "I can't breathe." I clutched the material on my stomach, pulling at it. My mum looking at me worried, my dad let go of my arm.

"Okay, lets go in the side room," Vanessa said, her eyes on Brooke, Brooke smirking at her. Vanessa ushered me into a side room where Ava was standing. My eyes widened, darting from her to Vanessa to Brooke.

"What's going on?" I asked.

My mum, dad and Chris walked into the room, closing the door behind them.

"Don't be mad at us," Ava said quietly.

"Why would I be mad at you? What's happened?" Panic now shearing through me, apparent in my voice.

"Because of me." I heard Taron's voice crash through me, he walked out from behind a wall.

"Taron," I whispered, the air leaving my lungs.

"Luna," he said before rushing towards me, scooping me up in his arms, nestling his face into my neck, inhaling my scent.

He pulled his head up, looking at me in the eyes before covering my mouth with his. The charge running through me, the fire in my soul alighting once more, I felt as if my heart started beating again.

Our lips unlocked as he placed me down, I couldn't believe he was here.

"How? Why?" I asked confused, looking for a seat. My father pushed a chair up behind me and helped me sit down.

"When your father told me I had to leave you," Taron

said, crouching down in-front of me, taking my hands in his as he rubbed the back of them with his thumb. My eyes shot back to my dad, narrowing on him.

"Hear me out," he said, bringing my eyes back to his. "The evening your father warned me away, he told me he was being threatened. I said I would help him, but he pleaded, saying that you, and your family would be safer without me. The unknown source who was threatening him demanded that I left. They wanted rid of me." He sighed, his dark eyes glazed.

"Before I left the table, your father handed me my cash for looking after you in Hawaii, but inside the envelope was also a note. A note asking for my help. He couldn't agree there and then as he would have risked all of your safety. I have been working tirelessly with your father, Ava and the police," he said, his eyes batting up to Ava and smiling.

My dad came beside me, squeezing my shoulder. "I'm sorry for everything, Luna, especially because I had to force you back into Josh's arms, and what he did to you..." His voice trailed off when Taron stiffened, his eyes blackening.

"What did he do?" Taron shot up.

"Taron, please, sit down. I'm fine. I'll tell you all about it soon," I hushed, grabbing his hand and pulling him back down to me.

He closed his eyes, taking a few deep breaths before

flicking them open again, the darkness leaving, pulling me into his chocolate pools.

"What happened after you started working with the police?" I asked, palms sweaty, now getting conscious of the time and my father's deal with the Cameron's.

"I won't go into detail as we don't have time, but we found out who it was. It all made sense once I knew, the time the patio door was open in Hawaii, the evening I came back to the room and your room was ransacked and the time I saw the figure running out the door, the threats to your father..." He trailed off. "Before I continue, tell me what happened," he begged.

I sighed, dropping my head, closing my eyes.

Taron placed his thumb under my chin, tilting my face up to him. "Tell me," he said softly.

"Josh took advantage of me, the first night I met him after you left. He was rough, and marked me badly with bite marks..."

I suddenly realised that Chris, Ava, Brooke and Vanessa were all in the room. Taron's eyes went black, his breathing raged. I didn't say anything more, my heart raced in my chest at a hundred miles an hour.

I jumped in my skin when I heard someone banging on the door.

"Luna!" I heard Josh shouting. "Open the fucking door. Don't you embarrass me or my family and make our wedding late." He thumped again hard. "Luna," he growled.

Taron eyed my father, my father stared at me. All he did was nod his head and Taron was up like a shot. He ran for the door, pulling it so hard I was scared it was going to come off its hinges.

He grabbed Josh round the throat, pushing him back and smashing him against the wall. Josh winced and moaned at the pain from the impact.

"You no good fucker," Taron spat as I jumped out of my chair. "I'll fucking kill you for what you did to her."

"Taron, put him down," I yelled, confused and still not sure what Taron had been talking about.

"Tell her and apologise," Taron growled.

"Tell her what?" Josh spat in Taron's face, ignoring the apology bit. Taron didn't flinch. His eyes bored into him.

"You know fucking what," Taron hissed through his teeth, his teeth gritted as all his anger was projected into Josh.

"Let me go." Josh's voice was smaller as Taron's grip got tighter.

After a moment, Taron dropped him to the floor like discarded rubbish. Carlisle came running in to see his son as a crumpled heap on the floor, gasping for breath.

"What the hell do you think you're doing?" Carlisle's voice boomed at Taron, making him turn on his heel as he swung his fist into Carlisle's nose.

"Shit," Carlisle screamed, blood pouring from his nose.

"Fucking tell her." Taron kicked Josh in the ribs, hard.

"Taron," I heard an unusual man's voice call from outside the church. Turning my shocked face, I saw Josh's work captain, Landon, walking up the stairs with a couple of police officers behind him.

"Thank Christ," Josh cried out. "Landon, arrest him," he barked his orders.

"Sorry, Josh, I don't take orders from criminals." He smirked down at Josh. "Arrest them," he ordered as the two police officers pushed their knees into Josh and Carlisle's backs, cuffing them.

"You do not have to say anything, but it may harm your defence if you do not mention when questioned something which you later rely on in court. Anything you do say may be given in evidence," Landon called out as the police officers pulled them up, walking them towards the car. Josh spat at Taron's feet as he was dragged away.

"Thank you, Taron, David." Landon stepped forward, shaking Taron and my dad's hands.

"Can someone tell me what's going on?" I asked, tear marks streaked my face. I hadn't even realised I had been crying.

After the girls and Chris had made sure everyone had

left and apologies were said, we all sat in the side room.

"Can you explain now?" I asked, feeling utterly exhausted.

"Of course," Taron said, tucking a bit of my hair behind my ears and giving me a soft smile. "I gave your dad a burner phone, so we could make contact when needed, and also so I could make sure you were still okay. I had a burner phone too. I turned my phone off once you left my home, after you spoke to Gloria." He sighed.

"I only turned it on last night as I knew I was safe to do so. Your father had some suspicions in regard to the threats. I contacted the police and explained that we believed that one of their cops had gone rogue."

"Josh," I whispered.

"Unfortunately so. We had some clues to why it was him, but we needed the police's help in catching them. He never received a threat before your wedding, it was all part of the plan to throw you off the scent. Once he knew we were getting closer to finding out it was him, the threats started on your father again. It was all a ploy to inherit your father's wealth. Once you were married and legally bound, they were going to kill your father and make it look like suicide. And, because you and Chris were the sole inheritors of your fathers will, you both would have received every penny. That way, Josh and his father had enough money to last them a lifetime and more. It was Josh who I saw in Hawaii. I'm sure there was more to their plan than what we know. The police bugged Carlisle's office, that's when they made the discovery that they were going to kill your father. They won't be set free for a very long time, you are all safe now," he cooed as he pulled me in for a cuddle.

I was shaking, the shock of everything all came crashing on top of me. My mum was crying, Chris was raging. The girls all just huddled together stunned.

Taron kissed the top of my head. "You're all safe now, baby," he said, wrapping his arms around me.

Chapter TWENTY EIGHT

We all arrived back home, and I have never been so grateful. I had a long soak in the bath once we were home. I needed to get out my wedding dress, I felt constricted and trapped. That's how I felt when I knew I was going to have to marry Josh. But now, I felt free again.

My head was fuzzy from the overload of information. Once out the bath, I slipped my juicy tracksuit on, tying my hair into a messy bun on the top of my head.

As I walked into the room, my heart sang when I saw Taron sitting on the chaise lounge, waiting for me.

"Hey," I said, my voice silky.

"Hey." His voice was gruff as he stood.

"God, I have missed you," I said throwing myself into his open arms, my head on his chest, listening to his steady heartbeat.

"I missed you, Luna, so much." His mouth was on top of my head, brushing his lips softly in my hair, before kissing me. "As much as I could stand here, kissing you, we need to go downstairs," he whispered before covering my mouth again. Our kiss soft but filled with need and want.

"Stay the night," I pleaded after breaking away from him.

"Luna," he whispered. "I am never leaving your side again."

We all sat in the lounge area of my parent's house. My dad looked like he had aged in the ride home from the church, I think the realisation of what could've happened to him, to us, had hit him hard. I stood, wrapping my arms around his large frame then leant up on my tip-toes to kiss him on the cheek.

"It's okay, Daddy," I said, trying to soothe him.

"I know, my darling, it's just been a very long, exhausting few months," he said before taking a mouthful of whiskey.

Ava and Chris were snuggled up on the sofa, Brooke and Vanessa were sitting together in an armchair, my mum was sitting in my dad's sherlock chair and Taron and myself were sitting up the other end of the sofa.

I nestled into his body, his protective arm wrapping around me, pulling me as close as he possibly could to him. We sat amongst light chatter, trying to move on from today's events and focus on the here and now. We were safe, that was the main thing.

The girls were staying here tonight, and to be honest,

I am glad that we are all together.

I kissed my parent's good night and waved to the girls as me and Taron retired for the evening.

Once we were in our bedroom, I closed the door, turning the brass key in the lock to make sure we didn't get any unwanted visitors.

"I'll be back in a moment," I said in a sexy manner as I walked into my walk in wardrobe. I slipped my shorts down and pulled my tee over my head, then opened my underwear drawer. I picked up a lacey black thong and slipped it up my legs, then grabbed a black corset out, wrapping it around my back and fastening it up at the front, my boobs spilling over.

I put my foot onto the bench in my wardrobe and slipped on my stockings. I looked at myself in the mirror, taking a deep breath before walking out.

His eyes were on me, hot and heavy.

"Fuck," he said, his eyes devouring me.

I sashayed over to him, where he was sitting on the bed, drinking him in.

He looked delectable.

He captivated me.

I pushed his legs apart with my hands before standing up in between them. I ran my hand up the back of his head, grabbing the nape of his neck and tilting his head up to look at me. His sexy smirk crept onto his face, making my want for him grow.

I was already wet for him, only him.

I lowered my face slowly, teasing him before pressing my full lips into his, pecking his lips before going in for more. Our tongues entwined with each other's, a moan leaving my mouth as I felt our connection fuse once more.

His hands were round my waist, pulling me onto his lap. I pulled my lips from his, his eyes hazily opening to look at me. "You're so beautiful."

I smiled, my eyes trailing up and down his body. He was wearing a fitted white tee, dark denim jeans and chukka boots. His stubble was now a full beard, his hair pushed back and styled. I loved the length, long enough to get my fingers in and grab, but short enough not to put it into a man bun.

I bit my bottom lip, as his fingers trailed up and down my bare thigh. His free hand reached up into my hair as he pulled it from its bun and let it fall down my back before he cupped his hand round the back of my head and pulled me into him, so our lips were together once more.

My hands fumbled with the button on his jeans, then popping the buttons on his fly, my smile appeared, which made him kiss my teeth. I grabbed the hem of his T-shirt before pulling it over his head, losing our connection. My fingertips ran from his shoulders, down his chest, running my nails through his dusting of chest hair before they continued down his stomach to the waist of his jeans.

"Take them off, Sloane," I teased, licking my lips.

He stood from the bed, taking me with him before he spun round and dropped me down softly. My greedy eyes watched him pull his jeans and boxers down at the same time, kicking his boots off and then discarding his jeans as he lunged towards me. Pushing my legs apart, I whimpered, his eyes on me, hooded and dark. Fuck, he was hot.

He hooked his fingers in my knickers, pulling them to the side, groaning when he exposed me. He rubbed his pad over my nub before gliding his fingers down into me, pushing deeper.

"Fuck," I hissed, the pleasure rippling through me like a wave.

He grabbed me round the back of the knee, pulling me down so my bum was on the edge of the bed. He covered me with his hot mouth, sucking on my sensitive bud then licked and flicked his tongue over me, then slowly gliding his tongue up and down me, my hips bucking forward as a moan left me.

He slipped his finger out, then knelt up, leaning across me and kissing me. I could taste my arousal on his tongue and it was hot. He hypnotized me, every single time. He teased his cock at my opening, slowly slipping it in then pulling it back out again. I could've come, it was that sensual and intense.

His hands were in my hair as he grabbed a handful and thrust himself into me hard and fast, tilting my head back before his mouth was on my chin, nipping at it.

"Oh, Taron," I moaned, my voice laced with lust.

He felt amazing, I could feel every inch of him as he continued to thrust into me. He stilled, looking into my eyes, our connection so intense I never wanted it to leave. Our souls intertwining with each other, after roaming with the lost souls for what felt like forever.

After a moment, he stood, hooking his fingers into the side of my knickers, pulling them down. He smirked down at me.

"You are fucking stunning," he said, in a low growl.

He leant down, grabbing my corset and pulling me up so I was sitting on the edge of the bed, then slowly unfastening each clip, pushing it away from my body, licking his lips before throwing it across the room.

"You won't be needing that." His teeth sank into his bottom lip. He grabbed my thighs, tightly gripping them, then kissed me again, his tongue invading my mouth. He pulled away slightly, running his lip along the inside of my lips before taking my bottom lip between his teeth and pulling it.

"Are you trying to make me come through sensual torture?" I giggled, gasping as he flipped me on my front, grabbing my hips and pulling my bum in the air.

I pushed myself up on my arms, looking behind me

as I felt the bed dip where he knelt on it, tightening his grip around my waist before pushing himself into me slowly, a delicious groan leaving his throat. The feeling of him filling me once more was like pure ecstasy.

He grabbed my hair, pulling it hard so my back arched as he picked up the rhythm of his thrusts. They were hard and slow, my insides crumbling with each thrust into me, until he slowed, letting go of my hair.

He pulled himself out of me, then pulled me onto my side as he cradled behind me, one of his hands splayed across my bare stomach, the other grabbing my thigh and lifting it up as he slid into me again. I leant up onto my arm, so I could watch him push himself in and out of me.

His hand moved from my stomach, up to my breast as he squeezed it gently, his lips on my neck as he continued slowly thrusting into me. The ache between my legs was getting too much, I was so close.

I placed my hand round the back of his neck and pulled his lips to mine, our tongues matching the pace of his thrusts as his hand slipped down in-between my legs, massaging me gently.

"I love you, Luna," he said into my mouth as I came crashing down around him, him following behind.

We laid quietly, the moonlight the only light coming through my windows. My hair was fanned out on the pillow, my head on his chest twirling my finger in his hair. The scent of me and him together was like a drug. I was completely intoxicated in him.

"What happens now?" I asked quietly.

"We never leave each other's side again." I can hear the smirk in his voice.

"Well, we will have to. You've got to go home, I have to go work." I sat up shrugging, my hair falling over my shoulder. He sat up next to me, looking down at my illuminated skin.

"Move in with me," he suggested, running his finger tip across my shoulder then down to my collar bone

"Really?" I asked. "We've known each other a few months, and most of those months we were apart," panic apparent in my voice.

He took my hand, holding it tightly. "Luna, I have lost one love of my life, I'm not going to lose you as well. We are meant to be together. It's me and you, baby." He smiled before dropping his mouth to my bare skin, trailing soft, petal like kisses across my shoulders.

It was sensual and passionate, setting my skin on fire. He wrapped his arms around me, pulling me close as he continued his trail, losing ourselves in each other again and again.

Chapter TWENTY NINE

I woke in the morning feeling totally, utterly, completely, madly and insanely in love with him. My smile was like I had slept with a coat hanger in my mouth all night. I turned my face to look at him, I couldn't describe just how much he meant to me in such a short amount of time. He stirred, his eyes opening slowly, he looked so cute and sleepy.

"Morning, handsome," I purred.

"Morning, beautiful," he said in a husky voice, draping his arm across me and pulling me into him, holding me tight then burying his face in my blond mane.

"Did you sleep okay?" he mumbled into my hair.

"I did, did you?" I asked placing my hand over his.

"I slept amazingly," he cooed.

"Good, I'm glad." A smile spread across my face.

We spent most of the morning in bed, I kept thinking about how different my morning would have been if the wedding had gone ahead with Josh. We agreed to sleep in separate rooms once married. We didn't want to be romantic in anyway, only at public functions. I was just grateful that all this happened before I said, "I do."

Whilst Taron was in the shower, I went to sit downstairs with the girls and my parents, I wanted to check in on my dad. I was worried about him, not that I wanted to let him know, but deep down I was.

"Morning," I called out as I got into the kitchen to my mum, who looked like she was cooking for the five thousand.

"Morning, darling," my dad and Mum said in unison. My dad was already in the dining room. I grabbed a cup of coffee, walking beside him and kissing him on the cheek before sitting down next to him.

"You all okay?" I asked looking at the girls, they all nodded and smirked.

"Yeah, we are wonderful, how about you? You look a lot brighter this morning, you have a certain glow about you," Brooke teased.

I knew where she was going with this. I raised my eyebrows, indicating for her to shut up. My dad wasn't stupid, he knew these things happened, but I was still his daughter, and this was something no dad wanted to hear about.

Brooke let out a giggle before taking a mouthful of coffee.

"Who's hungry?" my mum sang as she walked in

with her peony pink apron on, holding a tray full of sausages, bacon, eggs, toast, and a jug of hot beans. My belly grumbled.

She placed the hot tray down on the centre of the table. “Enjoy.”

I started plating up my breakfast when Taron walked into the dining room.

“Morning,” he said, his eyes on me instantly. The hairs on the back of my neck stood up at his presence. He pulled a chair next to me, placing his finger and thumb under my chin and turning my head towards him, so he could kiss me softly.

“This looks wonderful, Tabitha, and it smells delicious.” My mum blushed at his compliment as he started helping himself.

“Would you like a tea or coffee?” my mum asked, rising from her seat opposite him.

“Stay seated, Tabitha, I will go make myself one,” he said politely, standing from the table. “Would anyone like one?” he asked. We all shook our heads before he left the table and padded into the kitchen. Five minutes later he was back with a hot cup of coffee.

After breakfast, I went upstairs to get showered and dressed for the afternoon. When I had finished, Taron was sitting on my bed smiling at me, his eyes glistening. “So, are we going to move in together?” he asked.

“I want too, but I’m scared. Is it not too soon?” I

whispered.

"No, Luna, come on. Give me one good reason why we shouldn't?"

"Erm..." I went to speak but I realised that there wasn't a reason. At all.

"Exactly." He laughed.

"All my boxes are packed." I shrugged thinking of all the boxes in one of the guest rooms. "Oh, God, Taron, what if this all goes south again? If you fall out of love with me? Or just decide you don't want me anymore? I couldn't be unwanted by you. Not ever," I said quietly, standing in front of him as he undone my towel and wrapped his arms around my naked waist

"Luna, you will never, ever feel unwanted by me. I promise you. How could I fall out of love with you? From the moment I laid eyes on you, I fell so deeply. I was, and still remain, will *always* remain, utterly and completely in love with you, Luna Smith." His deep, brown eyes were on mine the whole time.

"Taron," I whispered, tears in my eyes as I took his face in my hands then kissed him with everything I had.

We spent the afternoon downstairs with my family, the girls left for home, all but Ava who was here with Chris. I was so happy that they were together. My heart was bursting that Chris had found someone special.

"Darling," my mum said as she walked into the lounge area with a tray of tea, eyeing my father who was sitting in his sherlock chair. "When did you want to unpack? There's no rush, but I'm assuming you are going to want your bits back where they belong. I know you unpacked a few items of clothes last night." She shrugged. "Like I said, there is no rush." She smiled as she started pouring the tea from the tea pot into her fine china cups.

"Well," I said, sitting up from Taron's hold and clearing my throat. "Me and Taron were talking last night..." I trailed off, feeling nervous. I felt Taron's hand rest on my thigh before giving it a gentle squeeze as he smiled at me. "We are going to move in together." I smiled at my mum, my dad's eyes popping from over the top of his newspaper.

"Oh," was all my mum could manage as she added the milk to the cups. "Well, okay," she said, handing out the tea. "Sugar is on the table." She smiled, standing up straight and brushing herself down.

"And, Luna," she said before she went to walk out. "I think that's wonderful."

Evening was soon upon us; Chris and Ava had left to go home. Me and Taron were chilling in bed, watching a film. I felt exhausted all of a sudden. The last couple of days had been mentally wearing.

We had decided that I would start moving boxes over to Taron's this week, and then settle in on Friday. I had to go to work this week, catch up with the girls and fill them in. I felt awful for just leaving them to it, but they knew there must be good reason for me to do so.

"Stay tonight?" I asked, lifting my head from my safe place on his chest.

"Of course, been in the same clothes for two days but..." He chuckled. "Your mum has washed them, so I am fine." He kissed me before I laid my head back down. I wanted him, I could feel the chemistry and sexual tension crackling between us, but I was wiped.

I woke, stretching my arms up and reaching the cream shabby chic headboard. I wondered whether I could take it with us, I loved my bed. Taron was already up and, in the shower, when I finally crawled out of bed. I couldn't get going.

"God, what I would do to be back in Hawaii." I sighed as he walked into the room.

"I know, it feels like a distant memory, doesn't it?" he replied, kissing me softly on my lips.

"Maybe one day we can go back," I said, smiling fondly at the memory.

"Hundred percent."

I dragged myself out of my bed and into the shower. Once I was done, I threw my leggings on with a tee and then walked down to the spare room to grab my converse.

"Okay, so I'm going to go to work for a couple of hours, check in on the girls and then I'll be back to start moving stuff over, okay?" I said to Taron. We already had the moving vans booked for when I was meant to be moving in with Josh, so my dad called them and just changed the location to Taron's house.

"Well, why don't I come with you? I have nothing better to do. I am on leave from work at the moment anyway." He shrugged.

"Oh, how come?"

"Carter is just having some down time with his wife Freya, so he gave me, and the other security guys a couple of weeks off."

"How's it going working for him?" I asked.

"Yeah, really well, I am really happy there. He is a good, fair boss." He nodded before bending down and pulling his boots on.

"That's good, I am glad." I smiled. "Do you miss being a one-on-one bodyguard?"

"No, not at all. Don't get me wrong, I enjoyed it, but then I met you. And the thought of having to go out and look after clients, mainly female, made me realise I didn't want it anymore. I called Carter when I got home from Hawaii and now I protect him and Freya, alongside James, his head of security. It's a nice family unit." He smiled at me as he stood up, pulling his tee out of his jeans and taking my hand. "You ready?"

"Just give me five," I said taking my hand from his and pulling out my stool at my dressing table. I brushed my hair before pulling it into a messy ponytail, then brushed some bronzer along my cheek bones, and a light pink matte lipstick on my lips.

"I like you in moving attire." He grinned as he wrapped his arms around me, pulling me into him as he nestled his face into my neck and kissed me before inhaling my scent.

"Oh, do you now, Sloane?" I teased, tilting my head back on his chest.

"Oh, I do," he said, his hand coming up to my neck and squeezing slightly as he nipped my skin. My heart raced, my arousal evident in my knickers from just his touch. I had to stop myself, pulling myself from him.

"Later, Mr Sloane," I cooed, running for the door before I fell under his spell again.

We hopped into the taxi outside my house and drove to the shop, we were going to get on the train, but it was so humid I didn't fancy being on a packed underground.

I loved the feeling I got whenever I saw my shop. I was immensely proud of myself. I put all my time and effort into it when I first opened it, knowing exactly how I wanted it to be.

Taron gave money to the driver as we pulled up and I hopped out the taxi, him following close behind me. I opened the dark green double doors, smiling as the scent of cake, coffee and flowers consumed my nose. It was one of my favourite smells.

I saw Tegan's eyes go wide when she saw Taron walk in behind me before a silly grin graced her face. I faced her, giving her a wink before walking towards the florist side to see Eva.

I walked out the back to see her filling a stunning vase of flowers, she was delicately putting white hydrangea's and pale, pink peonies into it, then filling the gaps with baby's breath. They were beautiful.

"Wow, Eva, this bouquet is amazing," I swooned, walking up close and bending down to smell them.

"I know, don't they look amazing?" she said, proudness in her voice, her eyes then moving to Taron. "Oh, hello," she said sweetly, tucking her brown hair behind her ears, her blue eyes sparkling.

"Hello," he replied in a smooth voice, extending his hand out to shake, which Eva took gladly, giggling like a shy school girl. I rolled my eyes at her.

"Anyway." I laughed. "Where are these off to?"

"They're a trial run for a wedding in a couple of months, I love the colours." The concentration etched on her face as she wrapped the ribbon round the stem after removing them from the vase of water.

"Well, Eva, they are honestly breath taking." I walked up and giving her a squeeze on the shoulders. "Well done."

I walked out of the back room and over to the coffee shop. "Coffee?" I asked Taron as he took a seat at my favourite table.

"Please." He nodded, pulling his phone out and tapping the screen with his thumbs.

I couldn't help but smile looking out at the busy tables. I felt incredibly lucky.

I turned the coffee machine on and started making two cappuccinos. "Hey," I called out when Tegan walked up beside me. "How's it going?" I asked her.

"Yeah, okay, we've been so busy lately," she said as she was prepping another cake order to go out. "One second," she called to the lady waiting at the till.

"Let me jump on, I'll run these coffees over to Taron and I'll be back, okay, hun?" I said.

"Yeah, fine." She carried on pulling cakes out the display cabinet as I walked off.

"Hey, just give me ten, yeah? Tegan is under it." I leant down, kissing his cheek before running back off towards the till.

"Sorry for your wait. Good afternoon and welcome to Cakes and Roses, what can I get you?" I shined my biggest smile at the customer.

Chapter THIRTY

I was at the shop a lot longer than I had anticipated, but I couldn't leave the girls on their own when it was so busy. Tegan ran the coffee area, Eva and Michelle ran the florist side and Jane just floated in between helping and cleaning.

"Sorry we were there so long," I said apologetically, my brows furrowing.

"That's okay, it's your business, Luna." He let out a little sigh. "That's why I left, I felt like a spare part there. So, I have loaded the van up with as much as I could, and they took it over to mine. I have just put it in the downstairs room for the minute, then when you are ready we will go through and unpack."

"Thank you," I muttered. "Do you fancy going out for dinner tonight? You have fresh clothes on, it'll take me a minute to change. We haven't actually been out, just me and you."

"That sounds good," he said nodding. "I am starving,

I've been a busy boy." He laughed.

"Oh, I know, baby," I cooed as I wrapped my arms around him, standing on my tip toes to kiss him.

He kicked back on my bed whilst I rummaged through my walk in, I hadn't a clue where we would end up, but I wanted something relaxed, not uptight. That wasn't my scene, and it definitely wasn't Taron's.

The weather had been glorious the last couple of days, so I decided on a white, mini smock dress. I loved the tiered layers; the sleeves were three-quarter length and a small 'V' neck line. I added a thin, gold chain choker with a small, solid gold circular pendant. I slipped on my black patent Doc Martens then pulled my hair into a messy bun and finished off with some gold-hooped earrings. I topped up my make-up, then changed my lip colour to a nude, natural matte colour.

"Ready, stud?" I called out as I walked into the bedroom. Taron's brown eyes looking me up and down, from head to toe.

"Oh, baby," he groaned as I sauntered over to him, swaying my hips and sticking my tongue out.

"Like what you see?" I said in a teasing manner, winking at him.

"Oh, I do, I really do," he growled. He grabbed my hand and moved it to his groin area as I gently groped feeling how hard he was.

"Not now," I whispered in his ear as I pulled my arm

away, hovering just above his lips.

He bunched the neck of my dress in his grip, pulling me towards him as he crashed his mouth onto mine, our hungry tongues entwining with one and other. “We need to go,” I muttered against his lips, using every bit of power in me to pull away, taking his hand and tugging him up. “Come, let’s go.” I smiled as we walked towards my bedroom door.

We decided on Shoreditch, it was the place to be for a relaxed, fun night out. They had quirky food stalls and things to do. I chose a restaurant called, Blue’s, it was a hidden gem.

From the outside it looked just like an everyday pub, but inside was dimmed with massive leather couches and a stunning, solid wood wrap-around bar. It reminded me of the bar in Hawaii, when me and Taron had just turned the corner in our relationship.

The lights were my favourite bit, they were grammar phones all linked together that had been made into lights. All the sofa areas were taken, so we sat on a small round table close to the bar, under one of the fabulous lights.

It was loud, and buzzing. There was a jazz band on the small stage in the corner of the pub, I was hypnotized.

Taron jumped down from the stool and walked about three steps towards the bar. I hadn’t even told him what I wanted, but I’m sure he would choose something delicious.

He came back with a strawberry gin cocktail, and a gin and tonic for him. I took a small mouthful, licking my lips. It was glorious.

"I've ordered us some bar food, I hope that's okay?" he said taking a big mouthful of his gin and tonic, rubbing his lips together and nodding to himself.

I stifled a giggle by taking another mouthful of my drink. "Yup, that's perfect."

After our easy dinner and one too many cocktails, we walked out of the pub and headed down the hustle and bustle of the London streets. I let go of his hand, running off in front of him and stopping in my tracks to face him, standing, just watching him walking towards me. The rush of love shot through me, I had never been so happy.

I stretched my arms out and spun round, ignoring everyone and everything around me. Only him, he is all I can see once I stop. Everything else is a blur around me. My breath was knocked out of my lungs as he pulled me towards him, so close but not touching.

"I am so crazy in love with you," I whispered, trying to steady my breathing, his hands round my face as he leant in to kiss me, but his lips hardly touching mine.

"I love you more," he said.

"Not possible." I shook my head, my eyes steadying on his, rubbing my lips together.

"Believe me, Luna," he said, his voice sounded pained, his eyes full of lust and want. "Come on, let's go."

He held my hand as we continued our walk down the streets.

We stopped outside a mini golf course, I loved mini golf. This was our first date, I wanted it to be fun and relaxed, and so far, it had been perfect.

Taron took the lead and got us two golf clubs and balls as we walked to the first hole.

"Ready to get your arse whipped, Sloane?" I said, cockiness lacing my voice, running my tongue round my top lip and teeth.

"Oh, you've got good talk, Luna, but I don't think you're going to win this one." He laughed, his head tipping back.

"Don't get cocky," I teased, grabbing my golf club off of him, stepping up to the first hole. I slowly bent down, showing him just enough to get his pulse racing as I placed the ball on the tee spot before rolling my body up, then lined my club up.

I stepped from foot to foot a couple of times, giving my bum a wiggle, knowing full well his eyes were on me the whole time. I pulled my club back, knocking it and getting a hole in one. I poked my tongue out, sticking my teeth into it as I did and pointing my perfectly manicured, black painted middle finger nail up at him.

"It's on," he growled.

After winning by ten points and rubbing it in Taron's face for as long as I possibly could, I wanted to go home.

The taxi took longer to arrive than I wanted. I was desperate to go home and lose myself in him again and again.

Once we were in the taxi, Taron shut the door, telling the driver his address. A pang of nervousness shot through me at the thought of going back to his place, the only time I had been there was when I went looking for him.

I didn't have time to think anymore as Taron threw himself onto me, his lips crashing into mine, hard. The pent up want and need over spilling from both of us.

He pushed me towards the door, my legs opening for him to lay in-between them, his mouth on my neck sucking, kissing and nipping. My hands were in his hair, tightening my grip. I wanted him now, here in the back of the taxi, but he wouldn't allow it.

The taxi came to a halt, throwing us forward slightly. Taron chuckled, kneeling back and throwing the driver the cash before opening his door and pulling me out with him, and then his hungry mouth was back on mine again as we backed through the black iron gate.

We reached the door, his lips leaving mine whilst he fumbled for his keys in his back pocket, pushing them into the lock and opening the door. I followed him through as he shut the door behind me, then his lips were on mine once more.

My hands fumbled with the hem of his tee, yanking

it over his head and throwing it towards the front door. I leapt up into his arms, a silly smirk on his face as my legs wrapped around him tightly. He walked me through to his kitchen, sitting me on the worktop.

He placed his head against my forehead for a moment, trying to calm his breathing. His hands smoothing down the side of my body, the thin, cotton material of my dress separating our skin from touching.

Once he was at the hem of my dress, he pulled it off, straight over my head then marvelled at the sight in front of him.

"You're stunning," he moaned as his mouth was on mine again, our tongues dancing together as his hands kneaded and squeezed my aching breasts before he pulled the material of my bra down and rolled my hard nipple between his fingers, sending a pang of pleasure straight through to my core.

He moved both his hands to my bare thighs, slowly moving them up towards my knickers and squeezing, licking his lips before pulling his bottom lip between his teeth, lifting his thumbs and running it across his bottom lip, his eyes dark and hooded.

I wrapped my fingers round the waistband of his jeans, pulling him towards me, closer as I unbuttoned his fly and pushed them down as far as I could. He pushed them down to his feet, my eyes moving down to his erection.

Within that moment, it was like a wild animal had been released from its cage within him. He pulled his boxers down, then grabbed my thighs hard, dragging me towards him. His hands yanked my knickers to the side as he penetrated into me hard, causing me to moan out. He kept one hand on my thigh, the other went back up to my breast as he continued his kneading and gentle tugging.

My hands gripped onto the edge of the worktop, trying to hold myself in place whilst he pushed harder and faster into me. His eyes went down to watch himself pounding in and out of me. I was ready to combust around him, but I was trying to hold off, I didn't want it to be over so soon.

He grabbed my chin, tilting my head up to look him in the eyes. Low groans escaped him as he picked up his pace, the sound of our skin hitting against each other. He pushed his thumb into my mouth, which I licked and then sucked, a growl escaping him. Feeling the glorious build up continue, I couldn't hold it off anymore.

"I'm going to come," I cried out as I bit down on his thumb, trying to stifle my moans as I came hard around him. It took him a moment after as I felt him throb and pulsate inside me as he came. Both out of breath and sweaty, we stilled for a moment before I leaned forward to kiss him.

I loved him so fiercely.

Chapter THIRTY ONE

Friday was soon upon us; all my stuff was now at Taron's. I didn't feel nervous, I didn't feel homesick. He was home. Wherever he was, I wanted to be. I hugged my parent's goodbye, kissing both of them on the cheek. I was grateful that our new home wasn't too far, I could walk or taxi it.

They walked down towards the kerbside where the taxi was waiting for us before hugging me and Taron again. My dad shook his hand, "Take care of her," he said, his eyes glistening.

"I will, David, until my last dying breath." Taron nodded, smiling at him then looked down at me. My heart and soul were aglow from just that one look.

He wrapped his arm around me from the side, pulling me into him and kissing the top of my head. "You ready?" he asked.

"Yup." I smiled up at him, then ran into my dad's arms one last time.

We walked up to the front door, Taron opening it and letting me walk through first.

"Welcome home, Luna," he cooed as he stood waiting for me to walk past him. I was so happy, I was smiling from ear to ear.

Early evening was soon upon us. I was unpacked, and everything was put away. Gloria popped her head round the bedroom where I was laying my nightie out on the bed.

"Hello again, Luna." She smiled as she sat down next to where I had put my pyjamas.

"Hello," I said shyly.

"I don't think we have been formerly introduced," she said softly, just as Taron walked through the door, snaking his arms around me from behind and cuddling into me.

"I used to be Taron's parents' house keeper, I had worked for them before Taron came along. Then, when Taron had just turned five, his parents were killed in a car accident." Her grey eyes shot up to Taron as she gave him a motherly, warm smile. "They didn't have any family, and in their will, they had requested that I become Taron's guardian. I never married or had a family of my own, so how could I turn down this beautiful, brown-haired, chocolate-coloured eyed boy?" she said, smitten.

"You couldn't," he answered her question.

"Obviously, Taron knew from a young age what had happened to his parents. I never sugar-coated anything, I don't believe in that." She shook her head, pushing out the pleats in her pinafore. "I think I have done a pretty good job bringing up this wonderful gentleman."

"You have," I muttered, turning my neck to look up at him, smiling.

"I tried to stick with the way his parents bought him up, we both had a lot of learning to do." She chuckled softly, her eyes turning from happy to sad in an instant. "I am so glad he found you, Luna. After Emerson..." her voice trailed off as her eyes found Taron's, looking for the confirmation that I knew about his wife.

He bowed his head ever so slightly, giving her the green light for the conversation to continue.

"After Emerson, I didn't think he would be able to love again. Trust me when I say, he hasn't seen another girl since her. Until you. I was starting to think it would just be me and him living in this big house for the rest of our days." She let out a sigh, then a smile as she stood up, walking towards us and taking my hands in hers.

"Thank you, Luna, thank you for saving him." Her eyes moved to Taron, her hand resting on his cheek. "You deserve nothing more than happiness, my darling boy." She sniffed, dropping her hand and walking towards the door. "If you need anything, then call. Now, Luna, I don't want you thinking I am a housekeeper, I left that job when

I became a mother thirty years ago. I'm not sure what upbringing you have had, and if you've had people wait on you hand and foot and be at your beck and call, but it's not like that here. I'm just Mum." She winked at me.

"Oh, Gloria, I didn't expect anything else than that," I replied, reassuring her of my morals and upbringing. "And, honestly, we never had housekeepers, my parents didn't believe in that. We came from money, we never wanted for anything, but my parents never believed that because they had a high pay cheque that they deserved to have people work underneath them."

"I'm glad to hear it," she responded before walking out of the room. I let out my breath.

"You okay?" Taron asked, he must've felt me relax.

"I am perfect." I nodded.

"And don't worry about Gloria, she doesn't hover around. She has the whole top floor. When I bought the house I had it converted into a flat for her. She has all she needs up there, but she gets lonely..." His voice trailed off. "I feel like I am the reason she didn't meet a husband and have a family of her own."

"Taron," I said wrapping my arms around his tensed body, resting my head on his chest, listening to his heart pounding in his chest. "You heard her, her job was to bring you up. You are her family. She doesn't want for anything else." I tried to re-assure him.

He craned his neck down, his breath on me as I

moved my head back to look at him. His thumb sat underneath my chin as he placed his lips over mine. His kisses were soft but passionate. Every stroke of his tongue against mine made me melt. I could never get enough of him, I never wanted to.

It had just gone eight pm, Taron had said he needed to pop to the shops and would be back in about thirty minutes, so I decided to run a bath and have a moment to myself. It had been go, go, go from the moment I found out about Josh and Carlisle.

We hadn't had any update from the police, but they did inform Taron that they won't be making bail which is a huge relief. I still couldn't get my head round that it was always him. His plan still made my blood run cold. If Taron had never found out what was going on, I could have been without my father, and the thought of that broke me.

I slipped into the hot bath, the vanilla and apricot bubbles smelt divine. My mind drifted to a young Taron, alone without his parents. My heart shattered for him, and I was so grateful that he had Gloria and didn't end up in an orphanage.

He has had nothing but hurt and grief in his short thirty-five years of life, no one should have that much loss. Life really isn't fair. First his parents were killed in a car accident, then years later his beautiful wife was taken from him. He had a photo on the wall in the lounge area of her, she had long black hair, honey eyes and caramel skin. She was Latina, and absolutely, breathtakingly beautiful. Taron went to put her picture away, but I wouldn't allow it. She was his wife, an important part of his life. I would never want him, or anyone to think that's what I would want.

It made me realise we didn't really know that much about each other; our connection and chemistry were so strong that we haven't felt the need to get to know the ins and outs of our lives. To be fair, we haven't even thought to get to know the basics. Upbringings, traditions, birthdays, likes and dislikes. Maybe that's what we should do tonight during dinner... Learn about each other.

I sank under the water into the huge, free standing tub to wet my hair. I lathered my hair with shampoo then smothered it in conditioner. It felt so dry. I cursed that I had missed my beauty appointment for my wax, looking down at my yeti legs and sighing. I grabbed the shaver out of my toiletry bag that was resting on the floor by the bath and started to shave.

Once out the bath, I rinsed it round then walked into our large bedroom, my bedframe looked so pretty in his room. We had moved his bed into one of the spare rooms. I didn't realise how big this house was, it had six bedrooms plus Gloria's flat upstairs. I couldn't ever envisage us moving, unless we decided to start a family and wanted to move away from the city, but then we had work to think about.

I shook my head, my mind getting carried away with something that I didn't even know was in our future.

I blow-dried my hair then slipped into my silky nightie that I laid out earlier. It was a warm evening, so I opened the bedroom window, pulling the blind up to let the air through.

I was so content, I had never felt so relaxed and full in my life.

-

TARON

I told Luna I had to go to the shops. I didn't. I took a deep breath as I walked up to her parent's front door, knocking then stepping back, waiting for David or Tabitha to open the door. It swung open, Tabitha standing there smiling.

"Taron," Tabitha called out, pulling me into her embrace.

"Hey," I said strained as she squeezed into me.

"All okay?" she asked, looking behind me for Luna.

"Yeah, all fine, just wanted to have a chat with David." I smiled as she welcomed me into her home.

"Oh, okay, he is in his study. Go into the lounge and I will tell him that you're here," she said as she wandered off down the hallway to the study, her heels clicking along the marbled floor.

I stood in the lounge for a moment, walking around and looking at the photos of Luna and Chris when they were younger. I smiled, picking up a frame of a white-haired little girl, her hair in pigtails. She was wearing a pink dress with her fingers in a peace sign. I laughed when I realised she was trying to be, Baby Spice. Her smile was still big and beautiful, even at that age.

"Taron," her father's voice boomed through the room. Turning on my heel, I put the photo back on the mantlepiece and he pulled me into a manly cuddle. Normally, I would never allow this, but they were my family. I had a bond and a connection with them.

"Is everything okay?" he asked letting me go, then wandering over to his decanters. "Drink?"

"Please." I nodded, taking a seat on the sofa. Sitting with my legs apart, my elbows resting on my knees as I fiddled with my fingers. He walked over, in his suit, he was always in a suit, then he handed me my whiskey before taking a seat in his sherlock chair.

"What do we owe this pleasure?" he asked taking a sip of the brown poison in his crystal glass, I mirrored him, wincing as the liquid burned my throat.

"I have something to ask you," I said, nerves now kicking in. I know he isn't going to say no, but the nerves are still ripping through me.

"Go on," he said, his stern face breaking into a small

smile, his lips curling upwards slightly.

"David." His name came out strained, my anxiety creeping up inside. I closed my eyes a moment, taking deep breaths, holding my breath for five then letting it out again. "I, erm..." I coughed. "David," I said, blowing the air out of my cheeks, rubbing my sweaty palms along my thighs a few times.

"David, would you please give your permission for me to marry your daughter? I want to give her the wedding, and the husband she deserves, but I won't if you won't allow it," I said quickly, taking a big mouthful of my whiskey once I spilled the words out.

"Taron..." he said, his voice trailing off. "Of course you can. Nothing would make me a happier man than you marrying my daughter. After everything that's happened, after everything you have done for us," he said, placing his glass on the side table before standing up and walking towards me.

I stood, meeting him in the middle of the room as he pulled me into a hug, patting me on my back.

"Tabitha," he shouted. "Get in here, woman." He laughed as he called her.

"What is it, dear?" she asked, running in with her marigolds on.

"Taron has asked for Luna's hand in marriage." He beamed at her.

"Oh my Christ." She threw her bubbly, marigold

hands up to her cheeks. “I can’t believe it,” she screamed as she ran over and threw herself into me. “Oh, Taron, this is wonderful. Our Luna is going to be over the moon. When are you doing it?” she asked, pulling away from me, now cuddling into David.

“Tomorrow.” I smiled, putting my hands in my pocket.

“Do you have the ring?” she asked excitedly.

“I do, I’ve had it since we came back from Hawaii,” I muttered, grabbing the black box and placing it on the glass coffee table in the middle of the room. Tabitha gasped when she saw it.

“Oh my god, Taron,” she whispered, walking over and staring at the ring in the box. “She is going to lose her mind over this ring.” Her eyes sparkled at the diamond in the ring.

“I know,” I said smugly. “Only for her.”

“Are you going out to do it or staying home?” she asked.

“Staying home.” I smiled.

“That’s what Luna would want.” She nodded then walked back towards David.

“Thank you, I thought that.” I bent down, picking up the box and folding it together before putting it back in my pocket. “Now, I need to hide it for another night.” I chuckled as I grabbed my glass and knocked the rest of the whiskey back. “I better be off, I told Luna I was going to the store." I winked at them.

"Oh, wait," Tabitha called out as she ran out of the lounge. I threw David a puzzled look, but he just rolled his eyes and shrugged before drinking the rest of his whiskey.

She came running back in, still donning her pink marigolds. "There we go, take that with you." She handed me some camembert, a loaf of crusty bread and champagne. I looked down, my mouth falling open slightly.

"Er, thanks?" I said not quite sure on why she had given me it.

"Luna loves camembert and bread." She shrugged. "And the champagne, well, just because."

"Thank you, Tabitha." I smiled as I held onto the bits she gave me. "Any chance of a bag?"

"Oh, yes, one moment."

I couldn't help laughing, David joining in as she ran out the room again. I think it was the marigolds that were getting me.

Within moments she was back with a big, plastic shopping bag. She took the items out of my hand and started packing the bag for me. I was about to ask her to stop, but David looked at me, holding his hand up and shaking his head, basically telling me I would be wasting my time.

"Thank you," I said as she handed it back to me.

"Anything for my future son-in-law," she squealed

then started to cry. “I am just so happy,” she said, wiping her eyes with her marigold shielded fingers.

I walked over to her, taking her in my arms and hugging her.

“I’ve got to go,” I said as I let her go. “I’m sure Luna will call you tomorrow,” I said as I walked out the lounge and down towards the front door, David and Tabitha following me. I let myself out, turning around to wave.

“Bye, David, Tabitha.” I smiled, they waved back. Tabitha was still crying when David shut the door. I let out a relieved sigh as I started my journey home, hailing a cab.

Now it was time to get home to my girl.

Chapter THIRTY TWO

LUNA

I sat in the kitchen, waiting for Taron to come home, helping myself to a cold glass of white wine. Gloria wished me goodnight just as I was coming out of my bedroom. I heard the front door go, smiling when I heard his footsteps coming down his tiled hallway.

"Luna?" he called out.

"In the kitchen, baby," I replied, jumping off the stool and grabbing him a glass, then pouring him a glass of wine.

"Hey, beautiful," he said as he came up close to me, kissing me.

"I missed you," I purred as I lifted myself up onto the square island in the middle of the kitchen, watching him.

"I missed you too," he said as he started unloading his bag, my wandering eyes wanting to see what took him so long.

"What did you get?" I asked.

"Camembert, bread and champagne." He turned the top half of his body round to see me, winking.

"My favourites." I smiled at him.

"I was thinking," he said as he put the oven on and walked over to me. "We should spend the evening talking, we hardly know anything about each other, yet we live together." He laughed.

"Hmm, I suppose we do need to talk." I nodded.

"I think it's important," he muttered.

"Oh, it is," I said as I grabbed the bottom of my silk night dress, pulling it up. "Now, let's see if you can focus," I said confidently as I spread my legs, revealing myself.

"Fuck," he whispered as he stood between my legs, his finger slipping straight into me. Using his free hand he pushed me back, flat against the island, kissing my neck, moving his hot, wet mouth down to each of my breasts, releasing them and sucking my nipples softly.

He continued licking and kissing down my stomach, dipping his tongue into my belly button, gliding it towards the apex between my legs. He softly kissed the inside of my thighs whilst his finger was still pushing inside me, slowly.

"You're soaked," he said through a smile, pushing his tongue between my folds, flicking and sucking on my bud as I moaned, my pelvis bucking up to his face. I ran my fingers through his hair, grabbing it, pulling his face into me more. I could feel my legs trembling as he continued the same rhythm with his finger and tongue.

"Taron, stop," I begged, tugging his head up.

His mouth glistened with my arousal. I sat up, moving from the island, pushing Taron towards the sofa in the kitchen then dropped to my knees as I pulled his jeans and boxers down, letting them sit at his feet. I stood, straddling over him. I smirked down at his hard cock before slowly lowering myself down onto him, a low moan left my lips as he filled me.

I thrusted my hips back and forth, quickly. "Taron, fuck," I hissed, my orgasm building.

He groaned as he tightened his grip on my hips, then thrusted into me, matching my movements. I leant my head down to kiss him, then bit his lip as I continued rolling my hips on him, pushing him deeper.

I tilted my head back as the pleasure rocked through me, his hands came up, cupping around my face and pulling me back into him, his tongue stroking mine as he took back the control, hitting into me harder and faster, pushing me to my release as I came hard, an earth shattering orgasm pulsing through me, which left me trembling, my legs shaking as he came with me, his teeth on my lips as he found his release.

I stayed where I was, panting, sweaty and in complete bliss.

"God, I love you, Taron Sloane," I muttered as I

nestled down and laid my head on his chest, listening to his racing heart.

"Not as much as I love you, Luna Smith." His neck craned down, and he kissed the top of my head before his muscular arms wrapped themselves round my small body, pulling me closer to him, holding me so tight. I never wanted to leave his arms.

This is where I am supposed to be.

Where I belong.

An hour later, we were sitting with a melted, gooey camembert, fresh warm bread and an ice cold bottle of bubbles. We were sat on the sofa in his kitchen, Taron sitting facing forward, I was sitting with my back against the arm of the sofa, my legs draped over his. His soft fingertips were moving up and down my shins.

"I love camembert," I said as I leant across to the coffee table, pulling a bit of bread off the chopping board, dipping it into the cheese before taking the lot into my mouth, grinning as I chewed.

"I have never had it before, until tonight," he said, taking a sip of his champagne. I looked at him shocked. How could he never have had camembert?

"So, Mr Sloane," I said once I had finished my mouthful, washing it down with a big gulp of bubbles. "What do you want to know?"

"Okay, top of my head... When is your birthday?"

"Fifteenth of January." I smiled, watching his face

drop.

"I missed your birthday." He sighed.

"That's okay, I didn't do anything spectacular, just got a year older, making me the grand old age of twenty six."

"That's not old," he scoffed before laughing.

"It is to me," I scolded before breaking into a laugh with him. "Okay, when is your birthday?"

"Sixth of June," he responded, raising his eyebrows before taking a mouthful of his champagne.

"Ooo, so we get to celebrate your birthday together, only a couple of weeks left," I said as I wiggled my arms a bit too excitedly, the champagne spilling over the edge of my glass. "Oops," I said, wiping it up with my hand. "So, that makes you thirty six this year, doesn't it, Grandpa?" I teased, winking at him.

"Grandpa," he bellowed as he pushed my legs off of him and crawled up in-between them before tickling me. "I'll show you, Grandpa," he shouted as I laughed from his tickles. "And I love that you are still naked underneath that, free for me to touch and taste anytime I want," he purred before tickling me again.

"Taron, stop," I laughed out, sounding like a plea. He did, but he hovered above my lips before kissing me. A slow and passionate kiss. I wrapped my arms around his neck, my glass still in my hand, but I didn't care if I spilt it. I was too lost in the moment.

He pulled his lips from mine. "Back to talking." He smirked as he sat back, crossing one of his legs.

"Fine," I sulked, sticking my plump bottom lip out as I scowled at him before giggling.

"Okay, favourite colour?" he asked.

"Black," I said quickly.

"Black? What sort of colour is that? Out of all the colours in the world, you choose black?" he asked confused, his brows furrowing, his eyes narrowing on me.

"Don't judge, you asked what my favourite colour was." I shrugged. "Yours?" I asked, now even more intrigued.

"Yellow," he said, his voice a pitch or two higher.

"Huh, I can't even come back with a sarcastic comment. Yellow is a pretty decent colour, I suppose." I chewed the inside of my lip.

"Plus, it's in one of my favourite memories of you," he said, his eyes glistening at me.

"It is?"

"Yup. The day I had to zip you up in the yellow sundress. You looked so beautiful in it," he gushed.

"Thank you." I blushed. "I liked that memory too, only up to the part where I was unwanted by you, and you went all cold and bodyguard like again."

"Only because I was trying to protect myself," he explained, his hand reaching for mine as he interlocked our fingers, lacing them through one another.

"I know," I whispered, bringing his hand to my lip as I kissed it, smiling at him.

"Favourite film?" I fired at him, trying to pull him from his thoughts.

"Oh, tough one... Die Hard." He nodded confidently, his face screwing up as he did.

"Die Hard? Really?" I rolled my eyes at him. "Typical man answer."

"Alright, what's yours?" he asked defensively.

"Pretty Woman, or Father of the Bride. Love both." I nodded. "Oh, and Grease."

"Alright, to be honest, they're not too bad." He chuckled. "I was going to ask favourite television series, but I already know the answer to that, so a bit pointless, you *Gossip Girl* junkie."

"Oh, God, I do. I really do love it." I sighed thinking to my fictional television series. I've watched it so many times, yet it is still my go-to.

"I know you do."

"Okay, next question. Favourite food?" I asked.

"Oh, that is a tough one for me," he said rubbing his short, trimmed beard with his finger. After five minutes he was still umming and ahhing.

"Oh my God." I laughed. "Taron, it isn't that hard."

"Alright, what's yours?" he asked.

"Lobster," I spat out quickly.

"Damn, I do love lobster," he said patting his belly.

"Okay, okay, I think, if I had to eat one thing for the rest of my life..." He looked into the kitchen. "Nah, I can't do it. I would rather starve. I can't choose, I love everything." He threw his hands down in defeat.

"Taron," I choked out, I couldn't stop laughing, holding my belly as it was starting to hurt. I ran my fingers under my eyes, wiping the tears away. I don't even know why I was still laughing, it was more his facial expressions and how hard he was having to think about it.

"You finished yet?" he huffed.

"Mmm hmm," I said, biting the inside of my cheek, trying to stop myself.

"Okay, next question. Favourite animal?" he asked.

"A horse," I said, finally able to talk without giggling. "You?"

"Dog."

"What type of dog?" I asked.

"German shepherd." He smiled. "Would you ever say no to a dog? It could be a deal breaker," he teased.

"Nope, I love dogs. Just not as much as horses." I grinned at him.

"Anything else you want to know?" I asked.

"Children, do you want them?"

"I do, yeah, not now, God, not now. But yes, I do. What about you?" I asked, my heart was racing in my chest, nervous that he wouldn't want children.

"I do. More than anything." His eyes felt like they

were burning through me.

"Is there a deadline for you?" I asked, nibbling the skin on my thumb.

"Within the next couple of years." He smiled, his face relaxing again.

"That works for me." I leaned across and kissed him. "Where can you see us in five years' time?"

"Good question," he said, pulling me into him for a cuddle. "Hopefully married," he said first. My heart was bursting and singing. I would love nothing more than to be his wife.

"Us sitting here, or in a new home. But I mean, us, sitting like this, talking, enjoying each other's company, me still undecided on my favourite food, a couple of kids running around." His lips kissed the top of my head.

"That sounds like an amazing five year plan, what about work?" I asked.

"Work is work, I am grateful for every day I wake up and I have work. To be honest, I have never told anyone this, but I don't need to work. I came from a very wealthy family, but I couldn't sit at home twiddling my thumbs all day. I went into my line of work to protect people, if I could stop five people dying like my parents and Emerson, then I knew I was doing my job right." He squeezed me a little tighter. "Your turn."

"Waking up to beautiful you every day." My green, big eyes looked up at him. "Children, a new home and maybe an expansion on my shop."

"So, we are both singing from the same song sheet then." He laughed. "That's good."

"I was thinking," I said, sitting up slightly. "Shall we have a party for your birthday?"

"I haven't really got any mates," he said, pulling his brows together.

"Well, how about a little get together with my lot? They are your family and friends too."

"Can I think about it? I have been so used to just having myself and Gloria to think about, it's going to take some time for me to adjust." He laughed.

"Of course, baby, sorry, I just get a bit carried away."

"No need to be sorry, princess."

My heart fluttered at his nickname for me, my memories flooding my mind of when he used to say that to get a rise out of me, a nickname I used to hate, and now he says it because he means it, and I love it.

-

My first night with Taron, in our home, was everything I hoped it would be. We spent the evening talking and trying to get to know each other a bit better. It's strange how our connection was so strong, yet we barely knew one another. But, that didn't change anything, the love I had for him was so strong.

I woke up to the sound of music. I couldn't work out if I had dreamt it or if it was actually playing. The song sounded familiar, I knew I had heard it before and then it hit me. It was, *'Road to Nowhere, Release The Sunbird.'* It was the song that was playing when Blair and Chuck got married in *Gossip Girl*.

I turned my head to the side, to see Taron there, still in his pyjama shorts, his body out, down on one knee, holding a Harry Winston engagement ring. The diamond was easily a five carat, maybe more. It was a clear cushioned cut diamond, in a tapered baguette setting.

My hands flew to my mouth, my eyes brimmed with tears.

"Oh my God," I whispered as I looked into Taron's deep brown eyes, his eyes glistening with unshed tears.

"Luna," he said, choked. "My beautiful Luna."

I nodded, a smile spreading on my face quicker than wild fire.

"Marry me, please?" he asked, taking the ring out of its box and hovering it near my hand.

"Yes, a thousand times yes," I exclaimed then squealed as he placed the ring on my finger.

"Thank fuck," he muttered as he pushed me back on the bed, his lips on mine.

Our tongues entwined with each other, my hands in his hair as I savoured this moment.

I was his.

He was mine.

Chapter THIRTY THREE

He scooped me up, pulling me on top of him as our kiss grew more intense. I ran my hands over his bare skin, electricity running through my body. I stopped my trail when I came to the waistband of his pyjama shorts, lifting my hips up and pulling them down and exposing him.

He ran his large hands up the side of my silk night dress, lifting it up against my skin as I lowered myself down onto him, a quiet moan escaping me as I felt him fill me.

He followed with a low groan, his arms wrapping around me and keeping me as close as he could possibly get me, our skin touching. I tilted my head back as the pleasure rushed through me, his slow pushes into me, breaking down my walls, thrust by thrust.

He kissed my bare neck, his hand grabbing my nightie and bunching it up around my neck so he had full access to my breast as he started licking my nipples, flicking his tongue. Normally, I would want him to speed up, to pound into me, but this, this was perfect.

I slid my hand down my body, pressing my fingers gently on my sensitive bud, my hips starting to move with his slow movements. I looked down, seeing his hips pushing up into me, making me moan again.

“Look at me whilst you’re touching yourself, Luna,” he said, my eyes obeying him and flicking up to his brown pools.

“Fuck, you are so sexy,” he whispered, his pace picking up.

“Oh, Taron, I’m going to come, Taron.” I cried out as I came, him crying out my name as he found his own release.

I laid in between his legs, my head on his chest as we came down from our engagement sex high. I held my hand out admiring my ring.

“This is so beautiful,” I wailed as it sparkled in the sunlight coming through our window.

“I knew that was the ring you needed,” he confessed.

“Honestly, Taron, I am so in love with you. It’s just perfect.” I turned my face towards him, pecking him on his lips. “I need to call the girls.”

“And your parents, they’ll want to know that you said yes.”

“They knew?” I leant up, surprised.

“Yup. I didn’t go to the shop last night, I went to get your father’s permission.” He smiled up at me.

"You're such a God." I giggled, kissing him again. "Thank you, that means so much."

"Luna, I am a gentleman. Of course I would ask your father's permission." He winked. "Now, go call your parents. I'll go start breakfast." He rolled me off of him as he collected his shorts off the floor.

I sat up, staring at his naked arse. Fuck, he had a good arse. He walked towards his dresser unit and grabbed a tee, throwing it over his head and walking out the door. "Breakfast will be about twenty minutes." He smiled before walking out the door.

I flopped back down and squealed with happiness. I couldn't believe I was engaged to Taron. My soulmate.

I could have been in such a different place if he hadn't got involved in Josh and Carlisle's plan.

I am a firm believer that everything happens for a reason.

I reached over for my phone, scrolling down and finding my mum's mobile number and clicking dial. It literally rang once.

"Luna," she answered apprehensively.

"Mum..." I trailed off.

"Yes, darling, is everything okay?" she asked, I could hear the smile through the phone.

"It's more than okay," I said, smiling myself.

"Yes, David," she shouted down the phone. "Luna is on the phone."

"I'm coming," I heard him shout. I rolled my eyes, biting my lip.

"So?" I heard her ask.

"So?" I said back, trying to stifle my giggle.

"Well, did you say yes?" my dad shouted in the background.

"Of course I said yes. God, I love him so much. I am literally the happiest girl in the world." I beamed.

"You deserve it, my darling, honestly, you really do."

"Thank you, Mum," I muttered. "Look, I've got to go, I'll come over later, okay?"

"Mmm hmm," she said. "Bye, honey."

"Bye." I hung up, dropping my phone onto the bed.

I needed to eat, I was starving. I crawled out of bed then flew down the stairs to see my handsome fiancé standing at the stove. I walked up behind him barefoot, then wrapped my arms around him.

"What you cooking, stud?" I asked before kissing him on the cheek, smelling his scent.

"Eggs and bacon with hash brown and beans. That okay?" He turned his head.

"That's perfect, babe." I waltzed over to the kettle, taking it off of its dock and filling it up with water before sticking it back on and flicking it on. "Tea or coffee?" I asked.

"Tea." He flashed his pearly whites.

I flushed when I realised I didn't know how he took

tea. Damn, should have asked him how he liked it last night.

"Erm." I twiddled my hair. "How do you like your tea?" Crimson rose up over me.

"Milk, strong, no sugar," he said as he started serving up the breakfast. "How do you like your tea?" he asked.

"Milky, two sugars." I smiled as I poured the milk in first, then added the water.

"Oh no," he said as he placed the plates on the island.

"What?" I asked, panicking that I had done something wrong, looking round where I had started making the teas. Had I used the wrong cup?

"You're one of them, aren't you?" He shook his head.

"One of what?" I stammered.

"You add the milk in first, who does that?"

"Oh, stop it. Trust me, it tastes so much better because the tea bags don't get scalded, which makes the tea taste better." I bit my lip, smirking. "Don't judge before you taste, do you judge a book by its cover, Mr Sloane?" I asked placing his tea in front of him.

"No, I don't."

"Well then, try the tea. Tell me what you think," I said as I took a sip of my tea, groaning in approval. "Mmm, delicious," I said, my eyes narrowing down on him as he took a mouthful of his tea, his eyes going wide.

"Okay, baby," he said placing his tea back down. "Hands down, the best cup of tea I have had." He smiled, leaning across and grabbing my hand. "Now, come and sit down, eat."

After breakfast we made our way upstairs. Taron made the bed whilst I hopped into the shower. I washed my hair, conditioned it then wrung it out before leaving the shower, wrapping myself in a towel. I looked down at my nails, I needed to book an appointment to have them done. I made a mental note to call and book next week.

I walked into the bedroom looking for something to wear. "Are we going anywhere today?" I asked while flicking through my clothes.

"We are going for lunch." He smiled as he pulled his jeans on.

"Can I know where?"

"Nope," he said cockily before putting his tee on and styling his jet black hair, pushing it back.

"Oh, I don't know what to wear then," I sulked, walking away from my wardrobe and sitting on the bed.

"I know what you can wear," he said, walking over to my wardrobe hunting for an outfit. A little smile crept on his face as he pulled out the yellow dress from Hawaii. "This," he said, laying it out next to me on the bed then swooping down to kiss me. "Wear this."

I stood from the bed, dropping my towel.

"You are a sight for sore eyes, Luna, do you know that? And you are all mine," he said, pulling me into him, my naked body against his fully-clothed self.

"I don't think this is fair, Sloane, I'm naked and you are fully dressed." I closed my eyes, bowing my head down onto his chest.

"This is fair." He chuckled. "This is very fair." He pulled the towel down off of my head, dropping it to the floor. "Honestly, I could fuck you all day, every fucking day." He groaned.

"Do it then," I challenged him.

He growled, his hands running around and under my bum as he picked me up and slammed me against the wall. With one hand, he undid his jean buttons then popped his flies undone, pulling himself out and straight into me, hard and fast.

"So ready, so wet," he whispered in my ear, both hands back on my bum, squeezing hard as he continued to pound into me, my orgasm building intensely, quickly.

"Taron," I called out with a moan.

He hooked his arm under my knee and then lifted it over his shoulder as he thrust into me, even deeper. My mouth formed in the shape of an 'O' as he slowed his thrusts, looking down, watching himself slowly pushing into me and pulling back out again.

"Shit," he hissed. "I'm going to come," he growled as he pounded hard into me, my back hitting the wall. It hurt, but God, it felt good.

"Keep going," I cried, and he did just that until I came, crying out his name, his head buried in my neck as he came with me.

He walked me back to the bed, dropping me, we were both panting.

"You, Sloane, are a fucking God," I whined.

"Oh no, baby, it's all you." He kissed me before pulling his jeans back up. "Now, get dressed, beautiful, we have a lunch reservation."

I finished curling my hair, then ran my fingers through the tight ringlets, making the waves in my hair that I liked. Pulling my yellow dress up, I slipped into my nude wedges and dressed it with silver hoops and a necklace.

I dusted my face in a light cover of make-up, brushing my cheeks with bronzer then applyed a natural matte lipstick, rubbing my lips together. I applied some lip liner, not that my lips needed it.

I took a look in the mirror as I walked out from the dressing room and into the bedroom.

"Do I look okay?" I asked, turning around so he could do my zip up.

He walked over, pulling the zip up to secure me in. His arms wrapped around me from behind as he kissed me on the neck.

"You look more than okay," he said. "We've got to go." I missed his contact as soon as he took his arms away, and I begrudgingly followed him downstairs. I could literally stay in this room forever, as long as he was here with me.

"Hello, lovebirds," Gloria called out from the lounge area. Taron pulled me into the room with her.

"Morning." He smiled at her, leaning down and giving her a kiss.

"Morning, Gloria," I muttered. She was sitting on the sofa with a little leather bag on her lap. She was wearing a short sleeved, long dress that sat just above her ankle. "You look nice." I smiled at her.

"Thank you, lovely, so do you." She stood, straightening her skirt. "We ready?"

"We are indeed," Taron replied as he waited for Gloria to walk past him, then took my hand and walked us out.

When we were on the kerb, I stood waiting for the taxi when Taron popped through a side gate.

"Where we going?" I asked Gloria, trying to get it out of her.

"Not sure, love." She smiled, facing the road when I heard a car come round the corner. A black four-by-four Mercedes pulled up kerbside, winding down it's window down.

"Get in, ladies," Taron said in a charming voice, pushing his sunglasses up his nose. I stepped forward, opening the front door for Gloria to sit up front with Taron.

"Oh no, I don't ride up the front. I like to sit in the

back, thank you though," she said as she climbed into the back. I shut the door for her then climbed into the front with Taron. He leant over and kissed me on the cheek.

"I love you," he said as he looked over his shoulder to pull out onto the road.

"I love you," I said. He makes me giddy.

"Can I know where we are going yet?" I asked.

"Nope." He smirked as he turned the radio on, Lewis Capaldi's voice crooning through the speakers.

"Have we got far to go?"

"About thirty minutes, not too long for you to wait, princess." He tapped his fingers on the steering wheel to the music. I smiled, I loved seeing him so happy instead of so haunted like he was when I first met him.

"I hope not, surprises make me anxious," I admitted, and his eyes darted to me as if he had messed up. "But it's fine. I'm a control freak, it's normally me doing the surprises, not the other way around."

"Did I fuck up?" he asked, his eyebrows raising, his voice tense.

"No! God no," I said, mindful of Gloria in the back. "Oh, baby, you could never fuck up." I placed my hand on his thigh and squeezed it. "Taron Sloane, you are everything."

And he was.

Chapter THIRTY FOUR

We pulled up on a small side road, then off into a communal car park. I looked at him confused, not a clue where we were going.

"Do you trust me?" he asked, brushing his thumb across my bottom lip.

"Always."

"Good, let's go," he said, turning the car off and hopping out the car, opening the doors for myself and Gloria. He helped her out before closing her door. I smiled at how he was with her.

I shut the door and stood, waiting for instruction. He laced his fingers through mine as we walked slowly towards Convent Garden.

After a five minute walk, we stopped outside Clos Maggiore. It was a white townhouse building, a small black iron fence securing the front of the property. It had a red canopy that covered the front of the restaurant. If it wasn't for that canopy you would think it was a house.

I looked through the window, it looked closed

"You sure it's open?" I asked, hesitant.

"Oh, I'm sure," he said with confidence as he pushed the door open. "After you, Gloria," he said as he stood with his back against the door.

As I walked into the quaint restaurant, my mouth dropped open as I walked into the dining area. I had never seen a restaurant so pretty. My eyes widened as I admired the breath takingly beautiful dining room. The room was filled with flowers, greenery and twinkling lights. There was a stone fireplace that sat centre in the middle of the room. I stood in awe.

"You like?" Taron asked cuddling into me.

"I love."

"Good," he whispered in my ear, nibbling, making me squirm and giggle. "One last surprise," he muttered as I saw the waiting staff walk out with my parents, Chris, Ava, Vanessa and Brooke. Then behind them was Eva, Michelle, Jane and Tegan. I squealed as I ran to embrace my parents, hugging them both before greeting the rest of the line whilst I listened to their congratulations. They walked over to embrace Taron and introduce their selves to Gloria.

I turned around to face him, happy tears brimming in my eyes.

"Surprise," he mouthed.

"I love you," I mouthed back.

After a glorious lunch, I went over to sit with the girls

"So, how did he do it?" Ava asked, she was such a hopeless romantic.

"Well, as you know I am obsessed with *Gossip Girl,*" I said.

"Yes, we know," Brooke responded, rolling her eyes, her arm resting on the back of the chair, sitting with her legs crossed as she flicked her red hair over her shoulder. I scowled at her, narrowing my eyes.

"Anyway," I said, letting my eyes linger on her for a little longer then moving them back to Ava and Vanessa. "I woke up to a song, at first I couldn't work out what it was but I knew I had heard it before. Then it clicked. It was the song that played when Chuck was running down the steps at his wedding." I swooned.

"Anyway, as I went to sit up, Taron was there, on the floor beside me, on his knee, holding the ring."

Ava and Vanessa sighed a happy sigh in unison.

"Small gesture, massive thought process." I giggled, holding my ring up to admire it.

"It's stunning, you deserve it," Brooke cooed.

"Thank you." I felt a grip on my shoulder and turned to see Taron as he leant down to kiss me.

"Get a room," Brooke said, pretending to stick her fingers down her throat.

"Oh, be quiet, Brooke, you'll be the same when it's you." Ava rolled her eyes at her.

"I think it's so romantic, you two are such a beautiful couple," Vanessa said, her chin resting on her hand, her elbow on the table as her honey eyes went hazy.

"Have you chosen a date yet?" I heard Eva say as she walked up beside Taron. "Hey, girls." She waved, pulling a chair over from the other table and sitting down in between me and Ava.

"No, no date yet. All I know is, I don't want a big wedding. It's about me and him," I said, squeezing Taron's hand that was still on my shoulder.

"Well, at least you know who your florist and cake maker are going to be." Eva giggled.

"I know, lucky to be in the business we have, aye?" I laughed with her. "I already have my ideas for flowers."

"I can't wait to hear all about it," she said as she sipped a glass of champagne.

"I'm going over to my parents, will catch up in a bit," I said quietly, pushing myself away from the table and walking over to my parents table, with Taron. I sat myself down, listening to the chatter between my parents and Gloria and my heart swelled. It must be nice for Gloria to have someone other than just Taron. I was hoping this would be the start of a beautiful friendship between my parents and her.

"Congratulations, baby," my dad said, scooting his chair closer to me and kissing me on the cheek. "Plaza round two?" he asked.

I laughed. "Aha, no. No more plaza." I shook my head, sipping my champagne.

"No?"

"No." I placed my glass on the table. "Bad omen and all that." I laughed again.

"So where?"

"I'm not sure yet, we haven't spoken about it, I've been engaged about eight hours." I rolled my eyes in a humorous way. "But once we know details, we will let you know." I winked at him.

The rest of the afternoon was pleasant, but all I wanted to do now was get back home with my man and snuggle up on the sofa.

Once we were home, I went straight upstairs to get changed. I grabbed a pair of Taron's light grey tracksuit bottoms and one of his white tees. I needed loose, I was so bloated from over indulging in food. I took my bra off and threw it.

Taron was sitting in front of the tele in the lounge, flicking through the channels, a childish grin on his face when Die Hard graced the television screen.

"No chance," I said as I cuddled into him.

"It's happening." He laughed.

"Fine, I suppose it's the least I can do after what you have done today," I teased.

"Oh good," he said, pulling me close and laughing.

"Where's Gloria?" I asked.

"Next door for a cup of tea, her friend Jean lives there."

"Oh, okay."

An hour into the film, I was getting restless. I turned my upper body, facing him and smiling.

"What's wrong?" he asked, tongue in cheek.

"I miss your mouth."

"Is that so? And where do you miss my mouth exactly?" His eyes now on me instead of the television.

"I miss it here," I said pointing to my lips. "I miss it here." My fingers moving down my neck. "I miss it here." Now gliding them down over my breasts. "And I miss it here." I slid them down inside my tracksuit bottoms, blushing.

He didn't say anything, he threw the tele remote across the room and pushed me back along the sofa. His hungry mouth on mine, my insides fluttering at the feel of his lips. He pushed his tongue in, twirling it round with mine as our kiss deepened. Electricity coursed through my veins from his touch.

My hands were in his hair, fisting and grabbing as his kiss got deeper. His hand slid down my body as he pushed and bunched the tee I was wearing up round his neck. Pulling his mouth away before his wet, hot mouth was on my sensitive skin as he moved down to my bare breast before taking one into his mouth, squeezing it gently before sucking and licking on my hard nipple, a moan escaping my lips.

Once he was finished, he blew his warm breath onto my nipple, then moved onto the other one and carried out the same pleasurable torture. I couldn't hold off.

"Taron, I'm going to come," I cried out as he continued licking and sucking on my nipple. My orgasm crashed through me like a wave, my back arched at the intensity of it.

He licked his lips as he leant up looking at me.

"Satisfied?" he asked.

"Hardly."

I shook my head, pulling my tee over my face.

"Good, I want to make you come again and again. My mouth wants to taste every bit of you." He pushed my legs apart, running his fingertip down my core through the tracksuit bottoms, smiling. He was teasing me, I needed to feel him.

"I need you to touch me," I pleaded, panting. "Please."

"Happy to oblige." He bit his tongue as he wrapped his fingers round my tracksuit bottoms and pulled them down, yanking them off my ankles as he discarded them on the floor.

He sat back on his knees, pushing my legs apart and marvelling at the sight in front of him.

"I am so lucky." He groaned as he glided a finger

down my centre then pushed it deep inside me.

"Touch yourself," he ordered.

I did as he said. I ran my hand down my bare stomach and rubbed my fingers over my nub, slowly matching his rhythm.

"Luna, you turn me on so much," he said, rubbing his own hand over the hardness that was bulging in his jeans. I couldn't talk, his burning eyes watching me as he stroked my insides, crumbling with every stroke. My orgasm was building once more.

"Taron I'm close," I moaned as he slipped his finger in and out, gradually speeding up his thrusts into me as my insides shattered around him, and me crying out as the second blow crashed through me.

"Fuck," I whispered, and he pushed my legs closer towards me, still spread as he pushed his finger into my mouth.

"See how good you taste?" he asked as I nodded.

"My turn," he said as he shuffled himself down the sofa, his head in-between my legs.

A whimper left me before his tongue even touched me. He ran his tongue from the bottom of me, right to my nub before sucking and licking it. He glided his tongue between me, slowly licking me. He moved his tongue side to side over my soft spot, causing a moan to leave as the pure pleasure rippled through me.

I didn't think I could take much more.

I grabbed his hair, pushing my pelvis into his face. I couldn't stop myself, my hips bucking and rotating to his expert tongue movements.

"Shit," I whispered, arching my back and pushing the back of my head into the sofa as he slipped two fingers in me, stretching me in the most delicious way.

I tightened my grip on his hair as I sat up to watch him make me come undone with every stroke of his tongue. His fingers pulsed slowly into me. His dark brown eyes watched me as I watched him, I could see the smirk on his face.

"Don't stop," I panted. I was too far for him to stop, my orgasm on the brink of falling and making me tumble into a seventh heaven. He sucked on my bud whilst pumping his fingers into me quickly as I come, hard. Shattering and falling into oblivion.

He pulled his fingers out and sucked them clean.

"You are delicious," he groaned.

I sat up, closing my legs, my arousal evident down my thighs, but I didn't care. I pushed him back, undoing his button to his jeans and tugging them down. He sat with his back on the sofa as I pulled myself into a ball, taking him into my mouth, taking him deep then pulling him out and swirling my tongue at his tip, tasting his bead of arousal that sat there, my eyes batting up to him.

His hand squeezed my bare bum as he slipped a finger into me again, twirling it. I moaned with him in my mouth as he pushed in deeper. His other hand entwined itself in my hair, before he grabbed a handful and pulled me up.

I was now kneeling on the sofa, looking down at him, unsure why. He pressed the inside of my thighs, indicating for me to open them more before he cupped me and pushed another finger into me, his hot mouth on my hard nipples as he sucked and squeezed my breast.

I grabbed his wrist and shook my head as I straddled myself over him, him holding the base of his cock before taking me, moving my hips back forth slowly, then picking up the pace. I leant back, placing my arms backwards on his knees to support myself as I rotated and thrust my hips faster.

I looked at him, his teeth sinking into his bottom lip whilst watching me move on him. I felt myself tighten around him, he put one hand on my hip before the other grabbed my top, bunching my tee up round my throat where he wrapped his fingers with some firmness.

I grinned at him, loving every minute of it.

He gripped onto my hip tightly as he smashed his hips upwards, pounding into me. My impending orgasm was building, my eyes on him as his name slipped off my tongue as I came hard around him, him following behind calling my name.

I was in heaven.

Chapter
THIRTY FIVE

ONE YEAR LATER

“Are you sure we have everything?” I asked Vanessa as we landed at JFK.

“For the hundredth time, yes,” she exclaimed then laughed as she shut the boot of the large people carrier that was waiting outside the airport. Taron came up behind me.

“Are you still stressing?” he asked then kissed me on the cheek.

“Nope.” I shook my head then drew a ring round my head like a halo. “I’ll stop now, okay? I just wanted to make sure we had everything.” I sighed.

“I get that, baby, but if the worst comes to worst and we didn’t, I’m sure that we will get anything we need in the big apple.”

“I know.” I nodded, taking a deep breath as I climbed into the car. Mum, dad, Ava and Chris were in the car behind. Gloria, Ness and Brooke were in with us.

"It'll be perfect," he said, taking my hand and bringing it to his lips, pecking me on the back of the hand.

"I love you," I muttered.

"I love you."

We pulled outside The Empire, a door man greeted us then opened our door, letting us out. A porter walked up to us with a gold luggage carrier as he started unloading the baggage then walked away.

"Please be careful with the dress," Vanessa said running after the porter.

Me and Taron had to go to city hall to collect our marriage certificate that we had applied for months prior to our wedding. We decided to get married on the thirtieth of May, the day we got engaged.

We were having a family dinner tonight, before the big day tomorrow. We decided on an afternoon wedding, and only immediate family and the girls would be there. Eva, Michelle and Jane were flying out this evening then returning home the day after the wedding.

After our wedding we had to go home for a few weeks due to work commitments but then we were taking our honeymoon in October, in Hawaii, for two weeks, and I couldn't wait to go back there with Taron as husband and wife.

I flopped down on the bed in our luxury penthouse suite, I felt exhausted. It had been a long couple of days making sure we had everything and that all the legal bits were sorted. We didn't need that just as we were about to say, "I do."

"What time is dinner?" Taron asked.

"Seven." I yawned, stretching my arms out. "How come?"

"Fancy a nap?"

"Oh, Mr Sloane, I thought you would never ask," I teased as he jumped on the bed, wrapping his long arms around me and pulling me close, nestling into my neck.

I woke up disorientated, feeling extremely warm from Taron's arms. I reached out for my phone, it was five pm. I stretched then rolled out of bed, not wanting to wake him. I walked towards the large bathroom and into the walk in shower, I felt groggy. It was nice to be naked and free of my sticky clothes.

The hot water felt amazing on my skin, the pressure hard, which was nice. I washed my hair and left the conditioner on a little longer whilst I scrubbed my body with exfoliator. I had fake tanned a few days ago, so now I looked like I had a nice summer glow that I wanted to last.

I saw a sleepy Taron walk towards me, peeling his top off, pulling it over his head, revealing his body. I bit my lip as he slipped his jogging bottoms down his leg and stepped out of them as he joined me in the shower.

He dropped his head back, letting the water cascade

over him. I picked up my shower puff, smothering it in shower gel as I ran it up and down his torso, covering him in delicious smelling suds. He groaned in appreciation.

I slid round him, keeping my hand on his stomach as I washed over his back, having to tiptoe to reach his shoulders. I planted soft kisses along his back, then wrapped my arms around him from behind and placed my hands on his chest, feeling his heart beat in my palms. His head was bowed as the water dripped down his nose.

"You okay?" I asked.

"Yeah, babe. Just feels weird, you know, being married again," he admitted.

"I bet," I said quietly.

"I get scared that I am going to lose you." He turned around, cupping his hands around my face.

"You're never going to lose me," I promised. "It's me and you until the end, handsome." I ran my fingers along his stubble, then up into his hair as I desperately pulled him towards me, needing his lips on mine. Needing to show him how much I loved him and that I would always be by his side.

We walked hand in hand down to the restaurant where our wedding party was waiting. Taron was wearing suit trousers and a white shirt, I was wearing a black cocktail dress and black wedges. I couldn't wait to see him tomorrow. We had decided not to show each other our outfits, we wanted the surprise.

We were sat in a private area of the hotel on a large table. The bubbly was flowing, I normally loved a few glasses, but I wasn't feeling it tonight. I was feeling anxious, I kept worrying that something was going to go wrong. Taron squeezed my leg.

"All okay, babe?" he asked.

"Yeah, just feeling a little out of sorts. I feel anxious," I admitted.

"I'm not that bad, and if you're not sure there is still time for you to run," he said, his eyebrows raising, his voice serious as he draped his arm round the back of my chair.

"I'm not anxious about marrying you, God no. I can't wait to marry you. I feel like I have been waiting my whole life for you, Taron. I am anxious that something is going to go wrong."

"Baby, nothing is going to go wrong. And if, and it's a big if, but if something does go wrong, there is nothing you can do about it. It's out of our control, beautiful. But whatever happens, it will be perfect. I promise you." He leant in and pecked me on the lips, winking at me. I sat back as our dinner was served. Stuffed chicken, mash and asparagus.

Once dinner was finished my dad stood from the top of the table, holding his glass of champagne as he tapped his glass with his knife.

"Can I have a moment, please?" he said, waiting for the chatter to die down.

"Thank you," he said, placing his knife next to his plate. "I just wanted to take this moment to say a few words." He coughed, clearing his throat. "Ever since Luna was a little girl, she told me she wanted to get married in New York and I said I would do whatever I could to make that dream come true. Granted, the first time didn't go as planned."

People broke into a small bout of laughter.

"But this time, I know my darling daughter will be getting her dream, her fairy tale and her prince. It hasn't been an easy road for them, but we are here. I can't wait to watch them finally say "I do" to each other and watch them start their life as a newly married couple. So, if you would all join me in raising a glass to the nearly, Mr and Mrs Sloane." He cheered as everyone held their glasses up and clinked them together.

I placed my hand round Taron's cheek, turning his face towards me as I kissed him. "I love you," I whispered.

"I know," he said.

I woke the next morning, early and with a belly full of butterflies. Today was the day. I was finally marrying Taron.

He spent the night in Chris' room, I had my mum and Ava in here. Ava was already up, enjoying a cup of tea, over-looking central park as she cradled her little baby bump. I was so happy for her and Chris, and I was so excited to become an auntie.

I hopped in the shower, pulling my hair into a messy bun so I didn't get it wet. Once out, I dried myself and slipped into my white, silk dressing gown that the girls had bought me at my bridal shower. On the back was, "Mrs Sloane."

I walked into the bedroom and joined Ava for a cup of tea, my mum was also now sitting with her. I hear the door go, standing up and opening the hotel door to see Vanessa and Brooke standing there screaming.

"YOU'RE GETTING MARRIED TODAY!" She barged past me, Vanessa following. I stuck my head out the hotel door and looked down the hallway. It was early, all we needed was complaints.

I shut the door before making my way over to the table where the rest of the girls and my mum were sitting.

"Tea? Shouldn't we be drinking champagne?" Brooke snorted. "Well, apart from preggers." She nodded towards Ava as she took a swig out of the bottle.

"Charming," I heard Ava mutter under her breath. I gave her a sympathetic look.

I sat on Vanessa's lap as I drank my tea, they were all in light chatter, but I wanted to just sit and take a moment to think about our upcoming wedding.

Half an hour passed when I started doing my make-up. I clipped my hair away from my face before applying a light layer of foundation, then brushed my cheek bones with bronzer. I brushed my false lashes, making sure none were stuck together then applied a matte red lipstick, rubbing my lips together. I sprayed some setting spray, worried that it would melt throughout the day. Brooke had been practicing doing my hair for the last few months, I wanted one of the girls to do it, and she offered.

She poured me a glass of champagne as she stood behind me and started separating my hair into sections. "I can't believe how long your hair has gotten," she muttered.

"I know, it's really grown the last year." I smiled in the mirror at her.

"I must say, that red lipstick against your skin and big green eyes looks stunning." She smiled back at me.

I felt myself blush. "Thank you."

She twisted two pieces of hair from either side of my head before pulling them into the centre and securing with a kerbie grip, adding a fake rose to cover the clip. She took another chunk of hair a bit further down and carried on the same process. The loose hair that was left, hanging down my back, she curled into soft curls. She held a mirror behind, so I could see. It looked amazing.

"Brooke, thank you so much," I said, standing up and hugging her.

"It's the least I could do." She smiled as she sat down

to do her make-up. Her hair was in tight ringlets. Ava and Vanessa were helping each other into their bridesmaid dresses. All three of them were wearing black three quarter length tea dresses with light pink flowers scattered all over. Casual but pretty.

My mum started getting herself dressed. She was wearing a fitted midi dress with a shawl to wrap round her shoulders, I knew she got chilly even if it was melting outside.

I took a deep breath as I was trying to calm my nerves before slipping on my third wedding dress, but this one would be my last. I slipped the soft chiffon material up my legs, hooking the spaghetti straps over my shoulders. The bodice was thin laced with a nude chiffon sewn behind. The chiffon skirt flowed out from my waist. I slipped into my white converse, bending down to do them up. I walked into the lounge area, staring at myself in the floor length mirror. This was my favourite dress out of all three.

"Luna," my mum sobbed. "You look beautiful, my darling."

"Thank you, Mum." I hugged her, squeezing her tightly. "Love you."

"I love you too."

There was a knock at the door, Vanessa running to open it. Chris and my dad walked in, my dad embracing me. "You look like a princess," he muttered in my ear.

"Thank you, Daddy," I said, trying not to get upset. I

didn't want tear stained cheeks.

Chris walked straight in and kissed Ava, rubbing her growing belly.

"How's Taron holding up?" I asked anxiously.

"He is fine, all good to go. Gloria is just having a chat with him, seemed pretty personal so we wanted to give them ten," he said, smiling at me.

"It's nearly time," Vanessa said as she checked her phone.

"Okay, cool, let me pack my little bag with essentials." I smiled, grabbing my phone, concealer stick and bronzer and putting them into my little bag.

"Mum, have you got the marriage documents?" I asked as I applied another layer of lipstick before putting it in my bag.

"Yes, got them all here." She patted the front of her bag then dabbed her eye as a stray tear fell down her cheek.

Chris went back to the room to let Taron know that we had to go. He said he would text me once they were at Central Park. It was literally a five minute walk to where we were getting married.

Once Chris messaged we left the hotel. Tourists were taking photos of me and clapping as we walked through the lobby. Eva, Michelle, Jane and Tegan were waiting for us, Tegan with a cannon round her neck snapping away. We were going to pay for a photographer, but Tegan insisted that she took the photos.

As we hit the hustle and bustle of New York, I took a moment to look up at the sky out of the concrete jungle and took a deep breath. Excitement coursed through me as we started walking towards Central Park.

I stood at the top of the steps, my make-up and hair being checked over by Brooke one last time before I saw my husband-to-be.

Eva handed me my bouquet of white and yellow frangipani's, pale pink peonies, hydrangeas and white roses. I held them up to my nose, smelling then smiling at the frangipani's, flooding my mind with memories of Hawaii.

"I must grab the details of the florist, she's amazing." I winked at Eva before taking my place at the top of the steps.

The girls all walked down before me and huddled round near Taron, under the arches. I smiled when I heard, "With Me" by Sum 41, playing. The tears now brimmed in my eyes as I started my walk down the stairs that lead me to the Bethesda Fountain.

As I stood at the bottom, my dad came and hooked his arm round mine as we started walking towards the arch that sat in front of the fountain where Taron was waiting for me. His eyes drew up and down my body, a huge grin on his face.

He looked so handsome in his black suite, his crisp

white shirt with his collar undone. His hair was styled and pushed back, his dark brown eyes glistened as the sun reflected off the fountain.

My heart was racing in my chest.

As soon as I reached him, my dad kissed me on the cheek, tears flowing down his face.

"Oh, Daddy," I whispered as I placed my hand on his cheek, wiping his tears away. He took my hand and placed it in Taron's.

"Look after her, son," he said as he stepped back to stand next to my mum.

"Welcome, we are gathered here today to witness the marriage of Taron George Sloane and Luna Aria Smith," the registrar called out in front of our family and friends.

"Luna," Taron said, gripping onto my hands tightly. "I wasn't looking for love when I met you, I didn't want to fall in love again." I saw him swallow hard. "But then you came into my world like a hurricane, turning my world upside down, in a good way. Neither of us wanted to give into our feelings, neither of us wanting to admit just how deeply we fell for one another, but here we are. You're about to become my wife, and I can't wait to start my life with you. You are my everything, my saviour, my princess," he said before pushing a diamond, platinum band onto my finger.

"Taron," I mumbled, my heart pounding in my chest. "You infuriated me when we first met, pushing me away at every chance." My eyes were on his, his eyes darting back and forth from mine. "But my God, you blew me away. Completely sweeping me off my feet and showing me what real love should feel like. I feel like the luckiest lady in the world to have you as my husband. I will love you forever, never leaving. I promise." I pushed a gold band onto his finger.

"With the power invested in me, I now pronounce you husband and wife, you may kiss your bride."

"Three words," he muttered, his eyes boring into mine.

"Eight letters," I replied, smirking, then pulled my bottom lip between my teeth.

"I love you," he said, his hands coming up to my face as he kissed me, my hands resting on his wrists. The cheers echoed around the archways.

"Oh, one more thing," I mumbled as I dropped my hands from his and formed a heart with my fingers on my belly. "You're going to be a daddy."

This queen had finally found her king. Her king finally finding his saviour.

And of course we had to have the most iconic *Gossip Girl* saying in there.

Epilogue

TARON

February 14TH

I sat in the hospital room with these two little bundles on my chest, Faith and Hope. My beautiful twin daughters who were a couple of hours old.

I had everything I had ever dreamed of, a beautiful wife and two daughters. Yes, I was outnumbered, but my God, I wouldn't have had it any other way.

Luna was incredible, her labour started but soon went downhill. The doctor had pushed for a planned C-section, but she wouldn't have it. She was determined to give birth naturally, but her body couldn't do it. She was taken down for an emergency C-section, bringing our daughters into the world. I was terrified, but I had to be brave for her. I couldn't be weak when she needed me. She was always the strong one, and this one time I had to be strong for her.

The fear of seeing someone you worship in a situation where you are useless really hits you. There was nothing I could do apart from tell her to keep going and that everything would be fine.

And it was.

I looked over at my beautiful wife, who was sleeping, I felt so incredibly lucky to have her in my life.

My mind drifted back to our honeymoon in Hawaii. It was so nice being back as husband and wife and not denying the chemistry between us. It was the honeymoon we needed.

Work had been crazy but good crazy. I remember the afternoon we had a walk. We strolled along the beach in Hawaii, the intense sun beating down on us, the sweet air filling our nostrils. I looked down at my beautiful wife who was glowing, five months pregnant with twin girls. I loved that she kept it from me and told me on our wedding day.

It was the most perfect gift and moment.

After everything that happened with Emerson, I never thought I would be able to love so deeply, but here I am. The happiest I have been in a very long time, in love with the most beautiful woman and the mother of my children. My wife.

She came into my life just as I needed her. She was the lightness to my dark. I was her protector, she was my saviour. She was my soulmate.

We were pushed together for a reason, our souls

seeking each other out, until we finally found one another. I was waiting to find her, she was waiting to find me. The moments we were apart were the hardest of my life, having to lie to her to protect her and her family. But that was my job, to protect her. I was her protector.

Now, my job is to love her fiercely, and remind her every day how lucky I am to have her in my life. I may not be a bodyguard anymore, but I would always protect her, and now, protect my daughters, Faith Nevaeh Sloane and Hope Nevaeh Sloane.

We were a family, a family I had craved since I was five. Now I got to be the most perfect dad and husband to the three most important ladies in my life.

I would never take them for granted.

They were my life, my reason for existence, the reason for my survival.

I looked up to see my Luna stirring, her eyes searching the room as she focused on me.

"Hey, you," she said quietly.

"Hey," I said as I stood up, walking our tiny bundles over to her and placing them both in her arms, bending down and kissing her on her lips.

"I love you so much, Luna," I whispered to her, cupping her beautiful face then shaking my head gently, looking down at the girls then flicking my dark brown eyes back up to hers, her eyes shining like emeralds. I smirked before pressing my lips against hers once more, taking in her intoxicating scent.

"I will never tire of loving you, do you know that?" I said. "I love you."

"I love you more, Taron Sloane," she muttered, smiling up at me, that beautiful smile that attracted me in the first place.

"Not possible, princess." I smirked before covering her mouth with mine once more.

She had my heart for eternity.

She was my forever.

She was my Luna.

THE END

Thank YOU...

Thank you so much for reading Unwanted. I hope you loved Taron and Luna as much as I did. I was so nervous about this book going out, seeing as it's my first one away from Carter and Freya.

I would like to thank my amigos, Nikki and Lindsey. Thank you so much for everything, so grateful for our friendship.

Robyn, my sidekick. You have been amazing, thank you so much for all your help and being there for me when I need you. Thank you for doing my initial read through of Unwanted.

And I'm sorry for talking your ear off!

To all the amazing bloggers who share my covers and teasers. I am so grateful for the never ending support. You are all stars.

Leanne (Irish Ink Publishing), thank you again for the formatting and cover. You make my book look amazing.

Lindsey, thank you for editing my book.

If you enjoyed Unwanted, I would be so grateful if you could leave a review on Amazon or Goodreads and share amongst your friends.

If you wish to keep up with what I am up to then please follow my social media;

Instagram: http://bit.ly/38NEN4B

Facebook: http://bit.ly/38QuJYI

Reader Group: https://bit.ly/3dKAXfA

Goodreads: http://bit.ly/2HMUXPZ

Amazon: https://amzn.to/2HOJUpf

Bookbub: http://bit.ly/2SSvISD

Printed in Great Britain
by Amazon

55363081R00222